*W*hat the critics are saying...

ର

5 *Hearts* "... a delightfully seductive portrayal ... well-written, fascinating and complex characters ... every bit as kinky and sexy as you might expect. Unexpectedly, it is also a pleasurable love story..." ~ *Sensual Romance*

5 *Stars* "...could be termed "The Story of O-New Millennium Style" this tale takes an intense look at the relationship between a Master and his slave... an extraordinarily impressive story told in an erudite and sophisticated fashion. I recommend it wholeheartedly, but with a caveat - it requires you to go places you may not have ventured before." ~ *A Romance Review*

5 *Stars* "Julian Masters is truly a Master of his craft. Training to Pleasure is not simply a work of erotic fiction, or a walk on the dark side of fantasy, though it is vividly sensual. It is an exploration of human motivations and sexuality...every scene, no matter how shocking, has a purpose..." ~ *eCataRomance Reviews.*

JULIAN MASTERS

TRAINING TO PLEASURE

ELLORA'S CAVE
ROMANTICA PUBLISHING

An Ellora's Cave Romantica Publication

www.ellorascave.com

Training to Pleasure

ISBN# 1419952269
ALL RIGHTS RESERVED.
Training to Pleasure Copyright © 2005 Julian Masters
Edited by Mary Moran.
Cover art by Darrell King.

Electronic book Publication January 2005
Trade paperback Publication June 2006

Warning:

The following material contains graphic sexual content meant for mature readers. This story has been rated E–rotic by a minimum of three independent reviewers.

Ellora's Cave Publishing offers three levels of Romantica™ reading entertainment: S (S-ensuous), E (E-rotic), and X (X-treme).

S-*ensuous* love scenes are explicit and leave nothing to the imagination.

E-*rotic* love scenes are explicit, leave nothing to the imagination, and are high in volume per the overall word count. In addition, some E-rated titles might contain fantasy material that some readers find objectionable, such as bondage, submission, same sex encounters, forced seductions, and so forth. E-rated titles are the most graphic titles we carry; it is common, for instance, for an author to use words such as "fucking", "cock", "pussy", and such within their work of literature.

X-*treme* titles differ from E-rated titles only in plot premise and storyline execution. Unlike E-rated titles, stories designated with the letter X tend to contain controversial subject matter not for the faint of heart.

About the Author

❧

Julian Masters is forty years old, single and divides his time between his homes in the UK and Spain. His main interests are writing and the study of oriental healing arts and philosophy. He is also an enthusiastic amateur musician and naturalist with a deep concern for the environment.

Julian's novels explore his fascination with the mysteries of sexuality and love—where the sensual and spiritual worlds so often collide, when ideally they would combine and fuse harmoniously. In his first published novel, "Training to Pleasure", he describes just such an harmonious fusion as two people find the courage to first reveal and then explore their darkest desires. It is an intensely erotic story and yet never loses sight of the fact that eroticism is empty without tenderness, trust and love.

Julian's forthcoming novels will continue to explore this theme but on a galactic scale, as he indulges his lifelong love of science fiction to combine adventure, romance, wildly kinky sex and ultimately a love that bridges worlds and cultures.

Julian welcomes comments from readers. You can find his website and email address on his author bio page at www.ellorascave.com

Training to Pleasure

Trademarks Acknowledgement

~

The author acknowledges the trademarked status and trademark owners of the following wordmarks mentioned in this work of fiction:

Barbie doll: Mattel, Inc.

Chanel: Chanel, Inc. N.Y.

Chapter One
A Flame is Kindled

ઍ

Kate was neither desperate nor unhappy — it would simply never have occurred to her to apply such words to herself. She was successful in her work, reasonably well-off and worldly wise enough to know, since she had been in the employ of some exceptionally wealthy, and yet lonely and unhappy individuals, that the important things to cultivate in life were friendships and self-respect. She counted herself fortunate to be well-endowed with both.

Only a few months earlier even attempting to communicate intense feelings and intimate desires solely through the written word would have struck her as absurd. Emails and instant messaging had always been, to Kate's way of thinking, just tools that made her work easier and quicker. Yet, here she was, seriously considering meeting a man whom she hardly knew the first *ordinary* thing about. The kinds of everyday things you would know about someone just from walking past them on the street.

This had struck her as bizarre almost from the start of her explorations in cyberspace. The normal everyday mundanity of people's lives remained largely hidden and unmentioned, and therefore tacitly and often erroneously assumed, whereas the private and secret were flagrantly and sometimes even intrusively displayed.

Kate was inexperienced only with regard to Internet-based relationships. She had been involved in several long-term relationships, and had on two occasions — since leaving behind those dizzy teenage years when she had seemed to fall in and out of love every other week — even thought she might be in love with the man in her life. Sooner or later though, some aspect of his character or a mannerism had begun to grate and chafe, or some deficiency in the relationship had started to frustrate her, and she had realized that what she had thought of as love was really merely attachment to a familiar face and to a known and therefore comfortable routine of interaction.

Looking back, she divided the men she had dated into two basic types — the nice guys and the bad guys. The former were genuinely decent men who were financially secure, sensitive to her needs, honest for the most part and even able to hold a conversation when the mood took them. They were male friends who had become lovers, not because of any wild attraction but because Kate felt safe with them. Sadly it seemed inherent in the safety factor that their attitude to sex be unexciting, unadventurous, apologetic and invariably passionless. Their lack of confidence in themselves as lovers meant that Kate spent most of her time in bed preoccupied with ensuring their fragile egos did not get bruised. In such circumstances, she found it impossible to relax and just enjoy herself.

The latter, the "bad guys", were sexually much more confident, passionate and adept, and it was with these men that she had explored some mildly kinky sex and first discovered that she had an exceptional ability to submerge herself in another's pleasure. They were selfish lovers in that they rarely thought of her needs or pleasure, but somehow that did not matter since they were both enthusiastic and vocal in their enjoyment of her, and she found their passion infectious. Unfortunately, their selfishness was not limited to sex. After the first weeks of the relationship, during which time this kind of man gave every appearance of finding her fascinating, she would finally, and often against her better judgment, allow them into her bed. Thereafter, as if relieved of a burden, they would swiftly revert to whatever their normal pattern of life had been before meeting her. Instead of sex being the beginning of deepening intimacy, it was the end-point — conversation became a thing of the past — if it had ever been at all.

Sometimes when loneliness or sheer horniness drove her to it, Kate did not mind that so much. There was something refreshingly honest about a man who was so direct about what he wanted, but deep down she always felt, always hoped, that somewhere, with someone very special, there would be more…

This search had led to talks with girlfriends, who shared many of her frustrations, if not perhaps her tenacious optimism that one day she would find a man who had that special blend of sensitivity and intelligence combined with a raw, earthy and above all, *masculine* passion she craved so deeply.

On a visit to one such girlfriend, another personal assistant from the office at which they both worked, the tone of conversation had become quite daringly open. It had been late one evening, when they were both somewhat flushed and giggly from the two bottles of wine they had shared, that Kate had told her friend some of her most secret fantasies and shared her despair in ever finding a man who might fulfill them.

Kate's friend had run to her bedroom and returned with an armful of books. "There's only one place you'll find what you're looking for Katie…fiction!" She had dropped the half dozen or so paperbacks onto her lap, grinning. "One of those and a set of new batteries in your vibrator is all you need to set you right, girl!"

The friend, though well intended, had been quite wrong. Instead of pacifying the desires that had been brewing within her for so long, the books just set Kate on fire, and had made her even more determined not to settle for less than her ideal in the future.

Kate had expected the books to be the normal mild erotica, and indeed most of them were, but one book immediately grabbed her attention. Though having only the sketchiest plot, the author wrote with vivid and convincing intensity, painting images in her mind that invoked feelings and responses that surprised and even shocked her.

The characters seemed convincing and real to her as she read about their lives, needs and desires and, of course, their sexual adventures. As well as arousing her intensely, it offered her something far more profound. The book used a certain stylized vocabulary to describe the various types of sexual preference of the protagonists. Moreover, in referring to people as dominants and submissives, switches, tops and bottoms, it gave the impression that such distinctions were commonplace. That there was a whole world, an entire culture out there where people were unafraid to acknowledge and define precisely what they needed from a sexual relationship.

Though Kate did not feel she fitted perfectly into any of the too neat categories outlined in the book, she began for the first time in her life to seriously think that she might be sexually submissive...the first time she had been able to put a term to what she had fantasized about for so long, and that this might explain why her previous relationships had never fulfilled her. That maybe, if some vital part of her self-understanding had been missing, she could not possibly have been looking in the right places or even for the right kind of man.

Kate had always prided herself on being an independent woman, often despairing of girlfriends who seemed willing to throw away their careers or simply never even begin them after years of college, just to keep their man happy. So, she struggled to understand why was she so powerfully aroused by these tales of total submission and complete subjugation to another's will. The story described in vivid detail things that went far beyond anything she had done previously with her "bad" boyfriends, she was not even sure that some of the things described were even possible—if indeed they were desirable at all in real life.

Yet, despite what she had come to think of as the sensible voice in her mind, deep down Kate somehow knew that it was all possible if only she could find a man whom she could really trust. How she knew it, she was not sure—it was instinctive, even irrational. But for it not to be true would mean that there was a deep part of her, something central to who she was as a human being, that would forever feel misunderstood and alone—and that she refused to accept.

And so, she had begun to explore further, surfing the Internet, reading and researching. Sometimes, amidst the dross of crudely pornographic websites, she discovered hidden gems written by submissives, or dominant and submissive couples who shared their thoughts, feelings and experiences with a heartwarming honesty. It was these that more than anything else inspired Kate to continue her search. Clearly if another woman could find a man to love and trust to such a high degree, then so could she!

Gradually, she began to build a picture in her mind of the "scene". She "met" all manner of different people in a variety of Internet chat rooms. Clearly some people were just plain crazy or obsessed—maybe both! Others were aggressively proactive in what they called their "lifestyle" and were obviously very serious about it. Perhaps even too serious, as if nothing else mattered in life. But at least they were normally kind and intelligently informative when she had questions. Such people almost never tried to make her feel stupid and she appreciated that.

The vast majority of the people in the chat rooms seemed to be in pretty much the same state as herself—they were single and searching, lonely and curious—regardless of what they pretended to know and no matter what experiences they claimed to have had.

Indeed this cyber-world struck Kate as being not so very different from the ordinary world. There were those who were shy and withdrawn, never saying anything. There were those who were boastful and arrogant, loud and obnoxious. There were those who tried to manipulate her and take advantage of her relative inexperience, and then there were those who seemed to her genuine and sincere—"real" people whom she could easily get on with—or might have done if only they had not lived thousands of miles away. Had she been able to meet them in real life, she would have most likely enjoyed their company and friendship.

Generally, Kate found that she learnt the most from talking to other women, especially those who had some real-life experience of being dominated. Over and again, from many different women from all over the world, she got the same simple message—

Do NOT wait for someone to find you! Search the profiles in the personals, find someone who seems to know what they are talking about, someone who seems sincere, and then get to know them really well. Ask lots of questions, learn all you can about them and establish the beginnings of trust. If he's for real, he will be patient, he won't be pushy or try to rush you. Arrange a safe meeting when it feels good for you. If in doubt, walk away!

It was this understanding that had caused her to take a second look at James' profile.

Master James. Experienced in all aspects of BDSM and D/s, but learning all the time.

Kate reread the profile she had by now committed to memory.

Trust is both the foundation and the cement of any worthwhile relationship, but especially one involving dominance and submission. Trust cannot be forced—it must be earned through experience. A Master is firstly his submissive's teacher, her guide and her trusted friend. If he is not these then he cannot be called her Master.

If you are the special girl I have been looking for, I will lead you down a path of erotic discovery, a journey into submission. Exciting and arousing you, and yet, ensuring your safety at every step.

The profile went on to say he was an engineer and described him as a single male, six-foot two in height, of slim and athletic build. His interests were listed as martial arts, reading, skiing, rock climbing and cooking. Which she thought an interestingly odd combination. But it was his mention of a

Master as a teacher that made her, after much indecision, write to him. Because, she reflected, that was exactly what she needed most. And if it came to nothing then she would at least have learned a thing or two.

And so, she had written to him...

Hoping. Wondering.

Curious.

Chapter Two
Synchronicity

ᔡ

James Courtenay sat before his computer just gazing at her photograph, mesmerized. Finally, after some moments, he remembered to breathe again. He leaned back in his chair and closed his eyes, her face captured in his mind. Making himself breathe more deeply, he reflected on the powerful feelings stirring within him.

Desire, certainly — very strong desire.

But there was also a tightening in his chest. Excitement? Yes, but perhaps also wariness, caution? Understandable since the last time he had felt such a powerful attraction he had been deeply disappointed and not a little hurt.

James dismissed the painful memories. The past was gone, those lessons learnt and he hoped Kate would be a big part of his future. This time things would be different.

The much greater feeling he recognized well. That sweet pain in the center of his chest, combined with longing, a sense of vulnerability that somehow brought with it a still deeper sense of inner strength. Tender strength — powerful gentleness. There were so many almost opposing feelings that combined, at least with regard to this woman, so very pleasurably.

James smiled. If he was not very careful, he was going to end up falling for this girl. Not just infatuation either, but the real thing. He could feel it, had begun to feel it some time previously, even before this particular photograph had arrived in his inbox.

The previous photographs she had sent had been very stylized, she had been too obviously posed by some kind of "professional" photographer — the kind that never spent more than five minutes getting to know their subject and consequently never captured them, the truth of them, in the frame.

By contrast, this one was just a snapshot, perhaps a lucky one, or perhaps taken by someone who knew her very well. Her complete lack of self-consciousness, her utterly authentic smile, the intensity of her gaze on someone out of frame, eyes widening in surprise…

Realizing that he had crossed his arms over his chest and had tensed up, James forced himself to relax and look again. This time more critically.

She was not pretty in the everyday sense. Her features were too irregular, her mouth too large, her nose slightly too long. Her hair was lovely, long, and dark and her skin lightly tanned, perhaps from a recent holiday. The harsh light of the flash had revealed a faint scar on her chin, perhaps a childhood injury?

Analyzing her features like this, however, would always fail to capture the whole—would, in fact, miss the point entirely. Such as the way her eyes matched the glorious smile that animated her face to reveal a straightforwardness, an absence of guile that he found extremely attractive.

No, James thought, *she was not pretty in the trivial, Barbie doll sense of the word*. Her face had too much character for that, but he found her exceptionally attractive.

Saving the photograph to his hard drive, James began to read the text of her message and by the time he had finished, there was a knot of excitement and anticipation inside him that no amount of deep breathing would get rid of.

* * * * *

Two months earlier they had "met" in an Internet chat room where people involved in dominance and submission gathered to discuss their shared interests. It was a conveniently anonymous way of getting to know likeminded people. That they were in the same room at the same time was pure synchronicity since James hardly ever bothered with them these days — it had been a sudden whim in a bored moment.

James had welcomed her into the chat room amidst a chorus of greetings from other dominants and submissives, and since no one happened to be saying anything very much, he had brought up her profile. This said very little about her except to hint at a willingness to learn, and at a curiosity about dominance and submission. When he closed her profile window to return to the chat room she had gone and a few minutes later he had left, too. There it would have ended except that the next morning there was an email from her in his inbox.

Dear Sir,

I have never written to anyone before, and I am not sure how wise I am to be writing even now. I read your profile and since you emphasize the importance of a Master being also a teacher and guide to his submissive, I hoped you would not mind my asking a few questions?

About me — I am late twenties, single and professional. I work as a PA — Personal Assistant. The rest you can see on my profile if you care to look.

I've been intrigued about submission, bondage and domination for a little while now. I have been trying to learn as much as I can. It all sounds exciting and arousing, it speaks to a deep part of me that has had secret fantasies for as long as I can remember.

But those are fantasies… In real life, I work hard and I am no one's doormat. In fact, when things really matter to me, I am really assertive, I won't tolerate being patronized or insulted. I mean, I see the abusive language the "submissive" women in chat rooms seem to put up with, even expect, and it just turns my stomach even when it's not directed at me.

So, I'm not sure that I'm what anyone would call submissive, yet all my fantasies involve my being overpowered, swept off my feet, bound and helpless… Perhaps I have a submissive sexuality, but not a submissive spirit? Is that even possible? This is so confusing!

I'm proud of the life I've made. I'm independent, and I respect myself and my achievements...it's not been easy! So why should I be aroused by thoughts of being controlled and subservient? It just doesn't make any sense to me...can you help me to understand?

If you are too busy to answer my questions, that's okay – I don't want to waste your time.

Sincerely,

Kate

James had smiled and spent half an hour he really did not have to spare replying, touched by the genuine tone of her writing. His interest was piqued by the fact that in her very first email to someone, she had struck right to the core issue of D/s relationships, however naïvely.

Dear Kate,

Perhaps some general pointers will help clarify things for you...

First, being submissive is something you do or don't do, it's not who you are and, further, being submissive is something you do with someone else whom you trust and respect. It is a special gift you offer only to that specific man whom you feel merits and deserves it.

Yes, the BDSM world is full of people who are heavily identified with being either dominant or submissive, but – for example – that is equally true for people who cannot distinguish between their professional role and their core identity, or the mother who has invested so much of herself in her children that she feels "lost" when they leave home and has to figure out who she is all over again...in other words, confusing what you do with who you are is a very common tendency.

My view is that your fantasies and desires are separate from your core identity, as is what you do when you explore them. However, perhaps paradoxically, through this exploration you can uncover, embrace and learn to love that "core you" in a way that never happens when these fantasies are denied and repressed.

Therefore, I believe that only truly strong women truly submit. After all, to surrender control of yourself, you have to first be in control of yourself — as much as anyone ever is! — or what are you giving up? What are you offering your chosen dominant? If you would obey anyone, acquiesce to the demands that any man made of you, how can he possibly feel any sense of pride from the trust you place in him or feel honoured by the gift of your submission and obedience?

A dominant man is not a domineering man — still less is he a control freak. A control freak is by definition deeply insecure. However in control he appears to be, deep down, he is frightened of life, frightened of women and probably even of himself. He seeks to impose his will through manipulation of another's vulnerabilities. He is threatened by another person's autonomy and therefore never seeks to empower those he claims to love, indeed he is quite indifferent to the negative effects he has since other people are not really real to him.

Like a very small child, he is demanding and liable to throw a tantrum if he does not get his own way. Indeed, on an emotional level, he may not have matured much beyond the age of four or five years old. Such adults are dangerous and best avoided.

By contrast, a dominant, at least as I define him, doesn't need to control. He is just extremely good at being in control and handles responsibility well. He's mature enough to know that you can't control life, that you have to go with the flow and yet he has a firm grip on those aspects of his life that can be ordered. The control he enjoys taking gives him a freedom of expression and, indeed, he mostly uses his control to free the self-expression of his submissive for their mutual enjoyment.

A considerable part of the pleasure for him, at least that which is not purely erotic, is in how honoured he feels by the responsibility and trust given him. That a woman who can perfectly well manage her life without him, chooses to surrender herself to him.

Why? For the same reason that any lovers are bound to each other — together they are happier than when they are apart. The only real difference as I see it, is that in a relationship involving dominance and submission, the couples' deepest sexual desires and honest emotional needs are communicated and acknowledged from the very beginning, which is not an unreasonable foundation for any relationship.

I hope that this helps at least as a starting point. I have deliberately avoided going into things in any great psychological depth. It would take something the size of a small book to begin to do the subject any justice. Please feel free to address any further questions you may have to me and I'll try to answer them as best I can.

Regards,

James

Kate's reply had been appreciative and grateful, and within a few days, they had exchanged several more emails, gradually sharing ever more intimate thoughts, feelings and desires, as well as everyday information concerning the nature of each other's work and interests. Apart from their powerful mutual attraction, they discovered many other things in common.

Slowly, during several chats via instant messaging online that went on late into the night, they began to reveal still more personal information that spoke of their dreams, hopes and fears, and in doing so, exposed vulnerabilities that in turn conveyed the trust they were beginning to feel towards one another. Despite the openness and intimacy of their conversations, at James' insistence Kate gave him no specific detail that would enable him to trace her to where she lived.

While accepting this, she was confused by it, thinking at first that perhaps forbidding her to divulge such information was his way of protecting himself from being obliged to reciprocate. But as time went by and they talked more often, she noticed that in fact he happily volunteered such information to her, and actively encouraged her to check him out. Eventually, she felt she needed an explanation and asked for one in an email.

James wrote in reply —

I am trying, in case things don't work out between us, to instill in you a strong awareness of the need to protect your privacy. This need not hinder in any way the process of our getting to know each other, but when we eventually meet, as I hope we will, the only thing I will know about your identity is what you look like from the photos you have sent and your cell phone number – which you can easily change.

After we meet, depending on how we feel and what the chemistry between us is like, will be soon enough for you to tell me more. It's actually quite hard for me to write this because I don't want to alarm you…I know I'm a good guy. But on the Internet, especially if you are a woman, a presumption of guilt before proof of innocence is definitely the way to go!

James went on to explain how safe meetings were arranged and how she would prepare a schedule of safe calls to a friend. He knew, of course, that it was entirely unnecessary with regard to him, but he knew equally well that the meeting of minds that chatting online represented need not, and often did not, translate into a physical and emotional attraction in real life. Her future safety was his concern, and he took his responsibility to an inexperienced submissive woman very seriously.

Chapter Three
Anticipation

ဢ

The exchange continued for several weeks, exploring in luscious detail some of Kate's fantasies as her confidence grew and she felt more and more able to open her secret mind to James. James never judged her, and while he encouraged her to express herself with complete candor and made no bones about the fact that the fantasies she shared with him aroused him to an exceptional degree, he was also concerned that through the process of revealing her desires, she came to a place of self-acceptance and self-understanding.

Often he would reciprocate by telling her of some of his earlier experiences with previous submissives, though he never boasted or showed off, indeed he mostly spoke of these experiences in terms of what he had learned from mistakes he had made. Kate was fascinated to learn how his understanding had developed over the years he had been exploring.

James' approach to relationships involving domination and submission, bondage and discipline was quite different from anything Kate had come across on the Internet. He explained that this was because of the years he had spent studying eastern esoteric sexual techniques as an extension of his training in the martial arts, which allowed him a fairly unique perspective. While never disparaging, he questioned some of the assumptions made by those who lived what they termed the "D/s lifestyle", most especially their tendency to see themselves as inherently different from what they referred to as the "vanilla" world.

During one online chat, they explored the subject in greater depth —

James: The simple fact is that *everybody* has sexual fantasies that involve at least some degree of sadomasochism. Of course, some people are so hung up about sex—even of the most ordinary kind—that they would never admit these fantasies to themselves, let alone describe them to someone else.

Kate: Oh, my god! But...hell that means my grandma has these fantasies!?

James: Oh, yes! Though, of course, many people like your grandma have them completely unconsciously. They might have some vividly erotic dreams, but they forget them the instant they wake up, because the gulf between their ordinary waking mind and their unconscious desires is simply too huge for them to bridge. That said, look beneath the apparently respectable veneer of mainstream romantic fiction—the kind of stuff your grandma probably reads—and there are all kinds of dark undercurrents.

Kate: Really? I always thought they were pretty dull.

James: I'm not saying they're overtly erotic! Only that when a heroine is kidnapped by some merciless pirate it is what is *not* said that sparks the reader's imagination and taps into illicit eroticism. Why do you think they're so incredibly popular?

Kate: I see. So the sadomasochistic fantasies are kind of subliminal?

James: Exactly! What people find acceptable is all about their upbringing and the culture they're born into. Various S&M practices have been around for thousands of years because there's always been a very thin dividing line between pleasure and pain. At best, they were always associated with a sense of the sacred. My problem is with how people nowadays tend to trivialize it or take it for granted.

Kate: You mean like in the fetish clubs?

James: Well, yes and no. They can be great fun and very liberating, I think it's a huge step forward for people to be open and honest about their sexuality. I just think it's a problem when sex becomes totally recreational and not treated with very much respect. I think that dilutes something that should be a meaningful and intimate experience.

Kate: I agree! But I think it's cool that people aren't so ashamed about this kind of thing. I mean it's got to be better than the days when women weren't supposed to enjoy sex at all!

James: That goes without saying—women in particular have been feeling guilty about their desires for far too long. That reminds me... If you look closely enough, then you often see that despite completely denying their sexual fantasies, people's sadism or masochism finds some sort of expression in their everyday life, though it's normally camouflaged as socially acceptable behavior.

Kate: Hmm...like a boss who bullies his employees? I've had a few of those!

James: Yes, exactly! He might be treating his staff extremely cruelly on a daily basis, but because he's in denial of his sadism, he'll justify his behaviour in terms of his profit margin, or the greater good or some other euphemism for making peoples' lives a misery. In fact, such people are incredibly skilled at justifying what they do, to themselves and to others...and most of the time the bully's victims are masochistic, submissive or "people-pleasing" enough to put up with it.

Kate: But why do people put up with that kind of abusive behaviour?

James: Because their need to please is unconscious. When a submissive recognises her need to please a chosen dominant or acknowledges her masochistic desires then she hopefully selects someone worthy of her trust. She submits to a specific individual and, at the same time, will often simultaneously stop being submissive in general. She stops being a "people pleaser" and starts being a *person* pleaser! But people in general put up with this sort of crap because they convince themselves that doing so makes them a good person.

Kate: A good person? I don't understand?

James: They define themselves by what they tolerate without complaint. The nastier someone's behaviour towards them, the more noble they feel in their suffering. When someone is really cruel to them then — as the victim — they get to feel really righteous as if proof of someone else's badness proves their goodness. Also, they feel like they've done some kind of penance for whatever it is they feel guilty about…normally the negative feelings they've kept bottled up for years.

Kate: Wow — that's screwed up!

James: Yes, but it's also very common — to the point of being almost ordinary. Our society is very screwed up when it comes to things sexual and emotional — just look at how comfortable we are with watching movies that portray people being killed in all kinds of graphically brutal ways, yet we censor images of people making love…

Kate: Okay, yes, I've always thought that was pretty crazy — but what about those people who are into S&M or those who live their lives as dominant and submissive, or Master and slave?

James: Well at least they've taken the positive step of acknowledging what turns them on and making their decisions conscious…which makes it less likely that they'll act out their desires unconsciously, at least in theory — but the rationalisations abound.

Kate: What do you mean?

James: Well you don't have to be a genius to figure out that if a guy can only get it up when a girl is completely helpless, he might just have a few insecurities! Maybe he has unconscious fears of being rejected or criticised — with the girl bound and gagged he's safe on both counts!

Kate: And even more if he makes up the rules on what she can and can't say and can punish her for displeasing him. That's a hell of a way to protect a fragile ego!

James: Yes, beneath the façade of being a regular "he-man"! What's critical is how aware people are of the choices they make, and the extent to which they've become jaded and desensitised. I mean if a guy can't see a pretty girl without wishing she was tied up — if that's the only time he feels confident — then that has to ring some alarm bells!

Kate: Do you think becoming jaded is inevitable? On the Internet I've seen some shocking things other people seem to take for granted.

James: No, not inevitable, but it is a real danger because of the way people tend to escalate things. For example a guy gets turned on when he imagines doing cruel things to girls. He probably spends a long time feeling really bad about himself — thinks there must be something wrong with him. Then he finds out that there are other people just like him — they call themselves "dominants" or "tops" or whatever jargon appeals to them — and that somehow, if he calls himself a dominant and finds a compatible girl, then it's okay for him to do his thing.

Kate: Isn't it?

James: Sometimes yes — it's fine — it's a step on the path of self-understanding, but people tend to confuse that single step with the whole journey. If no one gets harmed as they fulfil each other's fantasies, then it can be wonderfully intimate. Sadly it's not always that straightforward because what matters is not what you do, but the intention you do it with.

Kate: Sorry, you've lost me there — can you give me an example maybe?

James: It's just that you have to look at what the underlying motivation is and also at what the longer term consequences will be. It's just too lazy to say "well, I like it therefore it's okay" — people enjoy snorting cocaine, but that doesn't make it a wise thing to do on a regular basis, let alone make your life revolve around it.

Kate: So…

James: Let me finish what I'm saying please, Kate.

Kate: Sorry!

James: The problem comes from people getting desensitized to pleasure. At first just spanking a girl mildly is a wild rush for the dominant. He only just turns her bottom pink, but it feels great and she enjoys it and they have a great time. A year later, though, that's really tame. He's moved on to much more extreme things—now the beatings he gives his submissive leave bruises that take a week or two to heal. But he has to do that in order to feel the same or only very slightly greater level of pleasure he first felt from giving her a mild spanking. And it could well be the same girl—except that now she only gets turned on and is able to go deeply into her submissive feelings when the pain is really intense and the endorphin levels are really high. Compared to where they started, they've both become desensitized adrenaline junkies, but they think they're now more advanced!

Kate: But I've talked to subs that say they feel wonderful bearing the marks inflicted by their lover...

James: That's fine, and yes, she could feel that they're badges of the trust, love and mutual understanding they share—so long as they've found their own balance—the dynamic equilibrium that makes D/s work. The problem is when it just continuously escalates as people act out their bullshit on each other—sometimes doing real harm—and defending it in the name of D/s and their right to freedom of expression. Actually, most of the harm that gets done is emotional and not physical. Physical bruises do heal, but the wounds to the heart and spirit take a hell of a lot longer—if they truly ever heal completely.

Kate: I understand that...but how does it apply to D/s?

James: Like I said it's about understanding consequences, motivation and intention. Let's say that a girl has been brought up to feel guilty about her need for sex. That's incredibly common in our society where a randy guy is a *real* man, but a randy girl is called all kinds of vicious names—slut, whore, bitch in heat and worse. So this girl feels guilty about her lusty drives and is in a lot of conflict, then she learns about dominance and submission and figures she's a submissive. Now she has a category to identify with and learns that there are lots of other women just like her. She no longer feels alone or isolated, or so bad about herself—all VERY good things!

James: So she begins to explore, and eventually she finds somebody she likes and trusts enough to submit to. Pretty quickly, she discovers that if she is "punished" by her dominant then the guilt temporarily dissolves and she is able to enjoy all sorts of sexual fun without feeling bad afterwards. She's paid for her pleasure in advance with an equal dose of suffering, and after all, the only decisive step she took was to submit to him...everything else that happens is no longer her responsibility so what does she have to feel guilty about? And if she does feel bad, well, she can always provoke her dominant into punishing her a bit more. None of this is conscious, mind you—but if you step back and look at the pattern then you see it clearly. Do you see the problem?

Kate: She never learns not to feel guilty? She doesn't change deep down?

James: Exactly right. In fact unknowingly—probably—the dominant is actually perpetuating her guilty feelings. Certainly, he's doing nothing to resolve them because they're a major part of how he controls her. Of course, neither of them figure this out because, like most people, they can't see farther than the great sex.

Kate: That's really sad!

James: What is really sad is that in BDSM and D/s there is an amazing opportunity for self-healing, profound intimacy and deep understanding, as well as mind-blowing sex—but not if you use it as a way—as a justification for—acting out your most negative beliefs irresponsibly.

Kate: So I have to heal the part of me that wants to be submissive?

James: No! She does not need to be healed! There's nothing wrong with her! She's loving, sensual, kind and generous—she's wonderful, she's a beautiful part of you that can guide you on the path of your self-healing—of becoming ever more whole as a person throughout your life. What you need to get rid of are feelings of guilt, shame, embarrassment—all those things that make you feel bad about yourself, your body and the pleasures it affords you…

Kate: But James, I don't feel guilty or feel bad things about myself!

James: No you don't—because they're UN-conscious. That's what the word means, but they're there—all intertwined with lots of beautiful, wild and wanton sexual energy that's screaming to be expressed…and tries to find its way out through your fantasies.

Kate: Sorry, but I'm not convinced—I don't feel guilty about sex.

James: No? Don't be so sure. It may be true that there are many aspects of you that are guilt-free—conscious parts of you, but there are other aspects that hold on to these negatives until they're really resolved. For example, why does it turn you on to be tied up?

Kate: I don't know—it just does.

James: You don't think it might be something to do with being helpless?

Kate: Well, yes… I like that feeling…with someone I trust, of course.

James: Why?

Kate: Why what?

James: Why do you enjoy feeling helpless?

Kate: I don't know.

James: Well, when was the last time you were so powerless? At what other time in your life have you been so completely in another's power?

Kate: I've never been—Oh wait! Of course, when I was little!

James: Exactly! So the helpless feelings take you right back to a time before you learned to have any inhibitions. A time when as a baby you experienced your body as an ever changing kaleidoscope of sensations...before you learned to distinguish between sensual and sexual pleasure, and long before you learned to distinguish "right" from "wrong". When you're bound and helpless you are free—because you have no choice, you're resolved of responsibility for your response, so you don't feel guilty about it...not even unconsciously.

Kate: Wow!

James: Yeah, wow...once you understand that pretty much all D/s is about a very creative form of regression—about reconnecting to sources of pleasure deemed "wrong" or "bad" by our social conditioning—then you can really understand the motivation and, more importantly still, as a dominant I can really be clear about what my intention is. Since I know that it's ultimately all about remembering how to be completely sensually alive then I can guide my submissive through experiences that are both wildly erotic and very safe. For me D/s is a steppingstone, a framework—a temporary dynamic that allows me to create an incredibly trusting foundation and paves the way to much more intimately loving, though no less erotic, sensuality.

Kate: What do you mean by temporary?

James: I mean that as two people in the roles of dominant and submissive we explore the dynamic fully and completely. We relish every moment, we mine its depths for the nuggets of gold we will find, and we extract from it all the pleasure we possibly can—but that as we grow and evolve in our relationship, the enactment of roles will inevitably become less and less meaningful. After all, they only reflect limited aspects of who we are, and I want to be in relationship with the whole of myself, and love my lover for the whole of who she is, not just the part of her that is submissive.

Kate: That sounds lovely. Free to be ALL of who I am and not hide anything away...

James: Yes, it's worth everything, that kind of freedom.

* * * * *

There had been many such online conversations until one Sunday morning he woke to find a much more personal email from her.

Dear James,

I'm going to be honest with you and admit to something I feel bad about. When we began to talk, I thought that writing to you would help me to see that there was some obvious flaw in my character that explained why I need this so much. I thought that you were going to just bullshit me and in seeing through your bullshit, I would be able to get back to what I've always known as sensible and safe.

Instead, the opposite has happened. I realize there is no return to how things used to be. Remembering how frustrated I was, how deeply conflicted I felt, I wonder why I would ever want to turn the clock back? But if I'm to be honest...and I want to be with you...there is still a big part of me that does. Maybe I'm just scared.

Am I making any sense?

Of course, I realize that having opened this Pandora's box, I can't close it again. I cannot pretend the feelings and the dreams and desires aren't there, though sometimes I try very hard! Why? Because it frightens me! God, it would be so easy if you were some kind of psychopathic sex maniac! I could just dismiss the whole thing as crazy, and go get some therapy or something...but instead, you turn out to be the sanest man I've ever talked to, and you not only tell me it's okay to be frightened but even explain how such fears are inevitable, not even a bad thing to be feeling, and then go on to explain how such fears can be resolved and let go of. Every time I think I'm wrong or crazy, you give me a way to understand myself and accept who I am and the feelings I have.

Anyway, this has all been a prelude to saying that I would really like to meet with you, if you feel you want to, of course... I don't want to be presumptuous, but you've said you enjoy our chats and reading my emails, and you said you liked my photos – I've attached another one...just a snapshot. Does that sound good to you?

Kisses,

Kate

xxx

* * * * *

So now James sat, staring at her photo, and wondering how the meeting would be for them. There were two obvious ways of handling it, one sensible and cautious but essentially unromantic and almost devoid of eroticism. The other very much more romantic, potentially extremely erotic, but equally possibly disastrous if things did not work out the way he hoped they would.

In the former, they would meet somewhere public and just talk, they would have agreed beforehand that there would be little or no physical contact, however much desired, which would be the focus of a second meeting—a good way of building a sort of sexual tension, but not reflective of the degree of intimacy they had already established and begun to feel for one another.

In the latter there would be no rules governing what would happen beyond her consenting to whatever she felt like doing at the time. In other words, it would be almost indistinguishable from any normal "first date". The problem with this was that it set the precedent of the control being hers—the normal girl-boy head games where he made a move and she rebuffed him for the sake of appearances, perhaps sustaining this over several meetings until finally she gave in, thereby maintaining a status quo she clearly did not want.

Happily, there was a third way that combined the best of the two alternatives and hopefully avoided any of the negatives, at least with careful handling and a willingness from both sides to make it work.

Dear Kate,

Yes, of course, meeting with you sounds good to me. Wonderful in fact! I've attached a website address of a little place I've found about halfway between us. Have a look and if you like it then we can arrange a time…perhaps at the weekend? Let's chat on the phone a few times in the next week. This will be a good steppingstone towards our meeting and we will be able to say very much more than can be said by email anyway. However, this does depend on whether you are willing to accept the terms on which I will meet you…

As you might expect, there are certain rules that you must be prepared to follow when we meet. They are not anything too challenging, so don't worry, but they will create the necessary foundation for what I hope will be further meetings. More importantly, they allow us both to relax because we both know what to expect while making for an enjoyably erotic beginning.

Firstly, I will tell you what will not happen. I will not touch any part of you except for your hand to greet you when we meet, and your mouth to kiss you when we part. You are free to initiate whatever contact you like, but I am not. Though chiefly designed to help you feel completely safe, this self-imposed limit makes a lot of other things possible, as you will see!

To the meeting you will wear a skirt no longer than knee-length and a blouse and jacket. You will wear a g-string but no bra, stockings and not tights, and you will have shaved yourself completely below your neck. You will arrive before me, and you will sit at the bar to wait, ensuring that your skirt is not between the seat and your bottom when you sit down.

When I arrive, you will rise to greet me, and you will address me always as "Sir". From that point on, you undertake to obey everything I tell you to do immediately. On this occasion, there is only one penalty for disobedience…I will leave. Any instruction I give you will be repeated twice if necessary. If after I have repeated myself for the second time you still have not obeyed, then I will simply get up and go.

Since I am reasonably aware of what kind of experience you have, you may be sure that I will not be asking you to do things that will be impossible for you to obey, though you may find some of them challenging. This is vital to determine whether or not your need to submit and learn obedience can make the leap from fantasy to reality. Though this might sound scary to you, everything I have learned about you during our conversations online and in our exchange of emails leads me to feel very confident that you will enjoy yourself enormously.

If you agree to these rules, then send me an email and we can arrange when to chat on the phone.

James

xxx

There was no reply that day and by the following evening he had to stop himself from somewhat obsessively checking his email and also his voicemail since he had given her his cell phone number. He was feeling very down, positively miserable as the evening went on, by now sure that he had pushed her too far too fast, though he thought he had been patient.

Above all, he knew what an awful beginning to a D/s relationship it would have been had he agreed to meet for just a chat. *The fact was*, he thought as he smiled ruefully, he *was* a nice guy, albeit with a wicked streak a mile wide. But still, an essentially decent man who was utterly disinterested in playing mind games or covertly manipulating other people.

He shuddered as he thought of all those "dating rules". How many times a "good" girl was supposed to say "no" before saying "yes". How many times to let the phone ring so as not to appear to have been waiting anxiously for the call. What the proper interval should be between one date and the next...

Probably all well intended, he thought, *but hell if you were thinking about sleeping with someone*—he grinned—*okay, fucking them...*

He noticed how his own vocabulary had become caught up in the vernacular of "nice" Hollywood romance.

Then surely to god, you should be able to *talk* to them, have the courage to be honest and express your truth from the heart? He sighed, wondering if there was anyone out there who felt as he did. Sadly, it seemed he had misjudged her.

* * * * *

When her reply finally came sometime after midnight, and long after James had given up and gone to bed with a heavy heart, he was lying in bed trying to read a novel, though the words on the page just swam before his tired eyes. Then from the next room, his home office, he heard the chime of delivered mail and barely restraining himself from running, he rushed to his computer. He felt a surge of relief even before he opened it, and then laughed out loud as he began to read.

Dear James,

OH, MY GOD!! I can't believe I'm doing this! I have been totally unable to think about anything else since I received your email and typically I get two-thirds of the way through a lengthy and very jumbled, and overexcited reply to you when my screen freezes and everything is lost... I hadn't even written down your number to call you...so I thought I'd just have to wait until the computer gets repaired, but then I remembered about the local twenty-four hour Internet café – and here I am at midnight!

It has been intensely frustrating not being able to contact you...you must have thought I was running shy...what else could you think?

But in fact, I love your idea of limiting the degree to which we can touch, it makes me feel safe while at the same time my mind is reeling at all the possible things you might instruct me to do, even so, I'm sure you will surprise me! Can I ask you to be patient, though?

I will obey, if you don't ask me to do anything too terribly embarrassing in public, but I will have to conquer my fears first, so the only thing I struggle with is "immediate obedience" though I think even this is deliberate, isn't it? I mean the best thing would be for me to just do as I'm told, hesitating will only make it more difficult...and yes, I'm sure you will challenge me but equally sure you won't ask me to do anything impossible...

I'm just repeating myself, aren't I? I'll stop and simply say that I agree to your rules, and that I really like the look of the place you suggest to meet at.

What time do you suggest? Or should I say, "instruct" me to be there? I can be there anytime from noon onwards…

I hope you haven't given up on me!

Your very excited and "intending to be obedient",

Kate

xxxxxxxxxxx

Chapter Four
Sleepless Nights

ဢ

James could hardly stop smiling, often laughing for no apparent reason in the days that followed. They talked on the phone a couple of times, though he deliberately kept each conversation short, saying straightforwardly to her that though he would always be completely honest with her, his fear was that as an intensely passionate man his tongue would run away with him, diluting the moment of their meeting. They had exchanged so many dozens of emails and chatted for so many hours online via instant messaging there was little more to say until they met in person.

Communicating feelings was always fraught with the danger that one's words might be misinterpreted, but the danger was much greater when you could not see the expression on someone's face or hear the full tonal qualities of their voice, feel their presence and the immediacy of their response. *Though*, he thought, given the erotic tension that had by now been building slowly for months, that she would willingly obey him, he wanted to contain the energy until they were face-to-face.

This was also why he made no attempt whatsoever to dominate her over the phone, instead, simply clarifying, where necessary, his intentions and reassuring her on several points as to what he would not be doing. In a gently teasing way, he communicated to her that he knew very well how wantonly aroused she was feeling, that there would be no hiding behind coyness and "ladylike" appearances. At least, not as far as he was concerned.

* * * * *

The Friday night before their meeting was a largely sleepless one for both of them, though for different reasons. Kate had been feeling a knot of butterflies growing in her stomach even before receiving his email agreeing to meet with her. Those butterflies now closely resembled bats, as she lay curled up in her bed with her arms wrapped protectively around her middle, hugging herself and trying hard to quiet the tumultuous thoughts that raced through her mind.

Torn between arousal, anticipation, excitement and apprehension, she eventually got up at about two a.m. and turned on the computer. Starting at the beginning, Kate read through all their emails, hers and his, all neatly saved along with the photos he had sent of himself.

Kate found him enormously attractive. James' face with its deep laugh lines was not the pretty face of a boy. His features were an expression of what she knew from their conversations to have been a sometimes difficult life. Slightly graying hair cut short, thick eyelashes over startlingly blue eyes, a wide sensuous mouth and strong jaw.

His photographs revealed many aspects of him. In one, he was staring intensely at something off camera and the look was chilling, even a little intimidating, yet another photo, taken in the same room at about the same time, showed a mischievous smile and gave her a sense of approachable friendliness born out by their conversations and by his sometimes wicked sense of humor. Other photos that had obviously been taken on holiday abroad showed him to be muscular in the way of a natural athlete rather than the heavy musculature she associated with the bodybuilder type.

But it was as she reread their emails that Kate developed an insight that gave her a clue to the real character of this man who was in so many ways still a mystery to her. It was as she was piecing together the strands of his history, mostly concerning his relationships both personal and professional, in so far as he had mentioned the latter at all, when she thought she saw something of a pattern.

It was vague and she very nearly dismissed it as just due to her tiredness, but then once again he used the expression, "of course I had no alternative but…" She saw that, in fact, there were *plenty* of other alternatives, alternatives that he was obviously perfectly aware of, yet dismissed out of hand. For James there was only *one* way of proceeding—the way that matched his sense of personal honor, his sense of what the right thing to do was, which inevitably was almost never the easy thing.

However, to act contrary to his personal code was clearly not merely more difficult for him, it was just impossible. He saw the easy option clearly, but simply refused to consider taking it. Kate read more, and went back and reread again and finally began to understand.

He was romantic, but at the same time almost totally devoid of sentimentality, a rare combination. He was very conscious of the choices he made, aware that sometimes he made life much more difficult for himself than was strictly necessary because he refused to play other people's games and never by anyone else's rules.

A good example was from his early twenties—James had dated a girl who had recently been dumped by her boyfriend. James had been completely unaware that he was part of her devious plan to make her ex-boyfriend so jealous through flaunting her relationship with James that the old boyfriend took her back. James spoke in quite a heartfelt manner of how deeply in love with her he had been, while gently ridiculing himself for his ignorance and naivety concerning this kind of female.

Eventually, goaded by the girl's taunts, the ex-boyfriend had come to confront him. The man was aggressively drunk and determined to pick a fight. James had refused, one of his "of course I had no alternative but…" statements. Here James was alluding to the fact that he had spent all his youth in the disciplined study of a variety of martial arts. By his early twenties, he was running advanced courses in unarmed combat for the army and police force and was acknowledged by even these professional warriors as a man with exceptional talents. This Kate inferred from other things James had said—he was proud of his achievements but never boasted of them.

Consequently, the outcome of any such fight was a foregone conclusion. It was not that his personal code prevented him from fighting. He would do so without hesitation, but only to protect himself or defend another, and then only if there were no other alternative. Should he want to fight for the sheer enjoyment of using his martial skills he would take on someone his equal, not some drunken thug.

Since the ex-boyfriend was an idiot responding to the malicious wiles of a scheming little bitch, James felt more sorry for him that anything...she had made a fool of him, too, as he now realized. Concluding that they probably deserved one another, he had determined that at least she would no longer manipulate him and he certainly was not going to give her the thrill of being fought over. So, he had walked away and refused to have anything further to do with either of them.

What he did not say, but what Kate now saw clearly, was how betrayed he had felt and how very easy it would have been for him to win the affections, probably devoted affections, of such a girl...provided, of course, that he was willing to play the jealous lover and fight for her as often as she required. It was a classic example of how he refused to play by other people's rules.

In similar ways through the hours that they talked, though nothing he had said had ever been obvious, certainly never in the sense that he was seeking sympathy, he had quietly and with dignity shared more of himself than any man she had ever met. Hell, she knew less about some men she had dated for months! James was not afraid to be open with her, to share with her those things that mattered most to him, and yet at the same time, he retained this sense of untroubled poise. He would tell her about his worries and concerns so that she might better understand him, but he did not expect her to fix them for him, just to be there for him.

At an even deeper level than before, Kate realized that by some strange quirk of fate she had connected with a very special man. Perhaps too special? She felt all her old insecurities well up inside, the vulnerable fear that she might not be good enough for him. She quickly shrugged them off. She was too damn tired to indulge herself in painful memories and the still more painful feelings that went with them.

Sighing, she shut down the computer and staggered sleepily off to bed. She set her alarm for midmorning, grateful that fatigue had drugged her mind to insensibility and the promise of sleep rose in her like a wave. Her last thought before it engulfed her was, *Please...let tomorrow be the beginning of something wonderful.*

* * * * *

James' sleeplessness by contrast was neither anxiety-based nor remotely analytical of her character. He was deliciously tormented by the many images that swirled through his mind of how she would respond, how she would look, how she would move — tantalizing and frustrating — yet he savored the anticipation, and enjoyed the building excitement.

Grinning to himself in the darkness, his cock pulsing thick and heavy on his belly, he allowed the delightful images to flicker across his mind's inner screen.

Much earlier in the week, he had thought through what he would be asking of her, keeping to general principles rather than trying to form a rigid plan since so much would depend on her response. The essential principle was clear, and formed the basis of everything he did in dominating a submissive girl. Simply stated it was —

I will make you do everything you have ever secretly dreamt of doing, then make you want to do those things you have yet to dream of.

He thought he might have finally found a girl with the courage to dive deep into the ocean of sensual feeling...to walk the path of submission right through to its wondrous end — itself a beginning. A beginning that James longed for with every fiber of his being.

Tomorrow would tell.

Chapter Five
The Manor House

&

The next morning, about two hours' drive apart—two sleepy people struggled out of bed aided by the brilliant sunlight of a cloudless day and their extreme excitement. Kate had laid out her clothes the night before. Her morning's progress through showering and fixing her hair and makeup was smooth and organized...and in complete contrast to the bat-sized butterflies once more active in her stomach.

By comparison, James' preparations were anything but organized, since throughout his life clothes had never been high on his list of priorities. Though he knew how to dress well when he chose to, as he did this day.

Showered and shaved after his morning five-mile run, James paid much more than his usual attention to the clothes he wore. When he was finally satisfied he had hit the right balance between comfort and a certain stylishness—he loathed anything flashy or too fashionable, but enjoyed genuine quality—he went down to his breakfast.

James felt only a pleasant sense of anticipation now. Partly because he had disciplined himself against expectation, but also because he knew that the important thing was to enjoy the moment and the adventure of the day. If things didn't work out, then, deeply upsetting though that would be, he would worry about it when and if it happened.

They had agreed only to call one another in the event of some unforeseen delay, so by eleven in the morning, both were driving towards their mutual destination enjoying the sunshine and feeling the excitement mount steadily.

* * * * *

Kate pulled onto the gravel drive leading up to the country hotel and restaurant where they had arranged to meet. With plenty of time to spare, she sat in her car for a while, admiring the old Manor house. Formal rose gardens framed its south and west sides while acres of less formal gardens, woodland and parkland rolled away towards the north with the silver gleam of a river in the distance. The house itself, some three hundred years old, was ivy-clad and though originally built to impose itself upon the landscape, had been softened by centuries of weather and use, such that it seemed warm, friendly and welcoming.

Kate left her car and walked carefully across the gravel sweep of the driveway not wishing to trip in her high heels. Smoothing down her skirt as she crossed the threshold into the Manor brought some color to her cheeks. She had driven with her bare bottom against the sun-warmed leather of the car seat, anticipating what she would now have to do by instruction at the bar.

In the reception area, she told the young girl behind the desk that she was meeting a friend for lunch and would wait in the bar. Receiving directions and a friendly smile, she glanced at her watch, which showed she had plenty of time to freshen up. She followed signs to the ladies' room.

The room was well laid out with the necessary cubicles to one side, sinks and mirrors on the other. A somewhat unusual feature was that the wall straight ahead was entirely mirrored from floor to ceiling, and she could not help but stop and look at herself.

Glancing at the empty cubicles to make absolutely certain that there was no one else there, she turned back to the door and saw that it had a bolt. Smiling mischievously, she locked it and returned to stand before the mirror.

She had shaved herself as instructed several days earlier and kept herself smooth since then. It was the first time she had been completely hairless since she was a girl. The newly smooth look of her body fascinated her and she could not resist the temptation... *What a shameful slut I'm becoming!* she thought, laughing softly.

In the mirror, Kate saw the flush in her cheeks and made herself stand taller as she ran her hands down her body, momentarily opening her light jacket to feel her nipples prominent through the silk of her blouse, then smoothing down over her belly and hips before lifting her short skirt to reveal herself to the mirror.

Her theme had been blacks and whites, so while her jacket was white—her blouse, skirt, stockings and shoes were black. The g-string and garter belt were a startling white in contrast, especially against her lightly tanned skin.

Kate looked at herself critically, concerned and wondering if she would be made to exhibit herself so to James. She shivered in anticipation and hoped, really hoped that he would find her attractive. With an embarrassed smile, she remembered how often she had fantasized about being made to expose herself to her lover's gaze. But in all her fantasies, he was a faceless stranger, or perhaps some ruggedly handsome movie star, in any case, in her fantasies, he was always a man who passionately desired her...would James?

Kate let her skirt drop and turned to the mirrors above the sinks to wash her hands, and then freshened her lipstick while she cast a critical eye over her makeup. Satisfied that at least she looked presentable, she took a deep breath, unbolted the door and made her way to the bar.

At this time of day, the bar was almost empty. A young man, really still a boy, looked self-conscious in an ill-fitting waistcoat and bow tie as he polished glasses behind the bar. An elderly couple sat reading in companionable silence on easy chairs placed in the sunshine streaming through a large bay window.

Kate smiled at the bartender and asked him for a glass of white wine before settling herself on a barstool. She waited until he turned away to fill the glass before flicking her skirt out from beneath her, feeling the soft, warm, red leather on her skin, deliciously sensual. She called her friend on her mobile to let her know she had arrived safely and promised to call in a couple of hours time, though in this lovely setting she felt entirely safe.

She took a deep breath, wondering at her composure. She was not relaxed precisely, but neither was she agitated or anxious. Perhaps it was a false calm as sometimes happens before a storm.

At least now that she was here there was a sense of commitment, of no turning back, quite unlike the journey here when she had actually needed to pull off the road several times to muster her courage. She had sat quietly in the car and renewed her determination, quelling the rising panic in her stomach and mastering the urge to turn back.

While the road back home held no fears in the way the road before her most certainly did, the life choice it represented was terrifying — that things would stay the same as they had always been. Scary as it was, the choice to be here was a choice for change, for adventure and new experiences…

…and possibly much more.

Chapter Six
First Impressions

ହେ

James drove slowly up the sweeping drive to the Manor, enjoying the sounds of the crunch of tires on gravel and the soft growl of his sports car's powerful engine. It was a lovely day for motoring and an excellent day for walking through the Manor's splendid gardens and parkland after their lunch together...if all went as well as he hoped it would.

He had stayed at the Manor once before to attend a business conference. Bored with the conference, he had escaped to wander around the grounds whenever possible and so knew them well. He also knew that the hotel served excellent food in a beautiful setting. It was the ideal place for their meeting and for a moment he fantasized that years hence they would return here on anniversaries, laughing together as old friends as they remembered today.

James shook himself and let it go. He knew what he wanted, but it did no good to raise his expectations. He had been deliberately deceived in the past, and while he had never lost hope altogether, he had been deeply discouraged on several prior occasions by the duplicity of people he had met via the Internet.

It always amazed him that these people thought they could get away with it—as if their lies would not become immediately apparent at the first meeting. He had met women who had blatantly doctored their photographs, trimming years off their age and a couple of dozen pounds off their weight—women who had lied about their marital status, and then had the audacity to presume that he would trust them.

Yes, he accepted, the *real* person he eventually met was a nice enough person. Had they been honest with him from the start, they might have become friends and he had some measure of compassion for the insecurities that led such women to practice deception, but there was no way he could seriously contemplate going forward with a relationship begun with and founded upon dishonesty.

Consequently, beneath his effortless veneer of poise, James' heart was beating hard as he approached the Manor's front entrance. Since he was familiar with the layout, he found his way to the bar without assistance and stood in the doorway watching her for a while as he felt all his anxiety fade away. He stood there captivated by her, relishing the opportunity to observe her while she was unselfconscious and therefore her more natural self. Everything he saw pleased him enormously.

Kate was clearly lost in thought, sipping her wine. As she licked her lips, a delicate, yet such an innocently sensual movement, he felt himself harden instantly, he knew with complete certainty that he wanted to possess this woman utterly. She started, her eyes flicking to her watch, and then to the door as he entered the bar. She sat motionless as he approached, gazing at him.

James seemed even taller somehow than she had expected, though she knew he was over six foot from their emails. Kate felt quite tiny in his presence, he seemed to fill the room, claiming it and making it his own simply by entering.

His self-assurance was not the flamboyant flashiness of a man out to impress. James' whole manner was calm and quietly authoritative, yet there was something in his walk, in the way he held himself and the tilt of his head that spoke of an inner power and a strength carefully controlled. A strength, reined in so as not to overwhelm or intimidate, yet instantly available should he wish to call upon it. Kate's immediate impression was of a powerful cat, not the ponderous majesty of a lion, more the sinuous grace and lithe power of a leopard—dangerous, beautiful and exciting. Kate trembled inside. If James was the predator, then, held by his eyes, she knew how it felt to be his prey.

Remembering her instructions, she stood as he held out his hand to enfold hers—his touch was gentle and cool as he smiled down at her, his deep blue eyes washing over her.

"You are lovely, Kate," James said, the words uttered as a statement of fact that brooked no argument and permitted no denial.

"Thank you," she said, blushing, gazing up at him and feeling more than merely flattered. "Sir," she added, after slightly too long a pause.

"Bring your wine, we can talk much more privately in the restaurant." James gently let her hand go and turned, leading the way.

The restaurant was a large room with a high-raftered ceiling hung with chandeliers, now unlit in broad daylight, and many central tables covered in snowy-white linen. Most of the tables were bare except for elegant flower arrangements at each table's center.

James walked past these and through a pair of ancient wooden doors into a large conservatory with a profusion of plants, some clearly tropical, that formed natural arbors in which more tables were placed. Each arbor affording a degree of privacy and giving a delightful atmosphere of moist, cool, green lushness on such a hot, bright day.

There were no waiters, it being some time before luncheon was formally available, so he led her to a table and withdrew the ornate metal-frame chair gesturing for her to sit. James sat opposite her, turning just in time to see her half-rise and flick her skirt out before sitting again with a blush.

Knowing what she had done, but not wishing to draw attention to it, though he strongly approved, he sat back in his chair and inquired as to her drive, and made other such small talk to put her at her ease, allowing her to adjust to him. Finally, sensing her beginning to relax, he leaned forward and said with a teasing manner, "You know, Kate, if you think me too intensely ugly to bear, we can simply enjoy a pleasant lunch together..." he paused, looking at her intently, "...so last chance — do you choose to obey?"

Kate looked down at the tablecloth for a few seconds, and then up into his eyes, "I choose to obey...Sir. I have been obedient already, you know?"

"Yes, I do know, and I greatly appreciate not having to correct you. That would not have been a good start. But now, I think things should become a little more challenging for you." It was not a question. "If you have been as obedient as you say, then you should be wearing a g-string?"

Kate nodded, "Yes, Sir, I am." Calling him "Sir", which she had assumed would feel awkward, was becoming easier with each repetition. James generated an aura that simply demanded respect, despite his open and friendly manner.

James placed his elbow on the table and held his hand out, palm up. "Then you will remove it and give it to me now." He spoke firmly, but his eyes smiled as he watched her.

Her first reaction was to freeze in her seat, her eyes widening. Her hand gripped the stem of her wineglass tightly, but after a few moments she relaxed and said, "Permission to visit the ladies' room, Sir?"

Shaking his head, he said, "Denied, here and now." James' hand opened farther, willing her to obey.

Kate stood up quickly. For a moment, he thought she would bolt, but then she peered around through the foliage and, seeing no one, hitched up her skirt at the sides, tearing her g-string down as she sat, modesty preserved by the tablecloth. Leaning forward, she placed the soft, lacy cotton in his outstretched palm.

"Good girl," said James approvingly. He closed his hand around the g-string and brought his clenched fist to his nose. "You smell delectable," he said, inhaling the combined perfume of her musk and the Chanel she had scented her pubis with that morning. "One of my favorite scents." He left it up to her to decide which he was referring to.

Kate was blushing prettily, but smiling now, feeling the satisfaction of passing his first test with a certain finesse. He tucked the g-string into his jacket pocket, arranging it somewhat like a handkerchief so it was clearly visible.

"Do you know what a slut is?" James spoke casually as if he were asking the most ordinary question in the world.

Kate looked at him, sensing his playfulness behind the words. "Can I make a wild guess that I am one?"

James grinned. "Well, you are and you are not, there are several definitions. One definition is that of a woman who is slovenly dressed. You, however, have dressed with exquisite taste and you look charmingly elegant."

Kate smiled at him, enjoying the compliment, but knowing there was more to come. She raised a questioning eyebrow.

"On the other hand, a young woman who is wearing no panties in a public room cannot really be said to be properly dressed, can she? So, you fulfill part of that definition. A slut is also defined as promiscuous, but despite your torrid fantasies, that is not you. The final definition is that of a saucy girl, a minx, a wanton...and I think all of those fit you very well, don't you agree?"

"So that would make me at least a two-thirds slut?" she said laughing.

James laughed with her. "I suppose it would." He turned as a waiter arrived and, having ordered their drinks and watched the waiter disappear again, said, "In popular psychology, you hear a lot of talk about the 'inner child'. Most people misuse the concept or don't apply it properly, but I want to use it in a special sense...your 'inner slut'. I want you to really connect with her today. To be lewd, wanton and to break some taboos. She is not *who* you are, she is just a part of you that you have neglected for far too long. So today, and I hope for the next few months, you're going to get to know her really well. Get the idea?"

Kate nodded, and looked at him attentively, wondering what on earth was going to happen next.

"Sit forward on your seat, Kate," James instructed. "Good, now the wine waiter will be back in a moment so hold your wineglass in your right hand and let your left hand drop beneath the table." James watched as she obeyed. "Now touch your pussy and look at me."

As if in a dream Kate obeyed, her thighs moving apart to accommodate her hand. She gasped softly as her cool fingers touched the moist heat of her pussy. Desperately she fought the urge to turn her head, convinced that someone must be watching her, but she resisted even though her eyelids fluttered as his cool blue eyes held her gaze with their gentle, firm strength.

"Good girl." James nodded in approval. "Now run your finger slowly up and down your pussy lips, just dipping in to touch your clit with each stroke."

He watched her obey, her eyes becoming misty and her mouth opening slightly as her face flushed and her features softened with desire. She felt his control almost as if he were touching her.

"Now slowly push your finger between your pussy lips for me, Kate." His voice calm, firm and completely in control. "Feel your wet heat and slowly push deeper...look at me, look into my eyes," James corrected her quickly as her eyes began to close. "Now spread your legs wider and lean back in your chair a little more...good...now press the heel of your palm into your belly and pull your clit hood back, stroke her gently for me...good girl."

James watched her intently, delighting in her, incredibly aroused and pleased by her graceful submission, but he mastered the urge to smile, knowing she needed him to be stern and strict to pull this off. He noticed the wine waiter returning out of the corner of his eye and quickly warned her not to stop, to keep stroking herself.

The waiter arrived and to Kate's relief stayed on James' side of the table. He began the small ceremony of uncorking and pouring the wine for James' approval. James tasted it and nodded for the waiter to pour without taking his eyes off hers— watching the color mount on her face and her eyes flutter as she fought the urge to close them. When the waiter went to fill Kate's glass, James caught his arm saying, "I'll pour for the lady."

When the waiter had bowed and withdrawn, James filled her glass and said, "You may stop stroking now. Take your hand away from your pussy." He watched the struggle in her, torn between the urge to continue, to sustain this pleasure to completion, and the relief of returning to more normal behavior.

"Take your wineglass and touch all around the rim with your left hand." He watched her comply. "Now lick your fingers for me."

James reached over and took her wineglass. Giving her his own glass, he lifted her wine to his nose, savoring the combined bouquet before drinking as she licked her fingers.

"Good girl. You taste delicious, don't you agree?"

Kate's voice was husky with desire. "Yes, Sir." She said nothing more, her thoughts racing so fast that she could not think what to say. James sensed her loss of composure and sought to soothe her by directing her attention to more mundane things. He picked up the menus the waiter had left and passed one over to her, taking wicked pleasure in the abruptness of the emotional shifts he was demanding of her.

At first startled by the sudden change, she hesitated looking at the menu as if it were some alien object, but then her expression relaxed and she took it from him. They spent the next few minutes discussing the food, James suggesting things she might like and occasionally translating from the French the menu was mostly written in.

Once James had learned the kinds of food she enjoyed, he took the menu from her and asking her to hold out her hand, he gave her a small zipped bag he had taken from his pocket.

"You will go to the ladies' room and open the bag. Follow the instructions you find inside precisely, and then return as quickly as you can. I will order for you. Off you go!"

James smiled at her with a look she knew promised that this would be something still more challenging. He picked up her handbag and gave it to her to take with her, not wanting to trick her into staying. It must be her choice, freely made.

Bewildered, she hurried off, clutching the little bag, for the moment simply intent on reaching the sanctuary of the restrooms where she could be alone and compose herself. Kate walked quickly, not daring to look right or left, feeling sure that those who saw her knew everything, could see the sexual hunger in her body and read her thoughts.

Chapter Seven
Choices

ॐ

When Kate finally reached the mirrored restroom, again she bolted the door and leaned on the sink, staring at herself and breathing deep. After a few moments, she reached for the little bag and opening it, withdrew a small piece of folded paper which read—

You might be a little scared. That's okay, after all, this is all new for you. So, relax and enjoy the adventure. Everything will be fine. All you have to do is obey.

Inside the bag, you will find a specially fashioned piece of jewelry called a torc. You will notice that it is something like a small bracelet with two ball ends and a tag on a small chain. Read the inscription on the tag.

If you wish the inscription to become true in time, as I very much hope you will, then insert the torc in your pussy and ass and squeeze it closed so the balls grip you inside. The tag will dangle between your thighs.

Also inside the bag, you will find a small jar and a brush. The jar contains a combination of oils that are lubricating, warming and stimulating. Use the brush to coat each ball of the torc before insertion, then brush the oil into your pussy lips, clit hood and clit, ensuring that every inch of your pussy is well covered.

You will then return to me.

Kate took the torc from the bag. It was heavy and beautifully made, a smooth metal bracelet that was circular in cross-section, ending in two highly polished silver balls, one ball being slightly larger than the other. On the end of a fine five-inch long silver chain was a metal disc, which was engraved in cursive script that was delicate and so tiny that she had to hold it up to the light to read it.

Enslaved with Love
Bound in Obedience
Trained to Pleasure

Kate's heart fluttered as she read the inscribed words, reading them through again and again before once more reading the phrase from the note, "If you wish the inscription to become true *in time...*"

Her feelings were in turmoil. On the one hand, she was profoundly relieved he was not implying that he loved her, that would have been just too intense to deal with, as well as premature. After all, you couldn't fall in love with someone just through exchanging emails and talking on the phone...could you?

And then on the other hand, she was confused. During their hours of conversation they had often discussed the notion of whether it was possible for one person to ever really own another, yet they had also admitted that such an ideal struck a deep chord within them both, though they were fully aware of the paradoxes. To be completely possessed by another, to be utterly enthralled by them, claimed, enraptured, captivated and captive. When two people were so intertwined in their hearts and minds, who was the Master and whom the slave? Who was possessed by whom?

"If I ever owned you," James had said, "it would only be to set you free. Perhaps I could capture your heart, shackle your body in chains, but I could never own *you*, the essence of who you are is not tangible. To even attempt to do so would be futile, would be loveless, would be to deny us the possibility of something much more beautiful. Yet, if you were determined to enslave yourself whilst I was seeking to empower you, then maybe the complexities of who we are would be respected and love could grow."

Kate sighed. James never spoke in absolutes. He was so supremely confident as a man that he had no need to pretend to know something when he did not. His humility was his strength. He did not have all the answers, but then he wanted someone to love him as he learned, and he was absolutist in this—he wanted a life where love in all its many variants could flourish and grow.

Kate wished that she could just fast forward today and feel his arms around her, enfolded by him, safe and protected, cherished, adored... The longing in her nearly overwhelmed her for an instant and she choked back a sob.

Kate shook her head, trying to clear her thoughts. Did she want to feel his torc claim her at her core, to feel the tag brushing her thighs as she walked, feeling owned, feeling claimed...an overwhelming "Yes!" So why was she hesitating? She was missing something, but what?

Then she understood. Today he was giving her a preview, almost a free sample of all he had to offer to her. He was dangling a very specific sort of bait—a bait without a hook. She had to want it enough to hold it tight for herself, and she would only do that if she were the right woman for him.

With a flash of intuition she realized that this was something very important to him, something he would be enormously proud for her to wear, but only if she truly wanted it, that she wanted it with all her heart. That kind of *knowing* could only come in time, with a solid foundation of the ever-deepening trust that would allow love to grow and blossom between them. It could only come through the experience of him, through the experience of being his.

And when next she was given this to wear, he would be telling her that he loved her.

Kate picked up the jar of oil and the little brush, and having coated the balls of the torc liberally with oil, she walked to the chair in one corner of the room. Perching the cheeks of her bottom on the edge of the chair she took a deep breath and touched the smaller of the balls against the mouth of her bottom.

Kate gasped, but then clenched her jaw in determination as she pushed and willed herself to relax at the same time. The ball of the torc slid inside her suddenly, her bottom gripping it tightly by reflex. She uttered a soft whimper in anticipation, and then pushed the second ball inside her pussy. Though the ball was larger, this was a far more normal sensation for her, and she sighed with pleasure as it slid inside her.

Holding the shaft of the torc, she squeezed cautiously, gradually applying more strength, until the soft metal gave under her pressure and she felt the two balls grip her inside. Tentatively she stood, feeling the weight of the torc and the tag against her thighs. The internal pressure was gentle, yet exquisitely erotic.

After just a few steps, Kate had to stop, reaching out to the cool, tiled wall with her hand for balance and reassurance in case her trembling legs folded beneath her. But the momentary wave of dizzy arousal passed, leaving only a deep, aching glow inside her and the sense of being held. A sensation that was both strangely comforting and calming.

She sat once more and leaned back cautiously in the seat so that she could spread her legs. She dipped the brush into the oil and painted it over her pussy lips and clit, exactly as directed in James' note. Though her thighs trembled at the touch of the brush, so soft as to be barely perceptible, despite her heightened sensitivity, she resisted the urge to press harder and returned the oil and brush to the small bag before placing it in her handbag.

Kate unlocked the door, and as she walked back through the restaurant area and into the conservatory towards their table, she found she was walking with increased assurance. Somehow, strangely, having taken this further step into submission, her confidence rose and she walked taller, delighting now in the insistent weight of the torc. It seemed to center her, bringing her more into balance within herself so she felt she moved more gracefully, her limbs loose and relaxed.

Chapter Eight
A Fire Inside

&

As she entered the small arbor, she saw James' face light up with a truly radiant smile of welcome, and she realized, guiltily, that she had been gone such a long time he must have assumed she had bolted.

"Welcome back, Kate," said James. "I delayed our food, but it should be here soon now." He helped her to her seat and she sat cautiously, remembering to lift her skirt at the last second and relaxing only after she felt the torc slide a little deeper inside her with the pressure of the chair's cushion.

"I am so very pleased you came back… I was beginning to wonder if you would, but then I realize I gave you a lot to think about…didn't I?" James said, smiling his understanding.

"Yes, Sir, at first, I didn't understand, but now I think I do." Kate looked down at the tablecloth, toying with the cutlery as she thought through what she wished to say. "I've been thinking about today as a sort of test…in the sense that you might not like me, might not want to teach me, train me…but now I realize that it's a test of a different sort. After all you would never have given me the torc if you did not want to train me…if you did not want my submission."

He raised his eyebrows and looked at her attentively as she continued. "The real test is whether or not this is right for *me*, isn't it? You said so often in your emails that my submission was mine to give…so the test is discovering how deeply I need to submit, isn't it?"

James nodded. "Yes, and that's something you can really only discover from doing it…by, just for today, submitting to me and seeing how much you enjoy yourself, experiencing how the chemistry works between us in real life...then determining whether you want more and how much more?"

He paused as their soup was served, and then made sure everything was to her liking before dismissing the waiter. He then looked at her closely. Though maintaining appearances, she had been discreetly wriggling on her seat for the last few minutes.

"Everything all right, Kate?" he inquired innocently.

"Yes, Sir, I..." She looked up at him suddenly, whispering in alarm, "My pussy... Oh, my god!" She squirmed in her chair, her eyes wild as the full power of the sensations hit her all at once.

"Yes, I wondered when the oil would begin to work on you. You can probably feel it on your clit especially and inside your bottom, too?"

Kate was clutching her spoon hard, knuckles white and could only nod her head.

"You will also be feeling a powerful urge to touch yourself, I'm sure, but you must keep your hands above the table, Kate, and sit very still. Look at me, so I know you have understood. Good girl. Now tell me what you feel?" he commanded, his voice deep, soft and firm.

"It's like heat...burning and cold...and a tickle inside, Sir," she stammered.

"You would like to move, wouldn't you, Kate?"

"Yes, Sir, very much, Sir... I need to..." She sat rigidly stiff in her chair, trying desperately to control the urge to move her hips, though her pussy was already contracting strongly around the ball buried inside her and so was her ass.

"Kate, you can move as soon as you like, but you must ask permission first."

"Oh, please, Sir, can I move...please?"

"Not until you ask me properly, Kate. What is it you want to do exactly?"

She let the spoon drop to the table, her soup as yet untouched, and staring fixedly at the flowers in the center of the table, struggling to find the words he wished to hear from her, before summoning the courage to speak them aloud.

"Sir, I want to fuck my pussy on the torc...Sir, please!"

"And your ass, Kate?"

"Oh, yes, Sir, and fuck my ass, too, I need to move so badly, Sir...please...please..." Her voice was a plaintive whimper.

"You may move, Kate, just rock your hips forward and back...good...that feels better, doesn't it?"

She held the edge of the table and moved herself on the torc. Tiny movements were all she could manage without drawing attention, and though she was desperate to scratch this maddening itch inside, she had not forgotten that people might be watching her.

"Yes, Sir, it feels a bit better..." Her tone belied her words.

"Never refer to any part of your body as 'it' again, Kate. Your pussy is 'she', as is every part of you. Now I think you would feel much better if you could just tease your clit a little, don't you? Just soothe the need inside you a little more?"

Kate nodded vigorously. Her hand dropped beneath the table, but hearing him clear his throat she stopped, and very shyly glanced up at him before once more staring at the flowers.

"You must look at me when you ask for my permission, Kate. It's okay, you know...there's nothing hidden between us."

Tentatively she raised her gaze to meet his once more, very self-conscious.

"Please, Sir, may I...touch...touch my clit?"

"Yes, Kate, you may," he looked deep into her eyes, "I'm so very proud of you, you're doing so well and being so beautifully obedient."

James' words of praise coincided with the first touch of her surreptitious fingers on her swollen, aching bud. And she felt the pleasure jolt through her, not an orgasm, but something close to it...a release, and a part of her surrendered still more deeply to him.

"Thank you, Sir," she finally remembered to say as her fingers stroked and gentled the throbbing ache inside her core.

James smiled at her. "The oil's effect doesn't last very long, just continue stroking yourself for a few minutes more and try and eat your soup with your free hand...it will distract you a little."

Kate picked up her spoon and her hand trembling, brought a spoonful of soup towards her mouth. The delicious smell calmed her, and she realized how very hungry she was. "Oh, it's cold!" she said, as she tasted the soup.

"It's meant to be cold...it's gazpacho soup. I didn't know how long you would be, and I thought ordering you soup that was meant to be cold would be better than cold soup!" James laughed, and she grinned at him, recovering some of her innate mischievousness now that the sensations in her pussy had diminished to more bearable levels of tingling torment.

"So, Mister James...Sir...I trust you're enjoying yourself?" Kate raised an eyebrow quizzically, somehow now feeling very comfortable with him despite, or perhaps because of, everything he had put her through.

"Miss Kate," he replied, matching her mock formal tone, "I do not believe I have ever enjoyed a meal more...and we have yet to eat the main course!"

Kate paused with the spoon halfway to her mouth. "Uh-oh, that sounds like trouble coming my way!" She smiled, and provocatively shifted on her chair. "But so far, I am enjoying the kind of trouble you deal out...very much!"

James smiled happily across the table at her, wanting to reach out and take her hand — he laughed at himself — wanting to do *very* much more than take her hand, but that would do to begin with.

They chatted about inconsequential things as they ate — places they had visited on holiday, where they would love to travel to, time allowing. The conversation flowing freely and easily, as it had when they were chatting online and then on the phone, as if they had known each other for years. Both of them deliberately avoided subjects that approached things sexual in order to enjoy their food, yet despite this, the undercurrent of sexual tension was very strong.

When their coffee arrived, Kate decided to ask a question that had been on her mind for a while.

"Sir, I've heard so much about BDSM…and I already know from experience how much it arouses me to feel controlled, you know, I mean I told you already, that previous boyfriends have tied me up and stuff like that…the 'bondage and domination' side of things…"

Kate paused, a little embarrassed and searching for the right words. "…but it's the 'S&M' bit I'm not sure of. I told you I fantasize about being spanked, but I've no idea how much I'd actually like *real* pain…and I read all kinds of stuff about whips and torture and…god, some of it really made my stomach turn…and some of it really turned me on, almost despite myself… I mean I couldn't believe that what I was reading was having this arousing effect on me…but I couldn't pretend it wasn't happening anymore…"

Kate ran out of words not having been able to formulate a question.

James sipped his coffee. "So what you want to know is firstly where I stand on torturing girls, and secondly whether or not I intend to whip you?" He said this in a flat tone that shocked her, until she looked at him and caught the twinkle in his eye.

"Well, since you put it like that…" Kate laughed shyly.

"Okay. Well the first thing to understand is that what interests me is erotic intensity—*pleasure*—so if pain can be experienced pleasurably then it's not pain, sometimes it's called pleasure-pain. Since we're in a restaurant perhaps I should talk about food…"

James grinned at her. "Stay with me, okay, there's a point to this! Think of a curry or perhaps a chili dish. If it's *all* hot spices, it just kills your taste buds, it's hell to eat and after the first mouthful you push your plate away and drink a pint of water. Unless you're dumb, or intensely masochistic or possibly trying to be macho—" James' eyes twinkled at the irony, "—you won't go to that restaurant again, and you certainly don't trust that the chef knows what they're doing. By contrast, if the blend of spices and flavors is just right...not too much, yet not so little as to be bland and boring, then even though you know it's going to hurt a little to eat...it's so delicious you go back for more...and more!"

Kate laughed as his face assumed the expression of a man consumed with greed...greed and hunger that clearly had nothing to do with spicy food! She loved the way his handsome and normally stern features could so suddenly split apart in a smile that transformed his face.

James grinned at her. "So that's how it should be with pleasure-pain in S&M. The ingredients have to be just right and it *really* matters who's cooking! There needs to be just enough to make things spicy, hot and exciting!"

James became abruptly more serious with a lightning change of mood that Kate was recognizing as a sign that he was about to say something important.

"The key is what I call 'sensitization'—that means the purpose of pain is to enhance pleasure. It should make you *more* aroused, more passionate, less inhibited...more sensitive to sensual pleasure."

James paused and then asked, "Do you have any idea how masochistic you are?"

Kate shook her head. "Not much, I wouldn't think..."

He looked at her. "Hmm, I wonder... You enjoyed the little torment with the oil though, didn't you?" The question was rhetorical, though Kate's blush was answer enough. "Here, hold out your hand...we'll find out."

Somewhat hesitantly, Kate held out her hand and was surprised by the weight of the small objects he passed to her.

"Those are nipple clamps with small weights on them. Put them on now." He saw her look a little wild. "Yes, now…you're not wearing a bra, so just undo a button of your blouse and put one on each nipple…see they're sprung, so you just squeeze to open the jaws and then release to pinch your nipple."

Hesitantly, and with many an anxious look around her, Kate opened her blouse, her nipples already erect in anticipation. She shivered as the cold metal brushed the skin of her breast and gasped as she felt the rubber teeth of the clamp sink into her tender flesh. As she attached first one clamp and then the other, Kate felt the color mounting in her cheeks, more so as she felt their weight pull the tips of her nipples down against the silk of her blouse.

There was no immediate pain, just pressure, yet within seconds her nipples began to throb and soon they were more erect than seemed possible and the feeling reignited the molten heat in her belly and made her extraordinarily aware of the torc once more.

James told her to button her blouse and as her trembling fingers tried to obey, she saw him gesture to a waiter to settle the bill. This spurred her on, and by the time James was signing for the meal, she sat with her jacket hugged tight around her, once more gazing fixedly at the flower arrangement and trying valiantly to maintain her composure. The sensation in her nipples had turned to a burning throb, a pulsing that echoed and amplified the liquid vibration inside her and the tingling ache in her clit.

"Kate…" She looked up at him, her eyes wide. "Come on, let's go for a walk in the gardens."

Chapter Nine
The Rose Arbor

ॐ

To her relief, James did not turn to go back through the main restaurant and foyer, but instead led her out through doors that opened directly onto the rose gardens. He said little as they walked side-by-side along the neat little paths that zigzagged through the gardens, except to point out a particularly beautiful rose for her to smell and once or twice, when she felt her legs were turning to jelly, to tell her not to dawdle, which though said with mock severity, was belied by the wicked glint in is eye and his barely suppressed smile.

Kate was enormously relieved to find that the gardens were completely empty of any other visitors to the Manor — who were only now just sitting down to their lunch. Without the presence of strangers to keep her inhibitions in force, she felt wave upon wave of arousal course through her body. With every step, she was intensely aware of the torc moving inside her and the throbbing, aching weight on her nipples.

Kate was accordingly in something of a daze by the time they came to a bench so surrounded with trelliswork and climbing roses that it formed a natural blind. They were by now some hundred yards from the Manor house and it was quite secluded, but she felt so sensitized and vulnerable that the impenetrable foliage seemed like a sanctuary.

James guided her to sit on the bench and looking down at her said, "Here, Kate, you will need this." He offered her a clean, white cotton gentleman's handkerchief. "Sit down and wipe your thighs before your juices run down your legs." His words were deliberately calculated to cut straight through any attempt to deny her present state.

Kate looked up in surprise…how could he know? Despite all her fantasies and her earlier experiences with James, she had been shocked by the power of the feelings that raged through her body during the walk through the rose garden. The tugging weight of the clamps had seemed to link directly to her clit and the grip of the torc. The sensation a curious mixture of pleasure and pain, since her nipples undeniably hurt—they ached with an almost unbearable throb. Yet, the effect on her whole body was to arouse her extremely, and for the past few minutes, she had been increasingly aware that the feelings were becoming too intense to be endured without relief.

James stood in front of her as she sat with the handkerchief in her hand, squirming with discomfiture.

"Lift your skirt, Kate. Lift it right up—show me your lovely, hot, wet little cunt. I want to see how wet you are before you mop yourself up."

Kate sat rigidly. This was so sudden. In the restaurant she had always had the tablecloth to preserve her modesty, no matter what he had made her do, he had not actually seen her doing it. Yet even as one voice in her mind screamed "No!" another inner voice was honest enough to feel the still deeper melting inside as the force of his words and the total command in his voice caught hold of her. But still she hesitated.

"Kate, look at me," his voice was firm but kind, and she looked up at him through eyes moistened with the tears that were welling up in the confusion of her feelings. "I will tell you once more to lift your skirt. I know you want to obey me, but I also know this is difficult for you, so I will say this. You are very beautiful to me, you may feel shame at what I tell you to do, but there is *nothing* shameful in your arousal, only a delicious sexuality that I treasure and adore in you. Do you understand?"

Kate nodded her head.

"So lift up your skirt and be my obedient girl."

Her hands trembling, she picked up the hem of her skirt and lifted it slowly, making herself obey, her breath ragged.

"Good girl...how beautiful you are! Now lie yourself back a little and spread your legs wider for me...don't think about it, Kate...just do it...there, that's better. Now I can see how lovely your pussy is with her pretty pink pouting lips so swollen with desire and my torc gleaming between them."

James bent forward and blew gently, his face a few inches from her glistening mound. Kate groaned with desire as she felt his breath caress her supersensitive flesh.

"Would you like me to touch you, Kate? You must ask for what you want."

Kate turned her head to one side as her hips lifted towards him with a mind of their own, eagerly seeking his touch, desperately craving it.

"Please, Sir, please touch me," her voice tremulous with longing.

Again, his breath blew a stream of cool air over her heat and she moaned softly. But instead of his longed-for touch direct to her pussy, she felt his hand close upon her wrist and bring her hand to touch herself.

"I made a promise, Kate, so you touch yourself for me. Do exactly as I say." His voice was husky with lust, and he wondered at the self-control it took not to reach out those few inches and touch, even more — taste her — as he so strongly desired. James had anticipated this moment, and knew that were he to break his own rules Kate could never truly come to trust him, no matter how much she might say it did not matter when aroused beyond endurance as she was now. He had told her to ask for his touch because he wanted her to acknowledge her need out loud, to admit the need to herself in a way that could never be unsaid.

"Kate, spread yourself wider for me...yes, that's good...now touch your clit ever so lightly...just small circles...good girl...now a little faster." Kate moaned, and felt herself slip into another world within herself where only pleasure and the sound of his voice existed. Some part of her remained dimly aware of the gardens, the heady scent of roses, but it all seemed remote. James watched her intently as her fingers continued to flutter over her swollen bud. He saw the contractions in her belly, heard the rapid panting of her breath, and knew she could not stand much more of this without coming. He eased his rock-hard cock, now throbbing and aching so powerfully that it took all his self-control to remain focused on Kate.

"Take your hand away from your clit, lovely slut...no, don't argue, do as you're told...good girl. Now look at me." Kate turned her head and tried to focus on his face through eyes misted with desire. She saw him smiling and longed for him to touch her, feel his weight crush her. The gripping of the torc just served to aggravate her unfulfilled need to be taken by him then and there—it was driving her crazy. She gasped as she felt a tug at her core—he was holding the tag, pulling gently on its chain.

"Kate, you must never come without my permission...so ask me for what you want."

"Oh, please, James...please let me come... I need to come so much," she gasped, totally unaware she had said his name, so lost was she in her desire.

"Yes, Kate, you will come soon, first remove the nipple clamps...open your blouse." Her fingers struggled with the buttons and he had to stop himself from helping her, but finally, she had undone several buttons, and without any hesitation pulled her blouse open, revealing her breasts quite shamelessly.

"Please, Sir...take them off for me...not touching me...it's okay..." Kate whimpered as she felt the weights being lifted, her nipples pulled away from her body. A sweet, delicious pain...stretching...burning.

"Kate, you can touch again now...touch your clit for me, lovely slut, and come for me...come hard...give me all your pleasure now, Katie." His voice close to her ear was a deep growl of desire. She felt his gentle pulling on her nipples through the clamps and imagined him touching her, imagined the beautiful, thick cock she knew must be aching to plunge into her hot, wet cunt…and lost herself in pleasure.

No sooner had she started to come then James released both clamps simultaneously, and the rushing of blood back into her nipples triggered sensations that flooded through her to engorge her already swollen clit so she thought it would burst with the sweet pleasure-pain. As the image of her lewd display for James struck her mind so Kate's pleasure skyrocketed, her whole body arched in a spasm of ecstasy and she began to sob and cry with the beauty of the feelings that washed through her and melted her to a puddle of boneless lust.

A little stunned by the sheer power of her orgasm, James longed to hold her, but resisted the almost overwhelming urge to take her in his arms and gentle her as the spasms ebbed slowly away. Instead, he steeled himself, making sure there was still no one around, he drew down her skirt and recovered her lovely breasts, waiting patiently for her to come back down to earth.

She looked so very lovely to him. Her hair in disarray and the soft sheen of perspiration on her forehead, lips full and cheeks flushed. He was studying her when her eyes blinked open and she smiled a lazy smile at him.

"Mmmmm, that was lovely. Thank you, James…I mean, Sir." Kate attempted to look apologetic, but failed completely. She loved saying his name and no more so than now.

James grinned at her, and chose to ignore the lapse. "You are very welcome, Kate, I enjoyed your pleasure, you become exceptionally beautiful when you really lose yourself…and I think, from the wicked gleam in your eye that you know very well how much I want you."

James did not wait for a reply, satisfied to give her just so much…after all he could not reveal too much "Mr. Nice Guy" or she would start to take liberties. Abruptly he said, "Take your shoes and stockings off, we'll hide them here and pick them up on the way back. You can't walk in those high heels, and I want to take you down to the river. Come on, hurry up, girl!"

James turned and walked off towards a fountain where he soaked his handkerchief, and by the time he returned, Kate had struggled out of her stockings and put them in her handbag. Handing her the cool cloth, James took her shoes and hung them inside a thick bush out of sight, but easily recoverable later.

"Ready?" he asked. Kate had wiped her face and hands, grateful for the coolness of the cloth. The afternoon was turning very warm with soft, perfectly white clouds in an azure blue sky. The gardens were quiet and still except for the incessant busy humming of the bees around the roses—an idyllic English summer day.

Kate nodded, smiled, and ran a few steps to catch him up. Without asking, she took his hand, and momentarily surprised, he looked at her. "You promised not to touch *me*," she said. "I don't remember promising not to touch you!" She grinned at him, and he smiled and squeezed her hand gently.

"The point was really to show you that I can control myself," he laughed. "Though, god knows, you've sorely tested me today!"

"Yes, Sir, I know and I appreciate it. You've helped me feel very safe...safe enough so I could trust you and not be scared when you asked me to do all those wickedly sexy things for you. Well, not too scared anyway." Kate laughed, delighting in her sense of accomplishment—she had dared to submit and finally experienced her fantasies, and found reality far exceeded her expectations...at least with James' guidance.

James nodded, knowing he was being given permission to touch her and that he need not restrain himself any longer. At least, not so far as Kate was concerned. Her astonishing sensuality was intoxicating—her forthright passionate sexuality was like a heady wine to him, almost overwhelming. Little did she realize how very difficult he had found it to keep his hands off her! But then, perhaps she did, she was an amazingly empathic girl.

He recognized that she had already taught him a lot. Both with her willingness to trust him at his word, and now, when she was hinting strongly that an excess of caution combined with his tendency to make everything into a test of his will—a fault he acknowledged in himself—would spoil the beautiful spontaneity of this special day.

"I thought we'd walk down to the river, it's cooler by the water…and the view is something special," he said, struggling for a moment to control the welling up of emotion inside him.

They walked slowly, James taking off his jacket and slinging it over his shoulder and Kate trotting by his side, skipping occasionally to keep up with his long stride. Another hundred yards took them out of the formal gardens and into the parkland with its deer-cropped grass and stately oak and beech trees dotted here and there. The grass was fine and soft underfoot, and the land sloped gently down towards the gleam of the river, perhaps only half a mile away, but seeming farther in the summer haze.

Chapter Ten
By the River

 හ

They said little as they ambled through the meadows, for the most part enjoying a companionable silence. For Kate it was as if she were seeing the world through different eyes, perceiving and appreciating a loveliness that seemed fresh and vibrant, newly created just for her pleasure. A small flower that previously she would have walked passed without noticing, was now revealed to her in all its delicate beauty so that she must stop and examine it, so losing herself in its tiny, exquisite splendor that when she tore her gaze away, she found that she must run to catch up with James.

When they came to the river, James found an area of the riverbank with soft, short cut grass and spread his jacket down for her to sit on. He pointed downstream, and Kate gasped to see a majestic castle standing on the river's far bank—its lower walls were fringed with weeping willows and the sun glinted off high windows in the corner towers. In the sunshine, the castle was breathtaking in that quiet, subdued, balmy way that was so essentially English, speaking of a thousand years of untroubled solidity matched only by the deep water that flowed so smoothly that it reflected the battlements with mirrored perfection.

There was no shade, only some low bushes and bulrushes that shielded them from view, but not from the sun. James was hot from their walk and overheated to the point of exploding from the last few hours spent teasing, and in turn, being tormented by his hands-off proximity to Kate's enthralling sexuality. The water looked so inviting that with barely a glance at Kate, he quickly stripped off his clothes and without hesitating, dived deep into the cool welcoming depths.

Kate had been soaking up the sun with her eyes closed and had not even noticed that he was taking his clothes off. She thought the splash was him throwing something in the river and turned to say something, only to find him gone and a pile of clothes where he had been seconds before.

Though shocked for a fraction of a second, Kate very quickly realized what had happened, and she spun herself around on her bottom so that she lay on her stomach facing the river, chin resting on her hands to watch, saying out loud to herself, "Oh, goodie…girl's showtime!"

When James rose to the surface, he was nearly in the middle of the river. He turned and waved quickly, inviting her to join him, but clearly not commanding her since he did not wait for a response, as he immediately set off upstream.

Swimming powerfully for a while, he relished the wonderful coolness, before allowing himself to float and the river to take him gently downstream again.

The impulse to swim had been a boyishly spontaneous one, the water irresistible on such a hot day. Now he would have to deal with Kate when he got out, and he wondered how best to handle the situation. With a mental shrug, he decided just to see what happened, the important thing was that she felt *safe*— knowing when to let go of control was the art.

Kate watched and unconsciously bit her lip as he waded ashore. The sunlight reflected off the water pearling on his skin to make miniature rainbows, especially when he shook his hair. He had a beautiful body she thought, the smooth muscled, supple grace of a dancer or an athlete. As if hypnotized, she allowed her gaze to drop to his cock, long and thick despite the water's cold…and then suddenly he was standing over her.

"That feels so good…sure you won't take a dip?" said James playfully.

Kate shook her head and smiled at him, sitting up and then kneeling to stare up at him. Taking all her courage she said, "There is something I would like though…Sir." Something in the huskiness of her voice warned him, but he pretended a casual indifference.

"What's that, Kate?"

In answer to his question, Kate leant forward from her kneeling position and very softly kissed the very top of his foot. Then licking the beaded water from his skin, she worked her way slowly up his muscular calf, drinking from him, kissing his skin, adoring him.

James felt himself tremble internally, his cock hardening with every beat of his heart. He had not anticipated Kate breaking the "no touch" rule to this extent. He had wanted simply to tease her a little with his body—and perhaps get his own back for how crazy she had been driving him, confident in his attractiveness to women. Not really vanity, more an uncomplicated pride in himself.

He reached down and cradled her head in his hands, lifting her face up to look into her eyes.

"Kate…this breaks all the rules in a big way. Are you sure you want this now? No regrets?"

"Sir…James…I ache to give you pleasure, to touch you, to be touched…" Kate placed the palm of her hand over her heart. "And it feels right, *you* feel so right in here. Please, let me please you."

Kate turned her face into James' hand, kissing the palm. First his right palm, and then the left, in a gesture so deliciously feminine and submissive that James' defenses were completely undermined.

"Very well, Kate," James' voice was husky and deep with desire. "They're your limits to stretch. I think it's pretty damned obvious how much I want you…"

Kate giggled, but resisted the urge to take his beautiful, hard cock into her mouth immediately, instead, bowed her head to kiss his other foot, glorying in the exquisitely sensual subjugation of herself in this simple action. She reveled in her submission, in the power of James' presence and in how supremely safe she felt in giving herself to him.

When she had kissed and licked her way up to his mid-thigh, Kate sat back on her heels and looked up at him. "I would very much like to eat you, Sir."

James grinned down at her, and then teased her with a look of pretended confusion. "But, Kate...young ladies don't beg on their knees to suck cock...only a wickedly wanton little slut would do such a thing."

"Yes, Sir," she replied nodding happily. "But today, I am *your* wanton little slut so that's all right, isn't it?"

Without waiting for an answer, Kate leant forward to take the swollen head of his throbbing cock into her mouth and heard him groan as her tongue flicked around him. Relishing the pulsing of his blood on her tongue as he swelled still farther inside her mouth. Too soon, he drew away from her and as she mewed in protest he growled, "Wait you beautiful, insatiable girl," and lay down on the grassy bank, his thick cock slapping heavily on his smoothly muscled stomach.

Eagerly, Kate lay down too, so that she could rest her head on his stomach and then began to nibble and lick the very sensitive tip of him, teasing lightly until he groaned. Then she hungrily took him into her mouth once more while her nails lightly scratched his heavy balls. The taste of him, male, clean and strong overwhelmed Kate's senses. She began to moan, taking real pleasure herself, not just from the pleasure she longed to give him, but as if her mouth and pussy were one, and she could feel him sliding into her hot cunt as she worked her mouth on him. In fact, she was contracting her vaginal muscles and ass so strongly around the torc's balls that it was as if these twin mouths were seeking to suck the torc inside her.

Through the haze of her own arousal and the hunger that consumed her, she heard James' voice telling her what to do. For a second, she felt a flash of irritation, but then she understood that he was directing her to give him maximum pleasure, and she started to listen more closely and with it her urgency, which had in part been composed of a fear of not pleasing him, disappeared...and she relaxed into the moment. It was blissful, he had once again taken the burden of responsibility off her — she could not displease him because he would not allow it. She had nothing to prove. She had only to obey...and learn how to give herself ever more completely to him.

Gradually, a pattern emerged as she discovered what he wanted from her mouth, tongue, lips and throat...first hard and then soft. He would take her hair in his hand and guide her mouth, using her almost brutally, fucking her into the back of her throat. His voice telling her not to fight the urge to swallow when she gagged on his cock...and finally she understood.

When she swallowed the head of his cock she did not gag, he slid into her throat and the feeling of him transfixing her nearly made her come, sending a ripple of powerful hot pleasure right through her. Then as his pleasure reached a peak, his hand and voice would restrain her...would rein her in and make her serve *his* pleasure when her hunger to drink him down would have driven him over the edge for her own satisfaction.

Then he would direct her to licking, tasting the thick pre-come that pearled on the tip of his throbbing cock head, nibbling gentle bites into the shaft of his cock until she felt him pulse with pleasure. Scratching his balls lightly with her nails, or incredibly gently taking them into her hot mouth, to feel them dance upon her tongue.

Soon she understood and could anticipate his desires, and then all she heard was the heaviness of his breathing, his groans and gasps of pleasure as she experimented and learnt the unique pleasures of his beautiful cock. As she once more lifted her head to take him fully, she heard him murmur throatily, his voice resonant with the imminence of his passion saying, "Now, Katie...now."

Kate plunged her head down and swallowed his cock head, impaling herself recklessly, devouring him. And at the same instant that she felt his thick, hot jets spurt into her throat, she tipped over the edge herself, her belly molten, every part of her trembling powerfully as waves of orgasmic force washed through her again and again, until she collapsed onto him. Fiercely, passionately holding firm to him, as if his cock were her sole anchor in the storm of pleasure that flooded through her.

Chapter Eleven
Surrender

໔ဢ

Kate awoke slowly from a deep, dreamless sleep, aware that she must have lost consciousness, but happy, blissfully happy that despite her slumbers her mouth was still full of James' cock. A cock, which was even now, stirring back to life. She gently lifted her mouth away, but only to kiss the tip softly, and then the smooth hard muscles of his belly. She turned her head and saw he was sleeping, or at least dozing, and contentedly she settled her head to pillow on his stomach from where she could look at his cock and kiss him whenever she wished — which was often.

Her thoughts were tranquil, calm and easy. Without trying to analyze anything, she knew that an extraordinary process had begun. An unfolding of something deep inside that she had kept locked away in hidden places deep within herself. Places to which James had the keys, and that he knew intuitively how to find. In any other man, that would have frightened her, but somehow it did not with James. He unlocked these treasures within her, but in the same moment, he gave her back the keys, because ultimately, he wanted her to be able to open them all for herself...for their mutual pleasure.

Kate frowned and smiled, not completely happy with her metaphor, but far too sun-sex sleepy to be bothered about it. The point was, that the more she surrendered to James, the freer she felt. The demon of fear in the back of her mind that had been so busy on the journey to the Manor was exorcised as if it had never been.

Why this powerful internal shift? A voice in her mind said, *It's because you've a belly full of a beautiful man's come, you little slut!* and another voice laughed and said, *Maybe…nothing wrong with that!* But deeper down, she knew her contentment stemmed from the fact that she had absolutely no sense of being trapped or coerced by him. He gave her free choices — to obey or not…and the lesson was simple. Obedience brought her pleasure, exquisite pleasure combined with an ever-deepening sense of intimacy, of mutual understanding.

There had been many times when she had felt the rise of erotic fear throughout the last few hours — when he had given her instructions that had set her heart pounding in her chest, and elicited pleasure so extreme that she had wondered if she could bear it. Yet throughout, she had never once felt real fear…and that was because James' first priority was to make her feel essentially safe.

Kate understood then that a huge part of his need to dominate blended seamlessly with his need to protect. That surrendering to him was less about the obedience he demanded — though she trembled at the thought of what deliberate disobedience might bring — but about stepping inside the circle of strength he carried with him. Feeling enfolded in that strength and shielded by it gave her an elemental security that allowed and enabled her to embrace her innate femininity in a way that was new, fresh and exciting to her.

Paradoxically, she felt more powerful with James than she had felt with any other man. He did not play games, he made no secret of his desire for her and yet, at the same time, he was not ruled by his desires.

This is what people meant by "freedom through submission", she thought, and taking his cock gently into her mouth once more, she drowsily closed her eyes to be rocked to sleep by the smooth rhythm of his breath.

* * * * *

James woke to the delicious hot wetness of Kate's mouth around him and smiled contentedly. The weight of her head on his stomach told him that she was completely relaxed if not asleep. He reached out a hand to stroke her hair and she sighed around his cock, a half-asleep sensual purr that brought the blood flooding to his cock, hardening and lengthening vigorously, pushing deeper into her mouth. Inevitably, this woke her and she sucked him hungrily.

"Kate, no…" James chuckled, and pulled her off his cock. "Maybe later, I want to talk to you." She moaned and rolled over, head still on his stomach, but now looking up at his face. Her hair tickled his balls and cock so that he had great difficulty finding the words.

For a moment he just smiled at her, then propping himself up on his elbows he said, "That was beautiful, but it went a lot further than I was anticipating for today, not that I'm complaining!"

James looked down into her smiling eyes and continued. "I want you, Kate, very much, you know that…and if you don't know it then I'm telling you now. But you also need to know that I will have all of you—body, mind and heart…or not at all. As much as it is possible to possess another, I want to possess you." He stroked her face, tracing the line of her nose and lips with the tip of his finger, which she kissed.

"I want to be yours…James." Kate spoke quietly, her voice a whisper of desire and a much deeper longing. Then her expression changed, her face hardened as she faced some internal and as yet unspoken fear.

"I don't know if it is that I simply need to experience the feeling of being completely owned, controlled and possessed—to live that experience fully—in order perhaps to let it go, or stop tormenting myself with it. All I know is that for so long I have had dreams…dreams I've been so scared of trying to make come true because I knew, or thought I knew, that if I did then I would be terribly, horribly disappointed."

She smiled at him, her inner joy blazing from her eyes. "But today you taught me that my dreams *can* come true, that reality can be better than dreams…and…" Kate blushed. "I don't think you've even properly started with me yet, have you, Sir?"

James laughed softly. "I would love to make all your dreams come true, Kate, and better them if possible—and no, we haven't really started yet. There are so many experiences I want you to have...so much pleasure I want to share with you, but you know if I asked your permission to give you those experiences it wouldn't work, because you'd run scared." Kate lifted her head to protest, but James placed a finger over her lips.

"No, wait a minute, I'm not criticizing you...just think for a moment about what you've done today. If I had spelled out in advance everything I intended to do over lunch, would you have come here to meet me today? No, you would not...it would have made an erotic fantasy for you, but if you had known what was to happen in advance, *you* would have been responsible. But by agreeing to obey me within the limits we had agreed beforehand then *I* am responsible. You don't have to feel guilty about deriving wicked pleasure from the things I *make* you do."

James ran his fingers gently through her hair and looked deep into her eyes. "That's the magic of it. I make you do those things you secretly want to do, perhaps some things you don't even know you want to do...until you've done them. And that is why I want your complete submission, because only then can I guide you through experiences that will remove all your negative inhibitions and train you to surrender to extremes of pleasure. I want you to be my pleasure slave so you can learn that there are no forbidden pleasures, giving or receiving, so long as it is done with love and understanding."

Kate sat up, and turned to stare at the river. "I want to surrender to you, James, and I long to give you pleasure, to please you. I think most of me already has surrendered, crazy at it seems. But then this whole thing is so backwards, isn't it? On one level, we've only just met a few hours ago, on another we met months ago and on still another I've been waiting, hoping, for this all my life. However, it can't happen all at once, can it? Not just like that?"

James moved behind her and sat with his legs either side of her, easing her back against his chest and wrapping her in his arms.

"No, Kate, that's not what I meant. Building trust is a progressive thing. No…what I want is for you to do something similar to what you've done today. But for one week — a weeklong holiday we spend together…in the roles of Master and submissive slave girl. For that week, I want you to be mine to do with as I desire. Mine to torment, tease, command, instruct and punish according to the principles we have discussed at length online and with very clear objectives for your training — all the things you agreed would be extremely desirable to you. Give yourself to me for a week…then you'll really know." He grinned. "But whatever the outcome, I'm sure I can promise you an unforgettably enjoyable time."

Kate leaned farther back into him and turned her face up to look at him. She put a mock-serious expression on her face, which James was beginning to recognize meant she was about to tease him. She drew her legs up and spread them either side of his, lifting her skirt while at the same time looking wide-eyed and innocent.

"Sir?" she said making her lower lip tremble. "You didn't mention fucking…will there be lots of fucking? My poor, neglected little pussy soooo…" She got no further. James had moved to the side, and pushed her giggling onto her back then he deftly captured ankles in his strong hands and placed them on his shoulders. He pressed his hard cock up against the mouth of her cunt.

"Is so hungry to be filled and fucked?" James completed for her, laughing. Kate's answer was a sensuous writhe as she sought to impale herself on him. He let her legs drop and fell on top of her, pinning her hands above her head.

"I think my lovely slut and slave-to-be…that you're forgetting two things," James growled. Kate frowned playfully as if thinking. "First you have your ass and pussy full of my slave torc, and second you haven't kissed me properly yet. I'm sure a lovely lady like yourself would want to be kissed before she was fucked...only a little slut—" It was James' turn to be interrupted in mid-sentence as Kate's mouth clamped hungrily onto his.

James kissed her back passionately, his hands entwined in her hair, his mouth crushing hers. Loving the taste of her, and wanting her with every cell in his body.

He felt her scrambling between her legs, trying to remove the torc so he could enter her, but his hand clamped down on her wrist and brought it back above her head. "No, my beautiful wanton slut... I *am* going to fuck you. But not now, I have a better idea...and I'm going to make very sure you never forget the first time I fuck you, so long as you live!"

He gazed into her eyes and kissed her again, much more softly.

Chapter Twelve
The Hunting Lodge

&

James dressed while Kate did her best to tidy herself up, removing bits of grass and seeds from her clothing and hair, and rooting through her handbag to find her little mirror so she could touch up her makeup.

To her surprise, she heard him talking to someone else and was relieved to see that he had his mobile phone to his ear. She did not hear much of what he said, catching only the words, "free" and "lodge" before he had ended the call and turned back to her.

"That's fixed then...there's a shooting lodge about half a mile from here in those woods." James pointed to a stand of mixed woodland. "It belongs to the Manor but it's essentially the private property of the owner, along with the woodland that surrounds it. Fortunately he owes me a favor, so it's all ours."

James took her hand and they began walking towards the woods. "When we get there, I need to call the owner again and tell him how long we're going to be. When do you need to get back?"

"Well...I don't really have to be back, but I should call my friend and let her know what I'm doing." Kate grinned at him. "Though, perhaps not going into too many details!"

James nodded. "Okay...you should arrange to call her again in about three hours when you talk to her." He saw the look on her face. "Yes, I know you don't need to, but she doesn't know that, so you play by the rules until you've had chance to talk to her again face-to-face or she'll worry. I'll walk slowly on up ahead and you catch me up when you're done."

Kate found her phone and made her safe call. Her friend laughed as soon as she heard her tone of voice. Amidst girlish giggles and some teasing on the part of her friend, she arranged to call later, but had to fend off the many urgently curious requests for details because James was getting too far ahead…and anyway she did not want to discuss such things on the phone.

James had stopped to wait for her and she hurried towards him as fast as she could in her bare feet.

"I've just remembered something," she said. "My shoes are still in the rose gardens…can we get them?"

"Damn! Yes, of course, we must get them back for you." James thought for a moment. "Look there's no point us both going back to the Manor, so how about you walk on to the lodge while I go back and fetch your shoes. Just follow this path and ignore the 'Private Keep Out' signs. The path will take you straight there. The keys to the lodge are under a flowerpot to the left side of the door, so just let yourself in, and help yourself to whatever you want. It should be stocked up with food and drink. Once I've got your shoes I might as well pick up my car, so I shouldn't be too long."

Kate moved into his arms, he kissed her deep and long, a passionate promise of what was to come. Then with one last parting kiss, James reluctantly let her go, and they walked off in different directions.

As Kate approached the woods, she saw the first of the "Keep Out" signs nailed to a little gate. The gate was not locked and she stepped through it and into a very different world. Within the wood, the air was cool and still, and the trees cast a deep shade that was refreshingly chill after the heat of the surrounding meadows. The dark, moist smell of layers of leaves beneath the ancient oaks and beeches was rich and earthy, while the soft dampness of the path was a relief to her feet.

She walked on down the path and soon came to the lodge. It was a single-story timbered building with a gable roof and tiny windows with bars across them. As she moved closer, Kate saw that the windows were not as small as she had first thought—they were just very overgrown with the ivy and honeysuckle that covered every wall of the lodge, and had even climbed up to encircle the chimney. The lodge's front door was thick oak, studded with iron and the whole place seemed dark and unwelcoming. In stark contrast to the Manor house, the lodge looked like it could be part of the set of a horror movie.

Tentatively, Kate approached the door, absurdly she felt as if she were trespassing and she even looked over her shoulder in the hope that James would come. Telling herself not to be so silly, she lifted the flowerpot and picked up the heavy key.

The door creaked menacingly as she pushed it open, the sound setting the hairs on the back of her neck on end. Very cautiously, she stepped inside—even with the door wide open, she could barely make out the room, so dim was the light through the windows. Her hand searched for and found a light switch, and she was almost blinded by the startling contrast as soon as she had flipped the switch.

The lodge's interior was not modern, but it was very different from the dark and somber gothic she had expected and even dreaded she would find. The floor was antique pine with numerous thick rugs scattered haphazardly about. The walls were paneled in light oak, which gave the room a lovely warmth and a leather chesterfield sofa with matching chairs were arranged around a coffee table before a magnificent fireplace.

Kate wandered through the lodge exploring. There were only three bedrooms, a small kitchen and bathroom all leading directly off the central lounge area, but even so, the lodge was much larger on the inside than she had thought it would be. Two of the bedrooms had a double bed in an old-fashioned wrought iron frame, a closet, a chest of drawers, and thick rugs over bare, though highly polished, wooden floors. The remaining bedroom was much larger and had a king-size bed, a four-poster carved from oak with matching furniture and its own en-suite bathroom.

With the hunting prints and generally well-worn furnishings, the lodge's atmosphere was intensely masculine, there were no frills, no delicate touches anywhere. It was definitely a male preserve.

Having explored each room, she went back to the bathroom, feeling conscious of the effects of a hot day and very eager to wash and freshen up. Eyeing the shower cubicle she thought, *why not* and within seconds had stripped off her blouse and skirt and was standing beneath the powerful jet of water, relishing the force of it hammering into her back and shoulders.

Kate soaped herself all over, her hand hesitating as she touched her torc where it protruded slightly from between her legs. Though she had not been expressly forbidden, she felt it somehow wrong to touch herself without James' permission. The torc claimed her, marking her and especially her pussy as his, and the feeling of being so claimed sent a delicious shiver through her despite the heat from the shower.

Kate dried herself off and eyed her worn clothes with distaste, but then a wicked smile lit up her face. So, he wanted her as his slave girl? Then so she would be...kneeling naked and waiting for him when he arrived!

She hurried to do her makeup and fixed her hair as best she could, then, since she was feeling a little chilled after the hot shower, she found the heating thermostat and turned it up a fraction. Walking back into the lounge area, she eyed it from what James' perspective would be when he entered and cleared the coffee table in front of the fire of its ornaments. Then Kate put the largest cushion she could find on the table before climbing onto it to kneel facing the door. She bowed her head and clasped her left wrist in her right hand with her arms behind her back.

Chapter Thirteen
A Slave Awaits

ဆ

After a few minutes, Kate began to wonder how long she would have to stay like this. Realizing that she would hear the sound of his car arriving, she climbed down off the coffee table and went to hunt through the cabinets so she would know what was there and where to find it should James ask for something to eat or drink. She was just debating whether or not to fix herself a drink when she heard the sound of a car engine and rushed back to take her position on the cushion.

Excitement and arousal intermingled, the cool air made her nipples even harder and the melting liquid heat of her belly seemed to catch fire within her, causing her pussy and ass to tighten on the torc's balls. She trembled but tried not to look towards the door when it opened. It was only then that the horrifying thought struck her that, perhaps, it was not James at all, and her heart leapt to her throat.

To her enormous relief, she heard James say, "What have we here? A lovely slave girl waiting to serve her Master's pleasure!" He walked towards her, shutting the door behind him, and she looked up into his smiling and obviously delighted face. His smile lit her up inside, and she felt intensely happy to have pleased him so much.

Then his expression hardened as his eyes scanned her body with a laser-like intensity. "I see you have not been properly taught the positions of slavery, have you, little slut?"

Kate opened her mouth to speak, but James gently pressed a finger to her lips to ensure her silence.

"Sit up straighter, slave, thrust your breasts forward! They're beautiful! Be proud of them!... Good, that's better. Now knees farther apart!"

He pushed his warm, strong hands between her thighs, and with shocking ease, spread her wide. Then he stood back and examined her critically again, and gave a nod of approval. He made more small corrections — each touch, though gentle in itself, made her still more intensely aware of her body and her posture. As he minutely adjusted her position, she began to feel that he was molding her with his hands, as if her body were his clay and he was forming her into a living sculpture, a piece of art and somehow no longer her old self but a woman whom she was seeing clearly for the first time.

For his touch was not critical but enhancing. He drew her out of herself, and revealed to her a beauty that she had never thought to appreciate in herself before. The position was submissive yet never apologetic, it felt as if he were teaching her to proclaim what she felt in her heart — her desire, her pride in her body and the courage of her surrender. So that her back was straight and her head held proudly, her eyes level and not cast down. Finally, he took her hands and placed them behind her head, thereby lifting her breasts, and making her extremely aware of their soft vulnerability.

"Do not move, you are perfect just as you are!" James instructed, and walked away from her to the sideboard that served as the lodge's bar. He poured himself a small measure of one of the lodge's fine collection of single malt whiskeys and opened the sideboard's door to reveal a miniature fridge — similar to those found in hotel rooms — from which he took some ice to add to his glass. Then he returned to sit on the chesterfield and scrutinized her so keenly that the blush on her cheeks grew deeper by the second. She squirmed beneath his stare, and yet, felt immobilized by it, held deliciously, exquisitely bound by the force of his will.

"You are so very beautiful to me, Kate, but you are only just beginning to develop a sense of your own beauty, because you have always been frightened of it…understandably so in this day and age. After all what does it bring you? Only the unwanted, and very often, crude attentions of undesirable males, and the envy of other women. So, you have adopted a posture, mannerisms and behaviors that denies your sexuality and attempts to conceal your beauty as if it were something to be ashamed of. The beginning of real intimacy between two people happens when you can be unashamedly yourself—when you know there is nothing you need ever feel bad about, and that in turn begins with embracing, then learning to love and trust your body and its instinctive responses, so you become proud of every single aspect of yourself."

James stood and raised his tumbler, the ice tinkling as he swirled his drink before sipping the single malt appreciatively. Then he pressed the chilled glass to Kate's nipples, first the left and then the right. She trembled as the cold made her nipples stand still more proudly erect, but otherwise did not flinch. James nodded in approval.

"I would love to teach you, Kate. Some people would call it training you in submission, but really, it is not. I require your obedience only so that I may free something extraordinary inside you." James lifted her chin and looked deep into her eyes.

"I know you sense her…this extraordinary 'you' deep within, you occasionally see flashes of her in your dreams. She beckons you to come to her, to discover her and your true self at your core, yet you are scared of her. Scared to reclaim this lost part of yourself."

James looked into her eyes once more, his gaze unwavering, and yet, his eyes were gentle and filled with so much wisdom, kindness and understanding that Kate wanted to immerse herself in them, like diving into twin pools of crystal-blue water.

"I know you long to find her, Kate, but it will be a protracted and difficult process alone. There is a quicker way. However, it demands that you give yourself to me completely. No games, no jargon, not a superficial acting out of sexual fantasy that you drop as soon as things get challenging. I want you to enter fully into a role as my obedient slave, Kate. So that with my help, through not having the option of disobedience, you can become truly free…and then…well, then you will have a decision to make. For now, all that lies far in the future. First, we have tonight, then you have a few days to reflect on what you want, and then we will perhaps take that week together I talked about. Yet even that, will be only a beginning."

James took another sip of his whiskey and looked at her intently.

"Right now, you have only one decision to make. Do you wish to be mine for this night? To serve me as my pleasure slave until dawn tomorrow?"

Putting the tumbler down, James leaned forward and traced his finger very slowly from her knee up the inside of her thigh. He held his hand palm up, just hovering an inch from her pouting, needy sex and waited.

Kate's breath grew ragged, she could feel only the heat from his hand, and longed for more, so much more, the torment of his closeness was unendurable. "Please…" she pleaded. "Oh, please…"

"Kneel up, slave." James moved his hands so rapidly that her first knowledge of his intentions was the cruel, pinching pull to her nipples as he drew her upwards. Kate gasped and moaned, the pain brief but shocking, she had no choice but to obey.

"I am going to remove the torc now. Be silent and do not move an inch." James released her nipples and moved behind her. Then, tracing his fingers down the hollow of her spine from the nape of her neck to the V-curve of her bottom, he told her to lean forward and to thrust her bottom backwards.

The position was hard to keep with her hands still clasped behind her head, but she obeyed as best she could, though the strain made her muscles ache. Yet far more powerful, was the feeling of complete exposure, she knew that he must now be seeing her bottom mouth clutching tightly around the torc, her puffy, swollen pussy lips would be glistening with her juices. She could feel the familiar lubricious heat and knew how she must be responding.

Kate squirmed with embarrassment, a form of primeval panic welling up inside her as a shadow flickered across her heart. She felt nearly ready to bolt when she heard his voice murmuring, "So beautiful...so *beautiful*," as his fingers traced through the soft, wet folds of her sex, and the shadow was suddenly dispelled to be replaced by a delicious astonishment that her most intimate orifices could be so praised.

Stifling a moan, but unable to stop herself from trembling, she felt his finger curl inside the ring of the torc, and then another finger as he opened its grip upon her inner flesh and slowly began to withdraw it. Her bottom felt the pull and she tightened instinctively. "You must relax, Kate." His voice was both gentle and yet utterly commanding. Kate obeyed.

The torc's balls popped out and Kate moaned despite herself. She felt his fingers softly trace her pussy lips and instinctively she moved into his touch, aching for him. But his hand moved away from her pussy and instead grasped her shoulder to help her kneel upright once more. He came to stand in front of her again and looked her steadily in the eye as he spoke.

"Kate, I want you to submit yourself to me now. You have been obedient, delightfully obedient since we met, but this is a stage further. It is the first step in your training. I want you to offer me your body, for my exclusive use for the rest of today. With this submission you surrender all personal rights to your body and its pleasures, you will no longer speak, move or touch yourself without my permission. Further, you give me the right to instruct and punish you as I see fit, to inflict pain or pleasure on you, as I desire. From this point on your pleasure is secondary to mine."

James looked at her sternly and said, "It is your free choice, but once you have agreed, then from now until the stroke of midnight tonight you will be bound by your undertaking. At midnight, you may choose to remain mine until dawn, in which case you will make your phone call to that effect, or you will leave here. You have permission to speak."

Kate looked down, scared by his words, but thrilled by them at the same time. Yes, she admitted to herself, she had anticipated his arriving and perhaps carrying her into the bedroom, there to make love to her and satisfy the urgent needs that had been inflaming her all day. But while that would have been wonderful, it would also have meant that *she* had taken control. Her naked flaunting of her body, her acting the part of a submissive slave, would have got her what she wanted. James' way was so much better, and she loved the way he refused to be manipulated.

"Yes, Sir, I agree, please accept me as your submissive slave." Kate's voice started as a whisper, but ended more firmly as she found the inner confidence to assert what she desired.

James smiled at her and said, "I am going to lead you through a ritual of submission. You may revoke your consent at any time by repeating, 'I revoke my submission' three times, but unless you do, I will consider you bound by this ritual. Nod your head if you understand."

Kate nodded her head, and James instructed her to close her eyes. Almost immediately, she felt the soft touch of a blindfold being tied across her eyes and then felt his hands tracing the outline of her body, stroking the curve of her breast. His hands roamed freely from her throat to her inner thighs, touching every curve of her except for her nipples and pussy, wanting her to sink deeper and deeper into the aching longing for release.

Abruptly, his hands were no longer there, she shivered in anticipation of his next caress, but it did not come. Instead, she heard him moving around the room, and then, suddenly, what little light that had been filtering through the silken scarf wrapped before her eyes disappeared, and she was plunged into darkness.

A minute passed in silence, and then another. Kate suppressed the rising urge to call out, wanting the reassurance of his voice. Then she felt his hands at the nape of her neck and his voice telling her to open her eyes. She gasped and smiled. The dark room was now lit with dozens of candles.

Chapter Fourteen
Ritual of Submission

೮೧

James stood in front of her and told her to place her hands on her thighs. He had taken off his shirt and was holding a candle in one hand. The candle lit one side of his handsome face, casting the other into shadow and giving him an otherworldly beauty. The flickering light from the room candles reflected off the sculpted muscles of his broad chest and shoulders. Kate felt herself melt inside anew with longing for him, and knew she would do anything he asked of her.

He placed a candle on the table beside her and said, "Kate, you will now offer me your submission, beginning with offering me your mouth. You will say, 'I offer you my mouth, my pleasure and my pain. Yours to give or withhold as you desire.' Repeat that now," he commanded, his voice deep and authoritative.

Kate drew a deep breath and began. "I offer you my mouth, my pleasure and my pain, yours to give or withhold—" She had not quite completed her offering before his lips were softly against hers, sweet and sensual.

"I accept your gift of your mouth's pleasure," he murmured, his lips hovering over her mouth, and then he took her mouth with forceful ruthlessness and when their lips separated more than a minute later, she tasted the tang of blood on her tongue. "I accept the gift of your mouth's pain."

"Offer me your breasts, Kate."

Kate hesitated, knowing now what must follow, and yet, she felt the hunger inside consume her. She cupped her breasts and lifted them in offering.

"I offer you my breasts, my pleasure and my pain, yours to give or withhold as you desire." Kate felt each nipple in turn exquisitely kissed with the slightest nip of his teeth, just enough to send a delicious wave of pleasure through her body.

Closing her eyes and lifting her chest into his kisses, she gasped when she felt instead his fingers grip her nipples cruelly, pinching and pulling until she moaned. Abruptly he released her and her breasts bounced back, her nipples achingly hard. She thought it was over but then she heard him say, "I accept the gift of your breasts' pleasure," and his hand caressed the sensitive underside of her left breast, lifting it slightly. Kate's eyes flickered open, her lips parting as she shivered with pleasure beneath his touch. Mesmerized she watched him bring the candle before her eyes and then tip it slightly to allow just one drop of hot wax to fall directly on to her nipple.

Even as she cried out, she heard him say, "And the gift of your pain." His voice coming from the darkness behind the candle was almost formal, and yet, he managed to convey the pride he felt for her offering, as without conscious thought, Kate lifted her right breast herself in offering for the kiss of the hot wax upon her nipple though her lips trembled and her breathing was ragged.

James kissed each of her breasts softly and then her mouth as he whispered, "Thank you, Kate...now offer me your pussy and clit. Lie right back and hold yourself open with your hands. Do it now, Kate." Gently, he pushed her back until her spine was curved like a bow and her breasts, with their super-hard nipples both coated in wax, pointed at the ceiling. Her hands came down to spread her pussy lips wide as her breath came in shuddering gasps.

"I offer you my pussy and clit, my pleasure and my pain, yours to give or withhold as you desire." Kate's voice was tremulous, and near breaking towards the end. Then she felt his hot breath on her superheated flesh just before he caught her clit between his lips. Sudden, shocking pleasure ripped through her, jolting her entire body and making her belly spasm deep inside her core.

Dimly, she heard his voice say soft and deep, "I accept the gift of your pleasure." And then she felt his teeth gently close upon her most vulnerable flesh, not biting but slowly and with exquisite sensitivity increasing the force until pleasure flickered over the edge into pain and back to pleasure. Pain and pleasure intertwined.

His mouth suddenly withdrew, and then the swift, fierce pain as the wax fell directly on to her swollen clit—the epicenter of the earthquake that convulsed her so that she was only dimly aware of the sound of her own scream. A scream choked off as she felt his arms enfold her in his strength and his lips crush hers—whispering, as his lips moved to her ear, his acceptance of the gift of her pain. Then she felt herself lifted up and brought to kneel with her head bowed forward, her bottom raised, pussy lips pouting from between her legs.

"Offer me your ass, Kate," James commanded, ignoring her whimpers and moans.

Kate hesitated then stammered out, "I offer you my ass, my pleasure...and my pain, yours to give or withhold...as you desire."

Kate moaned loudly, but this time with pure pleasure as his hand cupped her pussy, parting the soft, wet glistening folds to touch and circle the entrance to her cunt. His fingers milked her cunt of her juices and spread them over her labia and then up to her ass so that slick with juice, his finger circled and probed until Kate's body betrayed her and she thrust herself backwards onto his finger. Yearning and aching to be penetrated by him however and in whatever way he wished. She panted her desire, moaning his name and pleading softly, her words a stream of wanting and need.

"I accept your pleasure, and now I will teach you the meaning of pleasure-pain my lovely slave," James growled, and began to knead her buttocks with his powerful hands, his strong fingers working her soft, supple flesh as her skin reddened.

James began to spank her, not too hard at first, just deepening the blush to her skin, before returning to his massage. As she knelt helplessly, his hands roamed her body, caressing her breasts, dipping into her sopping wet pussy, rolling around her swollen clit.

Then as her pleasure came on more strongly, he would spank her a little harder, watching her breathing, listening to her moans. His fingers and hands, playing upon her body as a musician would play upon an instrument—contrast and feeling, crescendo and diminuendo. The waves of pleasure and pain flowing one into the other, as the heat in her bottom sank within and connected with the fire in her belly.

Kate began to moan more loudly and toss her head. One part of her was aware of the feelings and powerful desires that coursed through her body but the awareness seemed to come as if from a distance. Watching with astonished, fascinated interest as this girl, who was her and somehow apart from her, responded to James' every touch, her bottom even rising to welcome the next delicious ripple of heat-pain-pleasure as his palm came down on her reddened flesh.

Another part of her was completely immersed in the sensations, swimming deep in the pleasure-pain currents so that the only important thing was where James' hands would touch her next—and that he did touch her. The pain, the only pain that mattered being the absence of that touch to her fevered and frenzied body.

Shuddering and moaning, Kate thrashed her head from side-to-side, her breathless pleadings unintelligible, yet her body's desires were plain from the way her back arched and her pussy dripped. Like a master musician who has played the audience to ecstasy through his virtuoso performance, James stood back to admire the effect of his work. She would never think so, but right at that moment, Kate looked more beautiful than any woman he had ever seen. Panting, skin glistening with sweat, her hair in total disarray—she was a woman completely released of the last vestiges of inhibition. Now he could take his pleasure with her and know she would hold nothing back...that she *could* hold nothing back.

Shedding his remaining clothes, James lifted the head of his cock to her pouting, dripping cunt and without warning plunged into her. Kate bucked and screamed as she felt him split her apart. She would have collapsed then but for James' strong hands holding her steady as he withdrew for the next thrust and then the next, savagely taking her with total focus on his own pleasure. Slowing and accelerating the speed of his thrusts and their depth, making the head of his cock explore every inch of her hot, wet cunt.

Far beyond any pleasure she had previously thought possible, Kate felt that she was holding onto the edge of sanity, a thought that would have terrified her ordinary mind. But now she was transported, far above such cares. More...she knew that if James took her over that edge then he would be there to bring her back, and so even as orgasm followed orgasm and his cock, impaling her, became her whole world, she let go and found herself floating free. Transfixed and transformed in the searing pleasure that engulfed her.

James slowed the pace of his thrusts, and then gently withdrew his cock ignoring her moan of protest. He walked around to Kate's head and grasping a handful of her hair lifted her head so that she could see his cock, with its shining, silken, smooth head just inches from her panting mouth.

"Kate...you may call me Master...and you will beg for permission to take me in your mouth."

Kate looked up through glazed eyes, her mind and emotions reeling. And yet, despite this, knowing that she had somehow passed the most essential test of her life...not through any effort on her part, but simply through being herself. Through throwing wide the doors of possibility and accepting utterly who she was to the deepest core of her being, and knowing that in James she had found a man, and a Master she could adore with every cell of her body.

"Master," Kate said the word and loved the sound of it, and said it again, marveling, "My Master, please may I suck your beautiful cock?"

Kate opened her mouth and her tongue flickered out to lick the bead of pre-come from his engorged cock head. She smiled up at him her eyes wide as she took him deeper and sucked their combined juices from his long shaft. But then withdrew to kiss him mumbling, "Master, mmmy mmmmaster," and then with eager greed, inflamed by her own words, Kate went to swallow him up again.

Chapter Fifteen
Initiation

ଛ

Far more quickly than he had expected, James was obliged to step away, withdrawing his cock against the insistent suction of her mouth. Her passion and even more, the delight, happiness and joy that radiated from her had very nearly undermined his normal self-control, and he wanted to savor her to the fullest.

"Follow me, slave, on your hands and knees." Though his voice sounded cold and distant, James touched her cheek with infinite gentleness, and in that one touch, communicated that he was with her, perfectly attuned to her despite the aloof role he played. Beckoning for her to follow, he walked towards the main bedroom. Kate crawled off the coffee table and hurried after him, grateful for the thick rugs beneath her knees. When she arrived, James was rummaging through drawers and so she knelt and, hoping it would please him, put her hands behind her head and tried to remember the posture he had taught her earlier.

James glanced at her, "Very good, slave...climb up on the bed and spread your arms and legs wide, lying on your back. Close your eyes." Kate did as she was told, centering herself in the middle of the enormous bed. Even with her arms and legs stretched out, her hands and feet were still a couple of feet from the post at each corner, while her head was even farther from the magnificent oak headboard.

James continued to search and eventually found what he was looking for in another bedroom. Returning he used the scarves to tie Kate's wrists to the posts of the bed, and then instructing her to arch her whole back up off the bed, he slid several thick pillows beneath her so that her head hung down facing the headboard. With her legs spread wide, her pussy became the highest point of her body, making her feel intensely exposed and deliciously vulnerable. A feeling that grew much stronger as she felt James grasp her ankles and secure each in turn to the posts at the foot of the bed.

Having ensured that the bonds were tight enough to stretch Kate's limbs to the fullest extent, and yet not so tight as to impair her circulation, James left her, saying only that he would be back shortly. He went outside and started hunting through the outhouses and sheds in which various equipment was stored.

After ten minutes of fruitless searching and with an exclamation of satisfaction, he finally found the length of rope he needed. He was good at improvising, but for Kate's first real experience of complete bondage, he would have preferred to be much better equipped. Yet, he could not possibly have anticipated that the day would come to this sweet conclusion. The sheer power of the chemistry between them was undeniable, far stronger than he had ever experienced with other women. Kate's passion, the delicious abandon with which she threw herself into her role and the exceptional trust she was placing in him, made him determined to make this an unforgettable experience for her.

Back inside the lodge, he collected various candles from the lounge area and after placing them around the bedroom he switched off the light. He threw the length of rope beneath the bed so that several feet protruded either side, and then began to fasten Kate's thighs.

Wrapping the rope around and around above and below each knee he created a wide surface area so that he could apply considerable pulling pressure without shutting off her circulation, and in this way Kate found her thighs spread wider than she would have dreamed possible.

James knew that the first automatic response of a woman's body as she approaches seemingly intolerable levels of pleasure is to try and close her thighs. He wanted Kate to know that she must take everything he gave her, for her to know this in advance with utter certainty.

Satisfied with the lovely spectacle Kate now offered him — her body stretched and helpless, James gazed hungrily at her. He mastered the almost overwhelming urge he felt to just take her immediately and went to search for some oil in the kitchen. Though any oil would do, he hoped there would be at least some olive oil and so was very pleased to find the much purer and lighter almond oil right at the back of one of the cupboards. It would be perfect.

The first Kate knew of this was the slightly cool sensation of the oil being drizzled over her breasts, and then down over her belly and along the top of each of her widespread thighs. Even then she had no idea what the liquid was until she felt James' hands on her thighs working the oil into her skin in long, firm, slow circles.

He began by slowly stroking up the insides of her thighs, at first featherlight touches and then gradually firmer strokes. Then he began to work the oil into her belly and up towards her breasts. At no time did he touch her pussy or breasts, not even allowing his breath to caress her skin. He would work around her pussy or breasts for several minutes circling his fingers tantalizingly closer until Kate's breath became ragged and she began to moan.

Then he would abruptly switch to another part of her body, perhaps her feet, her hands or shoulders. Places that Kate would never have previously associated with sensual pleasure. Yet, now with her attention totally focused on where James was not touching her, paradoxically he made every part of her body a superbly sensitive erogenous zone. His strong fingers explored her body, finding and releasing tension wherever they roamed — even in places Kate had not thought it possible to be tense. James even slid his hands beneath her arched back, his fingers melting her until she felt herself liquefy and begin to float.

But always he returned to the circling of her breasts, or outlining the V of her pussy and ass. Never touching, but somehow always moving closer, making the anticipation of his eventual touch build within her like a tidal wave.

For Kate, it felt like torment in heaven. She had given herself absolutely, and now she would be used and taken in any way James wished. For the moment, it was his pleasure to give her this sweet agony of denial, where the longer he deliberately avoided touching her dripping cunt, the more desperately she craved it. There was no choice. And in the absence of choice, there was release. Her inhibitions were as sandcastles to the waves of pleasure, crashing on the shore of her body.

Kate heard herself begging for his touch. For him to touch her pussy, fuck her cunt, use her, take her...please...please. Every time his hands neared her breasts or pussy, she writhed in her bonds as she sought his touch. A futile struggle, since she was so securely held. Her hands grasped spasmodically at her restraints as her hips rolled—her pussy, a hungry mouth, searching for succor. Nothing mattered but that the hot void within her be filled, and yet, she gloried in the utter helplessness of her bondage.

James knew she was more than ready for the fucking he had in mind, but he wanted to take her even deeper first. To bring her on and take her further than she had believed possible in her wildest dreams...and only then to take her and in doing so make her completely his own. He knew his powers and would use them all to make this lovely woman his willing slave. Yes, she would eventually emerge from her self-imposed slavery like a butterfly from a chrysalis, but first her submission to him must be made absolute.

He placed one hand on her belly just above her pubic bone and the other beneath her so that his fingertips touched her tailbone and the rest of his hand cupped her ass and cunt though without touching them. Then he started to raise his energy...the same energy that would in a martial arts context allow him to smash his hands through house bricks, now served him in this gentler art. As he breathed, his hands became incredibly hot, the heat penetrating deep—flowing from his hands into Kate, the sexual energy sinking into Kate's belly to stir sensations she never knew existed, never dreamed were even possible.

Her belly, cunt, clit and ass were on fire, and under James' hands, her mind came down into the heat to be consumed in the flames, and then rise like a phoenix from the ashes of her molten liquid desire…again and again. Not an orgasm—for James had not allowed her such release—but the intolerable pleasure of *becoming* her cunt, totally immersed within and identified with her sexual self, everything else remote and superficial by comparison. Kate's mind grounding into the sizzling intensity of her core, and finding a safety there like a ship in a hurricane finding itself in the eye of the storm. Peace, serenity and tranquility for moments that seem timeless before once more the fury of the winds of pleasure swept her away.

James placed the engorged head of his cock at the swollen, dripping mouth of her cunt and plunged inside her. Holding her hips, he fucked her pitilessly, knowing that there was not a single part of her that could now remain detached from the pleasure. She was subsumed by her own passion. As he fucked her cunt, James made love to Kate's mind, blowing her apart with the power of his thrusting cock while enfolding her within the sanctuary of his will and embracing her in the power of his love, now fully revealed and offered unconditionally. She had given herself to him and he had accepted, but now he claimed her for his own—he possessed her utterly in body, heart and mind and in the same moment he gave her his heart, his strength and his total trust.

The orgasm when it came was devastating. Sweeping away before it the debris of the past and all the pain and hurt of two lost souls, aching and hungering to find each other and failing, until this moment. United at last, they soared together, spiraling upwards on power currents of pleasure so strong that neither alone could have endured.

Chapter Sixteen
Possession

When Kate awoke, her bonds were gone and she felt James' arms around her. His one arm cradling her breasts and the other across her belly, his hand cupping her pussy, stroking her softly.

She turned within his arms and sought his mouth with her lips, wanting the reassurance of a kiss, disorientated and bewildered, yet hugely happy to be with him.

"Hello, my beautiful one," James said softly. "I woke you because you're a few minutes overdue to make your call. Do that, and then we can talk."

James handed her the phone, which now seemed an irrelevant intrusion to her. As Kate made the call, she noticed her throat felt raw and realized she must have been screaming. Her sex-soaked tone of voice and the happiness that bubbled within her were so obvious to her friend that the call lasted only seconds before she turned once more into James' arms.

James lifted her uppermost leg and opened her pussy lips with his other hand before sliding his cock easily inside her. Kate groaned. She loved to feel his hard length filling her so beautifully, and yet, she felt deliciously sore from her recent fucking.

Kate wriggled on his shaft, and squeezed him with her internal muscles. "You haven't asked me if I choose to submit until dawn...Master." Her voice teasing, ridiculing the idea that she might want to leave.

James held her to him more closely. "Kate, you are mine now," he said simply, knowing this was not a time for games or half-truths.

"You belong to me and me alone, as I am yours. That is what being your Master is all about. Deep down you knew this and wanted it, your inner voice has been guiding you towards this moment for many years. Do not take my word for it, my lovely slave. Search your heart. Tell me it is not true, if you can?"

Kate was silent for a long time, and then a shudder went through her entire body.

"It's true. I could not find what I have with you if I searched for a thousand years, I am yours." She paused. "But, James, that terrifies me...what if you get bored with me? What if—"

"Shhhh." James held a finger to her lips. "Dissolving your fears is what your training is all about, Kate. A Master does not train a submissive woman to submit, he creates the environment in which she is free to be herself...in any case, I don't *need* to train you to submit, I can easily make you obey me should I want to, but given your deep desire to please me that is hardly necessary."

James turned her head so he could look into her eyes, "No, I need to train you to be free from inhibition, free from shame, train you to pleasure. To do that, I require your enthusiastic and willing obedience, but your time as my slave is only a steppingstone to something infinitely more wonderful—the journey into each other's mystery. That feeling that you had the merest briefest glimpse of...but perhaps you don't remember?"

Kate's lips brushed his as she murmured, "How could I not remember the most astonishing feeling in my life when I am still trembling inside from the power of it?"

James smiled, and his hands stroked her skin. "I am so pleased...not everyone can endure the pleasure, you see...they slip into unconsciousness, it's like a safety valve for the mind when the pleasure gets too much to bear. But that's what makes you so special, I knew you would be able to...sooner or later." He grinned at her as he began to move inside her. "Though sooner *is* better!"

Chapter Seventeen
The Farmhouse

ഔ

One month later...

The estate car bumped over the rough country lane, now only a few hundred yards away from the large converted farmhouse that was their final destination. James drove with care, not wishing the bumps to trigger yet another burst of passionate cries from the naked slave girl who was securely fastened spread-eagled behind him.

Kate had not been given permission to come or even to speak, but this had done little to prevent her regular frenzied outbursts as the vibrators in her pussy, ass and the one taped securely over her clit brought her to climax again and again. James made a mental note to use smaller and less intense vibrators on the way back to civilization. But then thought that with a whole week of training, she would probably do a little better with her self-control, which at present was wonderfully poor. Such a wanton little slut! He laughed as a particularly large pothole sent her over the edge for the last time before they arrived. Even with his window open, her musk permeated the entire car—he had lost count of the number of times she had come, even though he was supposed to be counting them in order to deal out suitable punishment later. Though secretly, he was delighted with her extraordinary capacity for pleasure.

* * * * *

Kate had been waiting several hours earlier outside the train station. As instructed, she had traveled wearing only a light knee-length coat over her nakedness, the only other items of clothing he had permitted her were a pair of black hold-up stockings and the black stilettos she was struggling to balance on when he arrived, drawing the big, hired SUV up to the curb. In a misleadingly gentlemanly fashion, he had opened the rear door for her, but as she went to sit in the rear seat, she found it folded down and was obliged to crawl inside on her hands and knees.

"Lie down on your back, my lovely slave," James had commanded, and then he had closed the door and gone to take the wheel again. For a short time, they had traveled in silence. He occasionally had turned around to rub his thumb over her lips, pushing it between her teeth to make her suck on it, as she would have loved to suck upon his cock. Then he would once more turn his full attention to the road. Soon they were out of the city on quiet country lanes and he pulled over.

Getting out of the car, he opened the large, tailgate rear door and instructed her to kneel on the carpeted floor.

"Your training for this week begins here, Kate." James took a beautiful, silvered stainless-steel collar from its velvet bag. "This is a symbol of your servitude during this coming week. It represents a further stage in our relationship. While you wear it, you consent to non-consent, meaning I will not ask your permission to do anything I wish to you. You give me this power over you so that you may experience how I wield it for our mutual pleasure. This is the fastest possible way to build trust between us. You will ask me for it in full knowledge of the power you thereby surrender to me."

All that James now said had been discussed at great length in the weeks since their first meeting. At first, Kate had not really seen why it was necessary. She was his love-slave, pure and simple—she was his to command. It sounded overblown even when she said it to herself, but it was true for the most selfish of reasons—obedience to him unfailingly gave her exquisite pleasure.

She would happily wear the collar, both to please him and because the idea of it aroused her—that it would have practical usage in restraining her went without saying. But in her heart, she knew was already his slave — chained to him by far stronger bonds than mere steel.

In their conversations, James had explained that he wished to enslave *all* of her — that there were parts of her she unintentionally withheld from him, aspects of herself that even she did not know were there. Deeply buried, they were ringed around with defenses against intrusion and were therefore barriers to their deeper intimacy.

Such scars could only be healed with love, yet first, she must trust him sufficiently to allow that love in. It was not a conscious thing. This exceptional level of trust could only be earned and learned through experience…she had to walk out on the proverbial limb and find out that it held.

Inevitably, as she went deeper into her training, there would be situations in which all her primal fears rose to the surface. Occasions when against her conscious volition, her body, and her conditioned mind would recoil from that which he instructed her to do. In those circumstances, the collar would remind her that she had no choice — she had given the power to make choices to him.

The collar symbolized her general consent to everything he would ask of her in the coming week. Though traditionally a symbol of slavery, it was, in fact, far more a symbol of the profound trust they *already* shared, and her willingness to be guided ever more deeply towards ultimate freedom through the path of submission.

The many hours of conversation flashed through Kate's mind as she looked at the collar. James' understanding was profound, and yet she felt defiant — she loved him, surely that was all that mattered? She had not actually said those words as yet. "I love you" could be so meaningless, and she had heard it from so many men who so obviously had not the first clue what love meant. Actions spoke louder than words, and James had shown her from the very beginning his enormous capacity for love…now it was her turn to show him.

Kate looked down submissively and said, "Please, Master, I beg that you allow me to wear your collar and take me into your service as your submissive slave."

James leaned forward to fasten and lock the collar around her throat. Beautifully crafted, it clicked firmly into place with its large ring hanging down at the center of her throat. He attached a leash to the ring and ordered her from the car. "Follow me, lovely slave!"

The leash pulled gently at her as she struggled off her knees and stepped out of the car. Kate peered at her surroundings apprehensively. In the dim twilight, she could barely make out a rough stile set into the boundary wall and beyond that a dark wood. Feeling a more insistent tug, and not daring to dawdle, she hastened to follow him, her absurdly high heels hampering her every step.

At the stile, James straddled the bar and with seeming effortlessness, lifted her over it, and set her down on the other side. Then they were off again, him striding along, and her desperately trying to keep up and not disgrace herself.

The smell of damp woods assailed her, a light mist hovered eerily low on the ground and the trees were wide spaced between thick carpets of leaves. Had she been less focused on keeping her balance and not losing her shoes, she might have given more thought to where she was being taken.

In fact, James stopped in a small clearing only a hundred yards or so from the road. In a tone that brooked no discussion, he told her to strip and when she still hesitated, he roughly pulled off her coat and threw it away. Kate gazed after it in bewilderment. The next thing she knew her world had gone black.

To the muted noises of protest, more from shock than genuine fear, James hustled her over to two small silver birches growing parallel and about six feet apart. Had Kate been able to see anything at all, she would have been surprised to see him take a smooth, long pole from behind one of the trees and fasten it to each tree parallel to the ground at waist height with a few turns of strong rope that he had clearly left here for the purpose.

Since she was hooded, Kate could only stand trembling with both apprehension and cold as the chilly breeze hardened her nipples and brought her legs out in goose bumps. The earlier heat and wet in her pussy now began to feel achingly cold as she tottered on her heels. With a wry grin that she felt quite safe to reveal under the hood, she reminded herself that if she knew anything at all about James then she would not be feeling cold for very long.

Kate felt him take her arms and lead her a few steps, she squealed as the unexpected chill of the smooth pole touched her belly and again when he forced her to bend over it with her head down between her legs. Mercifully he removed her heels and stockings, and then she felt his hands grab her ankles to spread her legs wide so that now most of her weight was taken by the pole. Leather thongs securely fastened her wrists to her ankles and her leash was drawn through the eye of a peg he had placed in the ground earlier.

Without warning, James stripped away the hood and almost instantly she felt the pressure of his cock against her lips has he pushed himself into her mouth. Still breathing heavily from the shock of her sudden bondage, she hurried to open her mouth and take him into her. Rolling her tongue around his hardness, she tried to lubricate his passage deeper into her throat, though her mouth was dry with anticipation of what was to come. His hands rolled and pulled at her nipples sending bursts of heat directly to her clit.

Since James was kneeling to gain access to her mouth, she could feel his warm breath tantalizing the soft, moist folds of her pussy—she ached for his touch so desperately that her hips struggled to move back to contact his lips. At the same time, Kate frantically tried to take more of him into her mouth, wanting to feel him in her throat, wanting all of him, knowing she must take what she could when it was offered, since her needs were not going to be considered now that she was his slave. Or so she thought.

Having let her adjust to her new helplessness, and for the sensation of his cock in her mouth and the rough handling of her nipples to once more make her incredibly wet, James withdrew from her mouth. He ignored her mews of protest, which quickly turned to moans of lust as he plunged himself deep into her cunt. As always, the simple act of controlling her completely had made his entrance wonderfully easy. She was slick with juice, even though he doubted he had been fucking her mouth for more than a few seconds.

For the next twenty minutes, James fucked her. Sometimes so hard the pole creaked in protest as she bounced upon it, while she moaned and whimpered under his assault. Sometimes he fucked her slowly, letting her feel every inch of him as he slid in and out of her — as he toyed with her clit and slipped his thumb, lubricated with her own copious juice, in to her ass.

Twice, James withdrew to push himself in to her mouth, knowing that she loved the small erotic humiliation of being forced to taste herself on his cock. She licked him clean of their combined juices, before he resumed his plundering of her cunt. He took her for his own pleasure, but in doing so, brought her to orgasm twice, the second time her screams of pleasure echoed through the wood, so far gone was she that she had lost any concern for discovery.

Finally, with a satisfied groan, James came deep inside her.

When his cock eventually stopped pulsing, he withdrew and grabbing her hair, he lifted her head up between her legs, and made her open her mouth so that when his spunk began to drip from her swollen cunt, it dripped into her mouth or onto her face. She licked her lips appreciatively and opened her mouth wider, loving this new humiliation and the taste of him.

Leaving her for a brief moment, James walked to where he had hung his coat on a nearby tree and took a soft, wide-stranded flogger from the pocket. Then he began to flog her, never too hard and never too softly. The soft strands slapped her skin like a dozen tiny hands with each stroke. The backs of her thighs, her back, breasts, nipples and even the pouting lips of her pussy all felt their kiss as he worked on her.

Always just the right weight behind the stroke — varied dependent on his aim, as he brought her on relentlessly. Sometimes, he would stop to draw the soft leather up between her open pussy lips, frictioning her clit and caressing her ass. After a series of light, stingy strokes directly between her legs that took her breath away, he would turn the handle of the whip into a dildo to fuck her until she groaned and whispered to please, please be allowed to come. He denied her but resumed the flogging.

Only when James had brought her abruptly to a halt on the brink of orgasm half a dozen times, the last time only by being quite brutal with her nipples, did he insert the vibrators in her cunt and ass. He then taped a tiny clitoral stimulator over her swollen bud, her smooth, shaven pussy lips making for good fixing once dried of their slick wetness. Untying her, he led her naked back to the car. There he laid her once more on her back, but this time with her wrists and ankles shackled into strong, leather cuffs. Like this, she had traveled the two hours to the isolated farmhouse he had rented for her first week of intensive training as his slave to pleasure.

As he pulled up on the farmhouse's front driveway, Kate was terrified to hear voices asking if he need help unpacking the car and was he here on his own? The voices got closer and she fought the urge to struggle in her shackles, afraid that any noise would draw attention to her. James seemed to be taking his time! Chatting away! The devil would know how she was feeling — so exposed and vulnerable.

Ruefully, she admitted to herself that the fear of imminent discovery was melting her belly once more, even as her mind fought the sensation. Kate was astonished to discover yet another example of her wanton sexuality. She had never thought she might be an exhibitionist, it had never figured greatly in her fantasies before. Then she remembered James saying that for this week she must learn to trust and be guided by her most lewd and basic desires, not to question them or seek to understand why her body responded as it did. She must accept it, embrace the pleasure however derived, and try hard not to intellectualize what was happening. The answers and the understanding would come later.

Even so, she was relieved when the voices faded and she heard the crunch of James' approaching footsteps on the gravel drive. He helped her from the car after removing her shackles and vibrators, and told her to put on her stockings and heels. As he kissed her deeply, he took a pair of delicate steel cuffs, bracelets really, from his pocket and cuffed her hands behind her. Then picking up her leash, he led her into the farmhouse.

Chapter Eighteen
Slave Chains

ɛɔ

Once inside the farmhouse, Kate felt a wave of warmth engulf her. James had obviously instructed that the heating be switched on, ready for their arrival. Despite the time of year, the nights could still turn chilly, and he would undoubtedly wish to keep her naked most of the time. James told her to wait, and she stood obediently still, gazing around the hall as he explored the rest of the house to decide which of its many rooms would serve which purpose.

Returning to the hall, he took her on a tour. First he led her through to a large country kitchen with a wood-burning stove and huge oak table, an array of pots and pans intermingled with bunches of herbs hung on hooks from low rafters. It seemed charmingly rustic and hopelessly primitive until James opened cupboards to reveal modern appliances, such as a large refrigerator and microwave oven—cleverly hidden from view behind wooden fascias. Beyond the kitchen was a pantry stocked with everything they could possibly need for the week.

James led her back to the hall and from there to a large lounge with a roaring log fire, superfluous with the central heating, yet a glorious sight. The thick carpet and worn leather sofa and armchairs made the room seem to exude coziness. The adjacent dining room was strangely formal and austere in the otherwise welcoming house.

Upstairs, they came to a long landing with five doors. The first door opened into the master bedroom with its en-suite bathroom and obligatory four-poster bed. Three smaller bedrooms, each just large enough to hold a double bed, and a second bathroom accounted for the remaining doors.

Everything was clean and minimally decorated with only an occasional watercolor or pastel of flowers or local landscapes to relieve the bare walls. It was simple and delightful and, with so little of the owner's taste in evidence, already wonderfully private and intimate.

James led her back into the master bedroom, and cuffing her hands in front of her, he told her she had ten minutes free time to toilet and tidy herself, even shower, if she wanted, before he expected to find her kneeling at the foot of the bed in position one.

Kate rushed off to the bathroom to spend a frantic few minutes washing herself all over before she returned, desperately hoping she wasn't late. Not having a watch, she had no idea how long she had been. To her relief, she saw him smiling down at her. He was fastening ringbolts into the rafters above and around the bed — sinking the six-inch long bolts deeply in to the wood. She realized that she had once more underestimated him. If he wished, he could decide she had been twelve minutes or nine minutes, how could she possibly know?

Kate felt sure that he had requested the agent remove all the clocks from the house, and glancing round the room, she spied the circular spot on the wall where a clock had obviously once been. Very sly! Despite herself, she smiled back at him, loving that once more he had taken control of something she hadn't considered being reliant on until now.

Kate knelt quickly as James watched her — her knees spread wide, sitting on her heels, her breasts lifting and thrusting forward as she clasped her cuffed hands behind her head.

Presenting herself thus, she waited for him with her eyes cast down, though she could not help stealing occasional glances as he removed the chains, shackles, toys and a myriad of other unidentifiable devices from the large suitcase he had taken from the car's roof rack. The small suitcase that held his clothes and a few necessary toiletries for her was on the bed. If she had clothes at all, a fact she was far from sure of, then he had brought them for her.

Kate allowed herself the luxury of anticipating what the week had in store for her, and felt the heat begin to glow in her belly once more. It was such a perfect setting for her initiation as his slave. She hoped he would be gentle, and then she concealed a smile as her cunt melted as she imagined him being strict, masterful and erotically cruel.

While Kate was losing herself in dreamy erotic fantasies of what the week would bring, James was busy adapting the farmhouse to their needs. For the most part, he would rely on her obedience and genuine willingness to please him, but he knew that her sense of helplessness would be taken to a deeper level were she chained whenever possible. During the next few days, he wanted her to come to think of her bondage as naturally as she had clothes in her previous life. Her chains should not merely be the method by which he restrained her, but in their unyielding strength, become a form of security and safety as she went deeper and deeper into her feelings. He therefore wanted to place ringbolts, to which he could attach her chains around the house, and their placement required a little planning.

Kate would sometimes sleep at the foot of the bed on the sleep-pad he had brought for the purpose. It would be soft enough to be comfortable when covered with a faux fur, and he anticipated she would look stunning curled up on it.

A ringbolt was therefore required near her sleep-pad to restrain her by her collar while she slept, but with enough free length of chain to allow her to join him in bed should he permit it.

Then there were other bolts to fix. He wanted to be able to suspend her from wrist or ankle shackles for both punishment and discipline during the many hours he intended to play with her body. The most convenient location was the massive four-poster bed and James was relieved that it was made from sturdy pinewood — easily repaired and cheaply replaced should the owner take exception to having holes bored into its frame. Four bolts into the roof beams and four more bolts on each corner of the bed accomplished this easily, offering him a wide variety of options.

Instructing Kate to remain kneeling, he left with his small tool bag to fix further means of restraint around the house. In the bathroom—for he intended to shave and pluck her mound himself each morning. In the kitchen, so that she might be restrained either to cook for him or offer an erotic spectacle as he cooked, and lastly in the lounge before the fire where he intended to keep her during the day.

With these in place, James opened a door set almost invisibly into the paneling of the reception hall and descended down creaking steps into the cellar. The room covered most of the ground floor of the old house—large, brick arches supported the heavy beams of the floor above. Heavy flagstones gave the room a wonderfully dungeon-like appearance. He smiled wickedly as he made plans for her.

The cellar was almost empty except for an old boiler, which gave the room some limited warmth. There were rows of empty wine racks that spoke of the room's original purpose. He dragged a rough workbench to the center of the dusty, yet otherwise clean room, and drove bolts in to each corner of it and four more above it in to the roof beams. Still smiling, he checked the room for anything he might have previously missed, and then switched the single central bulb off as he left.

Out in the yard, with its surrounding outhouses and stables, he approached a large, heavy door and after unlocking it, he stepped inside. The rear half of the room was somewhat like a stable but instead of the usual wooden partition, it had steel bars that ran from roof to floor. The door into the pen was also made of steel bars and swung silently on oiled hinges as he pushed it open. Originally, the steel pen had been designed to hold a bull, so it would easily detain Kate should the need arise. James nodded thoughtfully and returned to the farmhouse.

Back in the master bedroom, Kate had obediently not moved. He walked in front of her and lifting her chin, looked into her eyes. His eyes were soft and gentle, there was no intimidation in them, but even so, they were penetrating and she could not hold his gaze, and looked down submissively after a few seconds.

James' hand brushed the velvet skin of her breasts, softly caressing her and then turning sideways onto her he smoothed his hand down to her belly. Lifting his hand away, he moved it farther down to hover over her pussy. She could feel the warmth of his hand even though he did not touch her, and her hips involuntarily tilted to seek the touch she craved. She gasped at the contact and felt him cup her, owning her and possessing her with just this simple gesture of his hand.

As always, the discipline of her position, her enforced awareness of her surrender to his will, the ease with which even his kindest gaze dominated her, all fused to have her aching for his touch and amazingly wet. He noticed that she had even been dripping down her thighs in expectation of his return.

"Tell me what you want, Kate?" His voice was soft, but there was no refusing it. Kate's mind reeled with images of desire, all the many things she had dreamed happening to her, the things that made her desperate with excitement, the things that made her heart seem to stop within her when she dared to think of them. From this complexity, she must find some simple truth that would communicate her need to him, even though she knew full well he knew it before she spoke.

"I want to be used, Master," she whispered. "I want to be your plaything and exist for your pleasure and to lose myself in lust…" Her words ran out, Kate hung her head confused.

"How do you want to feel?" Again she paused, trying to collect her thoughts, knowing that nothing less than complete, transparent honesty would satisfy him.

"I want to feel controlled, Master. I want to feel that I have nothing to think of except pleasing you. I want you to control my body utterly and dictate my every movement. I want to feel beautiful to you, sexy, sensual…and I want to feel safe, protected…and I want to feel able to completely surrender to you… I want…" Her flood of words amazed her and she faltered. James nodded in agreement.

"You *are* mine, Kate, you would not be so were you not beautiful to me, but I understand that is not the same thing as feeling so. But this you will learn. You will do nothing that does not please me, at least not more than once, because I will not allow it. As the week progresses, you will learn that whatever trust you invest in me will be returned to you a hundredfold in terms of your own fulfillment and the pleasure we share. When you are willfully disobedient of my wishes, you will be punished. In this, you will learn to feel also a great sense of security since I will never be unfair or inconsistent. Do you understand?"

"Yes, Master, thank you, Master," she answered quietly.

James let his middle fingers slip inside her hot wetness as he began to rub his thumb around her clit in slow, deep circles. Occasionally as he spoke, he would flick her clit with his thumbnail to emphasize some important point.

"I make a very special distinction between discipline and punishment. You will be punished only if you are deliberately disobedient when told to do something that is well within your experience and learning. The intention of such punishment is that you dislike it. It is not intended to be enjoyable or erotic, but to teach you obedience when kindness and patience seem to have failed. Discipline is quite different, it is a part of your training to pleasure — exploring trust, surrender, dominance and submission as I oblige you to experience and overcome your inhibitions and relinquish all shame of your body, and I expect you to enjoy it. Pleasure and pain are mine to give or withhold, but always to be enjoyed. Your *punishment* will always take the form of being isolated from me, to give you time to reflect upon your disobedience and discover the root cause of it if you can. Do you understand?"

James altered the movement of his fingers within her to press forward to the root of her clit and she gasped out, "Yes, Master!"

"Your training will also involve the earning and withdrawal of privileges. You start at zero in your chains and collar, silent and restricted. You may not touch yourself without permission, not even to scratch an itch. Your obedience and willingness to learn earns you privileges such as good food, clothing and permission to speak freely. The more privileges you enjoy the more freedom you have to serve me creatively, the fewer privileges you have, the more absolutely I have to control everything you do...so I *want* you to earn those privileges because controlling every little detail of your life is ultimately boring."

James looked at her, making sure she had grasped what he had said, wanting clarity in his communication and understanding between them.

Kate's lips parted to speak, but with his busy fingers inside her, she did not trust her voice and so nodded her comprehension, wishing he would stop talking and let her dissolve into pleasure.

"Now lastly, I will explain what you may say and what you will not say. You may ask permission to come at any time, you may ask for permission to speak at any time. If during the week you decide that you want your training to altogether cease, you will repeat your full name three times over and ask to be released from your training. Do you have anything to say?"

"Please, Master...please can I come?" she responded, her breath ragged. His precise statement of the rules that would govern her life for the next week having brought her to the edge of orgasm, despite the mild stimulation he was giving her.

"No, you may not," James said, a smile on his lips, but he slowed the circling of his thumb on her clit, and she sagged slightly with mixed relief and disappointment.

James' hand abruptly left her, and he went to his case and removed silvery chains linked to thick two-inch steel rings.

He clipped one end of the chain to her collar and let its remaining length hang down between her lifted breasts to fall between her parted swollen pussy lips. Kate gasped from its unexpected coldness. From a ring positioned between her breasts two short lengths of chain ended in nipple clamps. These he screwed firmly into place while allowing the joining lengths of chain to drape over her breasts in graceful curves. Kate moaned involuntarily as he tightened them on her rubbery-hard flesh. Her nipples immediately began to throb.

From the ring between her breasts, the main central chain went to another ring just above her pubis where it divided into three further chains, two long and one short. The middle short chain was also much lighter weight and one ended in a strange rubber-toothed clamp shaped like the teeth of a propelling pencil. It was this James used to clamp her swollen and juice-smeared clit, tightening it until Kate moaned so desperately that he knew she would come from its pressure alone if he continued.

The other two chains he drew down between her legs, ensuring that they passed between her inner and outer labia before bringing them up between her buttocks and around to her waist to fasten once more to the central ring at her pubis. A tiny padlock in the middle of her back maintained the constancy of the tension and kept the chain securely nestled between her buttocks and labia.

"Position two," James snapped the command at her like a whip. After a moment's hesitation that he chose to ignore, Kate was kneeling with her buttocks thrust up in the air, her head down and her arms stretched forward in front of her. Her position now drew the chains tightly between her pussy lips and, as the chains hung down from her body, they pulled at the clamps on both her nipples and her clit so that she moaned loudly when the sensation first struck her.

Not daring to look, but hoping that James would fuck her there and then, she knelt obediently, though she could not stop her body trembling with desire. She had closed her eyes and rested her forehead on the carpet in delicious anticipation of the feel of his cock surging inside her, and was therefore utterly surprised when a sheaf of paper and a pen was pushed beneath her nose.

"We have, of course, already discussed much of what is in that contract in our earlier conversations, but you will read it through carefully before you sign it, this is just to cover this week." James left her there to read, sitting on the bed soaking in the lovely image she presented — wet and wanton slave girl kneeling, desperate to be fucked and reading her own contract of submission. Wonderful!

Chapter Nineteen
A Test of Obedience

೩

Her hand trembling, Kate signed the contract and handed it to him. James' signature followed. Now perhaps he would take her? She hoped in vain.

"Right, I've been driving for hours and I'm very hungry! So go to the kitchen and throw something simple together for me, some soup will do… And be quick about it, and be obedient!" He drew her up by her hair and, making her stand in front of him, he lifted her braceleted hands to kiss her palms. Inhaling deeply.

James slapped her ass playfully as she scurried off and followed her downstairs to make himself comfortable in the deep, leather armchair he had spotted by the fire. He wondered if she would figure out the significance of him kissing her palms.

Kate ran down to the kitchen, her chains pulling tantalizingly at her nipples and especially at her clit with every step she took. Never had she been more aware of being naked. Her aroused but denied body was superlatively sensitive to even the gentlest of drafts, all her senses seemed more aware, colors were more vibrant, sounds more acute. She was free to move and yet deliciously restrained, controlled and yet free to express her joy in her sensual, sexual being.

In the kitchen, she began to open cupboards and quickly found bowls, a saucepan and in the fridge a carton of fresh soup. Putting this on to heat, she found a tray and began to lay it with cutlery and condiments then she realized she was rushing unnecessarily — she had time to pause for breath while the soup heated.

Kate looked down at her chains and stretched her body to make them pull on her clit and nipples, delighting in the feeling. Her hands strayed to her nipples, and then down to her belly pushing the cold links into her swollen, hot core—loving their cold, steely inflexibility. She lost herself in the sensations of warmth and heat that seeped uncontrollably from her cunt. The ache inside her was an itch that she must scratch. She could not endure the torment of not touching, even though touching would never be enough. A small voice within her mind protested in vain at her disobedience but was summarily squashed.

She needed to be filled, to feel James' hard length sliding deep inside her, stretching, claiming and possessing her. He was teasing her—he knew what she wanted! Why didn't he give it to her! Her hands smoothed her belly, her inner thighs, one hand easing fingers passed the chain to explore deeply inside her needy cunt, the other gently twisted her clit clamp. The perverse pleasure-pain of its grip at her center made her legs tremble, and she uttered a soft moan, breathy with desire. For long moments, she lost herself in delicious sensation.

Abruptly some part of her remembered the soup and she snapped out of her reverie, panicked that it might be spoilt. With relief, she noticed it just coming to the boil and she lifted it away from the heat.

Checking the arrangement of the tray, she poured soup into the two bowls and feeling extremely conscious of how she must look to him, she walked as elegantly as possible into the lounge, the steam from the soup condensing on her breasts.

She placed the tray on a small table by his chair and knelt by the side of it, ready to serve him, remembering to keep her knees spread wide. She waited for him to say something, hoping for some small praise for the elegance of her service or the speed with which she had done as he commended.

Instead, he came and knelt before her, intently studying her face and noticing the flush of her cheeks. Could it be from the heat of the wood burning stove, or was it something else that made her so prettily flushed? He took her braceleted hands and once more kissed her palms smelling the betraying scent of her arousal immediately. He lifted her chin and looked in to her eyes.

"Were you given permission to play with yourself?"

Kate flushed crimson at her discovery.

"No, Master." She lowered her eyes submissively though inwardly she was furious for being caught out so easily. With a hint of rebellion, she told herself she would wash her hands next time!

"And were you told to prepare food for yourself? Or did you think I might like an extra bowl?" James paused, and looked at her sternly.

"This will be difficult for you to begin with, Kate. You will do what you are told and nothing more. You will listen to the instructions you are given and you will obey them exactly. If you feel I have not thought of something, you must trust that I have, or at least ask for permission to voice your fears. If you catch yourself disobeying me then come to me, and talk to me about it. We will find a way to help you remain obedient so that you may always be happy in the knowledge that your submission is complete and you run no risk of displeasing me."

James removed her bracelets after unlocking them with a tiny key and returned to his seat, saying nothing for what seemed to her an age, but was perhaps only a few minutes.

"When I have eaten, I am going to explain your punishment to you. Go and stand before the fire, bend over and grasp your ankles and wait."

James settled the tray on his lap and began to eat with apparent indifference to the lovely spectacle of the beautiful girl so lewdly displaying herself to him before the fire. The act of composure, for it was an act, hid his mixed feelings concerning her behavior. Had she not played with herself, in truth, he would have felt disappointed. Both because he would have misjudged her astonishing sexual appetite and because it was vital she understood as quickly as possible that she was no longer in control. She could no longer act upon her desires, at least not while she was fully in role as his slave. She must understand this — it would make things very much easier for her in the longer term.

Even so, he would have been happier if she had done something less flagrantly disobedient, especially if she had not combined her disobedience with trying to deceive him, and preferably that she had done something unassociated with her delicious wantonness — perhaps if she had just eaten some of the soup, then the lesson would have been much easier for her to understand, and though the punishment would have been no less strict, it could have been much milder.

Finishing both his bowl and the second she had brought for herself as he idly flicked through an old country magazine, James waited for what he judged to be the right moment. Abruptly, he told her to come and kneel before him once more.

"You have disobeyed me and sought your own pleasure contrary to my explicit instructions. You must learn to appreciate that for the duration of this week, your body is my property and that the only way you may act with any freedom is with the clear intention of giving me pleasure. One of the many ways in which I will take pleasure in your body, and ultimately give you more pleasure, is to torment you with desire, to keep you permanently aroused, even desperate for release, and yet deny you until you are quite helpless with need." He leaned forward to grasp her chains dragging her towards him so that she was forced to shuffle forward on her knees.

"Tonight you will be punished because you must understand that I will have your absolute obedience. Your obedience is not conditional on whether or not it happens to be convenient to you. Most importantly, it is not for you to find inventive and clever ways to 'get away' with disobeying me. That is deception and it will not be tolerated."

James let her absorb the impact of his words and saw the conflict within her.

"You are perhaps confused? It was only a little thing after all, a brief lapse of self-control? I would agree with you save for one thing—you *knew* it was against the rules, and you did it anyway because you thought you would not be discovered. It does not matter *what* you did. It matters only that you tried to hide it from me."

James watched as the tears fell silently down her face, adoring her, but knowing that he must continue to drive this lesson home.

"In most cases in the future a contrite and honest sense of remorse for having disobeyed me would be adequate punishment in itself, possibly combined with a loss of privileges. However tonight, I think it imperative that you are punished very strictly so you learn the full consequence of any future attempts to deceive me."

Telling her to remain kneeling, he left the room and returned shortly with more lengths of chain and objects she did not immediately understand the purpose of.

"The first privilege you lose for tonight is the ability to walk upright. Because I'm being kind, I am going to allow you to wear these kneepads as we'll be going outside and *you* will be crawling."

He held the pads up for her to see before quickly fastening them into place with their loop and hook quick-release straps. "The second privilege is that of being trusted not to touch yourself so you will wear these short-chain wrist shackles. They will allow you to crawl, but once we have arrived where I'm taking you, the chain will be attached to your collar and make it impossible for you to touch your pussy or even your nipples."

James removed her bracelets and replaced them with the heavy steel cuffs then reattached her leash and told her to follow him.

Tears still running quietly down her face she followed him, frantically trying to keep up and quickly grateful for the kneepads.

Outside, the cobbles of the farmyard were wet and a soft rain drizzled down, a heavy mist was settling over the silent countryside. But the rain at least meant it was mild and except for the aching rigidity of her nipples, Kate was not especially cold by the time she had crawled across the yard to the stable. Her discomfort was within.

James led her inside and as he flicked a switch to turn on the single dust-covered light bulb, she saw immediately what was to befall her.

She was not allowed to hesitate, but taken quickly into the cage section of the bullpen and told to kneel while her wrist chain was fastened to her collar.

"This is a punishment, slave. I want it to be an effective one so there will be no repetitions. As they are, your chains prevent you from touching yourself, but you otherwise have some freedom to move. This is not acceptable." With this, James produced ankle shackles and picking her up threw her into a pile of soft, deep straw in one corner, then arranged her so she lay on her back with her head towards the corner, her wrists just beneath her chin, her eyes wide open in alarm at what he intended.

James put the ankle shackles on her and then drew each leg up high to attach the chain to hooks in the wall, repeating the process with her other leg so she lay with her legs wide open, her pussy glistening in the half-light.

Kneeling between Kate's legs, he slowly pushed a dildo between her pussy chains, using them to hold it in place at full penetration, and then took a timer from his pocket and plugged its wire into the protruding end of the dildo.

"This will cause the dildo to vibrate for one minute every half an hour. It is therefore obviously not for your pleasure, but to remind you of the pleasures your disobedience has caused you to forfeit tonight. You will remain here until morning. Do you accept this punishment, slave?"

Kate could only nod her head, not trusting herself to speak, and feeling very miserable indeed.

After carefully placing another small object high on a shelf, James left her. He padlocked the steel door and shut the outer one, and then hurried back to the farmhouse.

Once inside he fetched his laptop from his suitcase and booted it up. For a few minutes he fiddled with wires and tapped away at the keyboard until an image of her in the stable appeared on the screen and he sighed with relief that the technology had not let him down. Even in the dim light, he could see her clearly — as importantly, he would hear her should she cry out or become frightened. Punishing her was his responsibility, but then so was her safety and her essential wellbeing, and now he had the means to watch over her and ensure that her ordeal was no greater than she could cope with.

James sighed unhappily even though he knew that what was happening was vital to ensure that there was no room for miscommunication. As he poured himself a drink, he reminded himself of the many lessons learned from past mistakes, and knew this was the price you paid for clarity, for making responsible use of the power Kate had given him.

He knew that many dominants would have corporally punished a disobedient submissive. It was erotic, it was over quickly and it was the established method of correction, but James had come to believe that this was unwise. The risk was that the submissive would become attached to the pain in this context, and come to think that she must be disobedient in order to experience the erotic intensity of corporal punishment again — and this was not something he was willing to risk.

Of course, there were other dangers that were also avoided by punishing with boredom. James had talked with quiet a few submissives whose dominants had hit them in anger, used them as a punch bag in a manner he thought indistinguishable from abuse. The last thing James wanted was for Kate to be frightened of him, and the thought of her being physically harmed made him feel sick.

This way, though a little cold and uncomfortable, with a lot of time to reflect and in the sure knowledge that obedience would have kept her warm and dry and enjoying herself enormously in any number of wickedly erotic ways, he could be very sure she would think long and hard before trying to deliberately deceive him again. The simple truth was that her submission had to come from within her and could not be forced or threatened, but first, the silly little girl who thought she could get away with being "naughty" would have to be exorcised. James sincerely hoped that tonight would be enough.

* * * * *

Out in the cage, Kate was entirely unaware of the mini-cam and microphone and, believing herself quite alone, she finally allowed the tears to fall freely and her feelings to flow. It had been a bewildering few hours since she had first stepped into the car, so rich in intense pleasure and eroticism that she had had no time to digest what was happening to her. The conflicting feelings and thoughts churned within her and it was not long before the tears stopped and she lay there fuming—though she was not sure who she was angrier with—herself or James.

Why had he put her in here? All the erotic stories she had ever read described the wildly sexy consequences of disobedience—the spankings and floggings and the deliciously humiliating torments she had fantasized about for so long before meeting James. She lay there feeling let down, irritated and uncomfortable until the vibrator buzzed inside her for the first time. Its frustratingly mild stimulation reminded her that she had only been lying there for half an hour and suddenly the prospect of the coming hours hit her hard and she began to cry again.

When the tears finally stopped Kate, never much given to self-pity, decided to use the time as best she could. Though she could feel her legs gradually became more and more numb, the shackles that held her ankles were softly padded inside the heavy steel, and by wriggling deep into the straw she managed to get at least comfortable enough to think and wonder.

Slowly but surely as the hours passed by, punctuated by the minute-long irritation of the vibrator buzzing inside her, she began to pull together the threads of everything James had taught her about her training and what it would involve.

She had touched herself...she was bad and disobedient so she was punished...for touching herself...bad girls get punished...good girls get rewarded...she was bad...she disobeyed...she was punished...she disobeyed, she was punished...she touched herself so she was punished...no!

Kate smiled ruefully when finally amongst the tumbling thoughts understanding finally dawned. James had *not* punished her for touching herself, for being sensual and sexy! He had not even really punished her for disobeying him, but for *deceiving* him!

Her needs and sexual wantonness were not "bad" in his eyes, only the deliberate deception of touching herself, and then pretending she had not. She realized that had she gone from the kitchen and knelt before him, and told him what she had done, told him how she felt—helpless to control herself then the outcome would have been completely different! She would certainly have been punished for disobedience, but nothing like to this extent, and she suspected the reward for having the courage to tell James the truth would have been memorably erotic. How often had they discussed the importance of complete emotional honesty? Acknowledging how difficult it was and yet agreeing that it was the most desirable of goals to strive towards together.

So why had she not told him? Why had she tried to pretend, to deny what she had done? The answer could only be that some part of her thought such behavior shameful. Yet her wiser self knew that had she gone to James and told him of her need, he would have been delighted with her, perhaps would have told her to touch herself in front of him...and that could have led to all sorts of wonderful things!

And this now? This was to keep things separate! This was to ensure that she did not confuse feeling aroused and sexy in any way with being bad or wrong. He did not even want her to associate punishment with her being near to him! He had always said that the point of a punishment was to ensure that the offense was not repeated. *Well*, she thought, *there was not the tiniest part of her that wished to repeat this experience*! In the future, she would be obedient, willingly and with every ounce of her strength.

How many times had James told her that her submission was her gift to him? That it could never be forced. That forced submission was just abuse? It was then that she felt the deepest remorse, yet beneath it, she felt the underlying strength of determination never to willfully deceive him again, and never to feel ashamed of her needs and desires.

Chapter Twenty
The First Day Begins

ॐ

Dawn was breaking when Kate awoke to the noise of the stable door being unbolted. In the soft early light that streamed through the open door, she could dimly make out his face.

He bent to kiss her lips and whispered, "Good morning, my lovely Kate," and she felt a gentle tug on her slave chains, and then the sudden emptiness as he removed the dildo. He straightened and she felt his hands on her ankles as he released the shackles and lowered her legs to the floor, then his arms slid beneath her as he picked her up in the cradle of his arms, and carried her into the warmth of the farmhouse.

She rested her head on his shoulder as he carried her up the stairs and into their bedroom where he laid her down on the faux-fur bearskin he had placed on a small mattress at the foot of the bed. With deft hands, he removed her chains and clamps, pausing only to kiss each point where they had held her. She moaned at his touch, but it was too brief a sensation to be anything but a tender intrusion into the sleepy warmth that now engulfed her. Clipping her collar to the long house chain that would allow her access to the bathroom should she awaken before him, he wrapped her in the heavy fur and, kissing her once more, he left her to sleep.

Going to the bathroom, James arranged some items ready for later in the morning and made sure the fire was safe in the lounge. Then he, too, went to bed.

Several hours later, she awoke to the sound of his voice. Through sleep-bleared eyes, she saw that he had been up for some time. From his still wet hair and smooth chin, it was obvious he had showered and shaved, though he wore only a pair of jeans, his feet and upper torso bare.

"Wake up, slave!" he said, smiling down at her sleepy face. Kate watched drowsily as he removed her house chain and clipped the leash to her collar, and then she had to struggle inelegantly to her feet as he gave the leash an upward tug. James frowned in disapproval.

"No! That will never do. Lie back down again. You must learn to move with attention to grace and posture. In role as my pleasure slave, everything you do should be pleasing on the eyes and advertise your status and the pride you take in it. From lying, you will first push yourself up to kneel in position one, presenting your breasts to me with your hands behind your head. You will then on the command 'stand', raise your bottom, place your right leg before you while making sure you keep yourself open and exposed."

James took her ankle and placed her legs as he wished. One was folded beneath her and the other formed a graceful arc in front of her, which ensured full exposure of her pussy to his gaze. "You will then move your weight onto your front leg and stand with your hands still clasped behind your head."

He made her repeat the movement several times until, with a nod and smile of approval, he told her to follow him and led her into the bathroom.

Holding her leash, he pointed to the toilet and when she flushed crimson, he simply stared into her eyes. Kate realized she had no choice. Still blushing, she sat and after some hesitation, used the toilet. Next, he pointed to the shower and she eagerly rose to step beneath the powerful jets of water, grateful to wash away the remnants of her night in the stable.

James made her stand still with her hands clasped at the nape of her neck while he soaped her all over, before using a rough flannel over every inch of her skin until it began to glow. Telling her to drop her hands to her sides, he took the showerhead from its bracket to wet her hair as she tilted her head back towards him. She sighed with pleasure as she felt his strong fingers massaging the shampoo into her scalp and hair—it felt absurdly intimate to have him wash her hair given everything they had already shared. Then, as he knelt just outside the shower stall, he had her place her foot on his shoulder to give him easy access to her pussy as he gently soaped and rinsed her there. Finally he had her bend over, with her ass towards him until he was satisfied that she was thoroughly clean.

"I do not intend to make use of your ass today, Kate, but your morning cleanse will normally include an enema. I thought to mention it now since you may expect me to administer one soon. You can save your blushes! No part of your body is not wholly owned by me during this week, and if I want to fuck your ass then you're going to be absolutely clean."

Kate felt her legs tremble, and her heart was pounding in her chest as she stared fixedly at the floor. At once, both embarrassed and incredibly aroused.

The casual way James had assumed control over yet another intimate and previously private function made her shiver inside with helpless desire. Kate had been wet from the moment he had woken her and taught her how he wished her to stand and move, only getting more turned on as his hands roamed freely over her body in the shower, but this latest announcement made her melt completely so that she felt as if her bones had turned to water. Her fantasy was gradually, step-by-step becoming reality. Not one part of her would not be controlled and used for his pleasure and ultimate satisfaction.

Kate had some limited experience of anal sex, it held no great fear for her so long as she could trust her lover to be gentle and considerate as she knew James would be—yet to be kept prepared, to be constantly and instantly accessible to him in this way was to strip away the last remaining vestiges of her privacy and it shocked and thrilled her simultaneously.

James jerked her collar and led her across the room to the large old-fashioned enamel bath with its curved edge and ball and claw feet. He told her to get in and lie on her back, and then to lift her bottom up so he could slide a large waterproof bath pillow beneath her buttocks. Then he spread her thighs wide and used leather thongs to tie them widely apart to the bath's twin handrails. Once sure that she was comfortable, he grasped her ankles and lifted her legs below her knees so they draped to hang over each side of the bath. Her position was now perfect for the intimate inspection he had in mind.

Kneeling down beside the bath James ran a fingertip from her knee up the inside of her thigh to her cunt, then drew his finger slowly up between her pussy lips, splitting her open. With his right hand, he opened her farther and exposed her delicately pink nub as he leant over the side of the bath to kiss it gently then wash her with his tongue. Such was Kate's previous level of arousal that it was only seconds before her head was back and she was breathing hard, her face flushed as she moaned plaintively.

Abruptly James lifted his head away as he sensed the imminence of her orgasm and stood to fetch a razor and shaving cream. He lathered her pubis and labia then began to shave her, the razor moving rapidly and with great precision over the slight stubble that had grown since the previous day.

As he shaved her, he paused to play with her every now and again, bringing her on relentlessly, watching her and listening to her cries and moans with total focus—judging the exact moment when she could take no more, then immediately desisting so that her whole body shuddered with need and pent-up desire and her eyes beseeched him for release.

It seemed to her that every cell of her body was screaming and yet she could not bring herself to speak the words out loud. Somehow, this torment of pleasure felt like it must be endured to show him that she had truly learned her lesson of the previous night. James seemed to understand for he kissed her softly and stroked her face with incredible tenderness until the shuddering gradually faded to faint trembles.

Then James bent between her thighs once more and holding the cheeks of her bottom apart with one hand, he meticulously shaved her there as well. After sluicing her down with water cold enough to make her gasp, he began to work on the edges of her sex lips with a pair of tweezers, examining every tiny part of her for a stray hair. The sensation of brief discomfort when he found one was as nothing to the deep burning heat that was simmering inside her. The controlled and skillful manner with which he plucked and examined her made her feel as helpless as a child.

When James looked at her, he caught the soft-focused, trusting adoration in her eyes, and his heart filled so quickly that he felt it must burst with pride. Again, he kissed her softly on the lips and steeled himself to resume his task, filled with wonder at how much could be said without words.

Finally satisfied that she was hairless after running the tips of his fingers again and again over her cunt, just brushing the skin and driving her to distraction in the process, he untied her and told her to climb out of the bath and to bend over its side with her bottom facing the window. Able to inspect her pussy and ass more thoroughly in the bright sunlight that streamed through the frosted glass, he plucked a few remaining hairs and then told her to follow him back into the bedroom.

There he told her to sit on the edge of the bed while he rummaged in his case. After a few minutes he approached her with two smooth stainless-steel hoops and, telling her to lie back on the bed, he slid first one and then the other up her legs until they both nestled at the top of her thighs.

They fitted so snugly that Kate knew James must have had them made especially for her for they seemed to immovably weld themselves to her flesh, and yet she felt no discomfort. Rather, their hold on her felt intensely satisfying, as if something had previously been lacking and now she was complete—as if she had always been *meant* to be so restrained. In combination with her collar and the matching bracelets James clicked closed around her wrists, she felt strangely serene.

Peering curiously, Kate saw that the hoops were not quite perfect circles but slightly oval to better mold themselves to the curvature of her thigh and that on their outside rim they each had a small ring. It was to these rings that James fastened her wrist bracelets before helping her to stand once more.

Kate closed her eyes as a wave of pure lust washed through her, and she felt her legs go weak so that she would have fallen but for James' hands steadying her around her waist. The sense of her helplessness was so acute it took her breath. With her arms pinned to her sides, her palms against her thighs, she felt far more vulnerable than when James secured her with her wrists together behind her back, though she could not understand why it should be so.

He kissed her and then, warning her to walk carefully until she found her balance, he led her downstairs by her leash. Their first day together had begun.

Chapter Twenty-One
Intercourse

ဢ

James led her into the kitchen and helped her to climb up onto the big farmhouse table where he told her to kneel at its center. After a few adjustments to her posture that helped her kneel more comfortably, and yet ensured she kept herself exposed to his view, he began to make their breakfast. As he moved around the kitchen, he warned her to watch carefully to see how he liked it prepared. When the kettle had boiled and he had brought juice, toast, croissants, tea and a variety of spreads to the table, he sat in one of the sturdy carver chairs and began to eat as he talked to her.

"So what did you learn about yourself during your punishment, my lovely slave?"

Kate had been anticipating this question and wondering how to answer it honestly since she first awoke. But now that she heard it for real, she felt suddenly flustered and all her previously well-considered responses fled her mind. She dropped her eyes to the grained surface of the tabletop as if she might find the answer there.

"Kate, Katie...look at me. Good girl." She looked up to find James smiling at her encouragingly. "Take your time. It's okay. It's just you and me—learning about each other, learning about ourselves. What we learn, we need to communicate to each other. It's not a test, there are no right and wrong answers—so just take your time and talk to me."

She smiled and blushed, once more intensely aware of her bondage. Had she been clothed and sitting comfortably in an armchair, it would have been much easier to answer James' question, but to do so kneeling in front of him, like a centerpiece table ornament, felt like a double exposure of her body and her private mind. An intensely vulnerable feeling, of which, James was doubtless perfectly aware. Determinedly, she collected herself and tried to find the words.

"Master, I learned...eventually — " Kate smiled bashfully as she acknowledged the first few hours she had spent fuming at him for punishing her " — that you were punishing me for trying to deceive you and not for feeling horny and needing to touch myself."

James nodded and raised his eyebrows questioningly, knowing there was more.

"And then I had to ask myself *why* I'd felt I had to deceive you at all. You'd deliberately teased me until I was crazy with lust, you knew what I was feeling, you *wanted* me to feel that way, and you even warned me not to break the rules when you sent me to the kitchen. You knew what I would be tempted to do. The test was whether I was honest with you about my needs, whether I sought your permission. I didn't and that was wrong, but I didn't consciously decide to mislead you, it just happened that way..."

"I know that, Kate, we all have old tapes running in the background. Erasing them, or at least editing them is an important part of what this week is about." He paused and then asked gently, "But was it really about asking permission?"

Kate shook her head. "No, Master, it's about being honest about what I need and not being ashamed of it."

He smiled at her, delighted she had reached this understanding. "But you had come at least a half a dozen times on the way here in the car, even though you weren't supposed to. So what did you need? Be precise."

She frowned as she tried to think. She remembered standing in the kitchen, making the soup. What had she felt? Then she shuddered as the memory flooded her body with the same sensation she had felt last evening, the same aching need. Not just to come, but to be filled, stretched, *fulfilled*. To be fucked and fucked until the deep hunger inside her core was banished, satiated. And she had felt angry with James—sort of neglected by him—and that in turn had led to wanting to do something without his knowing, without his permission—and yet with all the silliness of a child wanting to be caught she had taken no steps to cover her tracks. Her behavior had been ridiculous given what she had so enthusiastically agreed to, and especially only moments after signing her contract!

But how, *how* to put all that into words? Words that James would understand? What would he think of her if she could make him understand?

James saw her inner struggle and held up a hand. "Perhaps if I say something it will help?"

He waited for her to nod and then continued. "You are a human being in an animal body. You have human needs and animal drives. Society, particularly the patriarchal society we have lived in for the last couple of thousand years, has evolved rules that prohibit and condemn the excesses of those animal drives, especially as far as the female animal is concerned— much more latitude is given to the male, as you know. For centuries western society has been afraid of female sexuality, probably because a bunch of celibate monks ordered our society for so long."

James paused and smiled. "Forgive me—I realize you already know much of what I'm saying, but I want to try and put it in to the context of what we're doing here, because *what* we're doing here is trying to liberate those primal sexual drives. We have to recognize and respect that we're going against centuries of traditional attitudes, which are so deeply engrained, that we have inhibitions about our inhibitions!"

He took a sip of his tea and looked steadily at Kate's pussy until she realized she had quite unconsciously drawn her thighs together as he was talking and he continued to stare until, blushing, she had moved them apart once more.

"All this means," James continued, "is that I already *know* that within you is a beautiful, sexual *female* animal. She is lusty and passionate, and unashamedly wanton. In total reversal of everything you've ever previously known, I will respect you *more* the more sluttishly you behave with me—because you are only going to behave like a slut with me and because I appreciate the courage it takes for you to reveal that side of you to me. Do you understand that, Kate?"

"Yes, Master. It's hard though sometimes..."

"Yes, it's very hard... If it were not, then you would not need me to dominate you, to control you, to help you learn through direct experience that she is a beautiful part of who you are. Of course, at the same time, you are an intelligent and sensitive human being who needs tenderness, understanding and love—as do we all. The myth is that being a sexual animal demeans our humanity, whereas the reality is that—used consciously—our primal sexual energy is an incredibly powerful resource for our growth as a human beings."

"Permission to speak, Master?"

"Yes, of course, Kate."

"Are inhibitions always wrong? I mean, I don't want to become a total slut..."

"No, of course, you don't, but that's just these old fears talking. Think about it. What precisely is a 'total slut', what and how do you imagine her? Presumably she would be someone who had lost all discernment, all ability to control her lusts?"

Kate nodded.

"Our fears almost always work generally—" he continued as he buttered some toast "—discernment and a positive sort of inhibition served you well up to the point that you chose to be mine. They worked to protect you from men *generally* until you could make a specific choice. They helped you select someone who was worthy of you, with whom you could be happy. A man whom you believe merits your trust. These are aspects of your innate intelligence, Kate, and I cannot and would not ever want to remove them."

James looked up at her to make sure she was following. "But the fear, the great fear, is that somehow by getting rid of specific inhibitions, along with shame and guilt, you suddenly become completely stupid—suddenly lose any ability to make wise and sensible choices for yourself as if you were losing your inhibitions by getting mindlessly drunk! In fact the reverse is true—you simply have more choices available to you whilst retaining your self-respect."

Kate smiled, feeling enormously reassured. The way James had of explaining things satisfied her constantly questioning mind, allowing her to relax deeper into the sensuality and feelings of her present role. Yet, he seemed willing and ready to answer questions, and she had one more that had been concerning her.

"Are things really so very different in the east? You've often mentioned how much you learned there...but I've heard about all manner of horrible things being done to women there..."

James nodded sadly. "Yes, you're quite right, and I have to be careful about making sweeping generalizations, too. The whole world has been largely patriarchal for a very long time and as we know power corrupts. If that weren't the case then you wouldn't need a homeopathic dose of the same medicine to sort this stuff out. However, few societies in history have been so ruthless in their condemnation of female sexuality as ours. Other cultures, especially eastern ones, at least respect the pursuit and enjoyment of sexual and sensual pleasure—see it as a foundation to human happiness rather than as something bad and sinful."

"And it doesn't matter that I have never thought of it like that?"

James shook his head emphatically. "No, because as children we absorb these attitudes and prejudices like sponges. Even if, as adults, we have come to think very differently, simply changing how we think is only the first step because it's about *feelings* not thoughts. The memories, the guilt and the shame are locked away deep inside, and the only way our psyche has to draw our attention to them is through our dreams and fantasies."

Kate frowned. "Does that mean that when I've lost all my inhibitions I won't fantasize about being your slave girl anymore?"

"Maybe...I don't know, Kate. I think it's more the case that right now you need to imagine yourself as my slave in order to permit yourself the feelings, urges and raw sexuality that arise through knowing yourself to be helpless. It's like you can experience them one step removed. I think in the future you'll simply feel much more at ease expressing how you feel and what you want as *yourself*. It won't be a fantasy, it will be real."

"I'll *really* be your slave?"

"If you want!" James grinned. "But no, I didn't mean that. I meant that your fantasies will be a creative process, using your imagination as the first step to making things real. You won't need me to *make* you do the things you secretly or even unconsciously want to do—unless of course that loss of control happens to be part of the fantasy. You'll simply come to me and say, 'Hey, James, I had this wicked fantasy and I'd like to...' and we'll talk it through and make it real for you."

"That sounds fun!" Kate moved her hips unconsciously as her mind went into overdrive. "I can think of a few already!"

"It will be, and of course you can," James laughed. "But first, let's live *this* fantasy fully. You are not a slave, but you are in the role of slave girl fully for this week. If you want to experience further weeks as my slave, or if I want you to, then we'll make that happen—there's lots to explore that we can't possibly do in just one week, or we might move on to other things. The important thing is that we keep growing and learning *together*."

His demeanor changed abruptly, and Kate shivered deliciously as she sensed him change gears and once more exude his natural calm authority.

"So my original question was, 'what did you need?'"

Kate looked down at the table. "I needed to be fucked, Master," she whispered.

"Needed?"

"I *need* to be fucked, Master."

"By fucked you mean you need your cunt to be filled with cock? Be explicit."

"Yes, Master."

"Say it, Kate!"

"I need to be filled with your cock...and I need you to fuck me senseless, to take me, fuck me hard, use me, I need you to fill me up with your come..." The words came out in a whispered rush.

James stood and leaned across the table to lift her chin so she was looking into his eyes. "Say it again, Kate, say it with pride."

As she repeated what she had said, he punctuated her words with kisses, his breath sweet and warm on her lips.

"Good girl," he breathed. "My lovely Kate."

His hands moved down her arms, over the bracelets that held her wrists tight to her thighs and then stopped, resting on the tops of her thighs, as he kissed and gently bit each nipple in turn.

"I want your hunger. I want you *hungry*, insatiable and yet constantly immersed in sensuality. I want to keep your pretty cunt dripping like a tap while your mind floats free, wandering, happily lost in a sexual haze."

His words seemed to bypass her ears and sweep down through her body to touch her pouting sex from within. She groaned, and her head fell forward into his shoulder.

Chapter Twenty-Two
Learning to Suckle

ଚଧ

James climbed up onto the table to sit beside her as she knelt. He drew her close with his arm around her shoulders so that she leaned into him, and he lifted her right knee and pushed it firmly outward until the sole of her foot rested upon the table. With her thighs spread wide, her pussy lips parted to reveal her glistening core.

He tore a small morsel from a croissant and dipped it into her pooling juice, letting it absorb, before he raised it to her mouth and placed it on her tongue.

Then he continued to feed her. First some fruit then a morsel of toast, a sip of tea, then another segment of fruit. Often, but not always, he let it soak in her flooding pussy before he fed her. Sometimes he made her take the fruit or bread inside her pussy to warm and saturate it whilst he fed her other tidbits until he judged it ready to be eaten.

Though unable to concentrate on the food, Kate still ate hungrily. She felt starved after her night in the stable, and she was still hungry when he stopped passing her morsels of food. Noticing the expression on her face, James smiled and helped her down from the table and told her to kneel on the floor.

He poured the remaining juice into a bowl and set it on the floor in front of her.

"Drink it up, pretty slut. Lick the bowl clean!"

With her hands bound to her thigh cuffs, she bent forward from the waist and was halfway through the bowl before it dawned on her that she was eating from the floor like a cat or dog. When she did think about it, she saw herself through his eyes — kneeling before him, her arms helpless by her sides and slurping from her bowl with the juice running down her chin. The image aroused her intensely for reasons she could not begin to fathom, and which she quickly decided not to question, for the simple truth was that she found it deliciously erotic.

Perhaps he would keep her like an exotic pet, bringing her out only for grooming, feeding, exercise and for her to serve his needs? Was it her animal self creating those images?

Her imagination was running away with her so wildly she did not notice James had moved until she felt a tug on her collar. Quickly she hurried to crawl after him, and only when they were in the lounge, did she realize that he had not told her to crawl on her hands and knees but had simply told her to follow. She flushed with embarrassment, and felt the now so familiar churning in her belly as she was forced to admit to the discovery of another level of submission within herself.

In the lounge, James made up the fire while she knelt waiting, her eyes cast down demurely while her mind raced, trying to absorb this new aspect to her submission. Would her body and mind betray her in other ways? Had they done so already in his eyes?

He jerked her out of her reverie by telling her to kneel between his legs. She noticed he was wearing specially tailored jeans, for his thick cock and heavy balls emerged not from the fly, but from lower in the crotch so that they hung at a natural angle between his legs. The design enabled him to walk around comfortably while at the same time it gave her easy access to him whenever he wished.

James removed her bracelets and replaced them with two wrist cuffs with just a three-inch length of chain dangling from each cuff. At the end of the chains were nipple clamps. He tightened the clamps on her nipples so that she was obliged to keep her hands close to her breasts. Should she drop her hands or move them too far, Kate would feel the pull on her nipples. James smiled as he relished how delightfully helpless she now looked.

Next, he took a ring gag from his pocket and, holding it up for her to see, explained, "This ensures I will remain in your mouth whether I am hard or soft and it very effectively binds you to my cock." He placed it inside her mouth and fastened the bindings at the back of her head. He smiled down at her, feeling intensely happy. She was so very beautiful to him and never more so than now when he knew she ached to feel the hardness of him inside her.

He pushed his cock through the soft rubber ring and into the hot wetness of her mouth, feeling her tongue immediately welcome him as she began to suck and lick.

"No, my lovely slave. You will not do anything but hold me. Occasionally, should you feel me softening, you may move your tongue around the head of my cock, but that is all. Now be good while I read for a while."

James settled himself back into the chair, drawing her head with him and forcing her to struggle forwards on her knees to stay with him, hungry for him as she was. His scent, the raw masculine taste of him on her tongue and his apparent indifference to her mouthing him drove her crazy as he continued to be absorbed in his reading.

How could he ignore her for some stupid book!? God, how she ached to be fucked, or even just to have him use her mouth so she could feel and taste his hot, rich cream on her tongue. If anything, this was more difficult for her to bear than anything else he had done to her, at least then she had been the center of his attention, now she thought of herself as just a soft mouth, a convenience. It shamed her, and yet, she felt the heat in her belly melting her from within.

As the minutes passed something inside her responded powerfully to this sense of becoming a sexual object in a way she struggled to understand. It was so impersonal and, though of course she did not entirely lose her sense of herself as a person, the sense became vague and hazy as it retreated into the background of her awareness, irrelevant to her for the moment.

She had no name for what replaced it except it was simpler, less complicated, a pure obsessive lust that drove out all the normal trivia concerned with past and future, and focused her entirely in the present. In this simplicity, there was an unexpected freedom, a sense of release, of feeling unburdened. Free not to concern herself with mental abstractions, there was no need to perform, no way in which she could or would be judged, instead she was free to immerse herself in the twin oceans of desire and sensation that comprised her unfettered sexual self. All she had to do was obey James' instruction to trust in her body's responses regardless of the source of the arousal and concentrate on the journey and not the destination.

As she knelt before him, Kate felt an impulse of calm surrender wash through her like a soft, heavy warmth that she finally identified as contentment — an acceptance of her position that combined fluidly with a gentle determination to accept the myriad sensations that swept through her without questioning them.

Her sense of James' cock inside her mouth instantly shifted with this acceptance. Where before it had seemed a demanding and invasive presence, now she felt that it was she who had captured his bounty, as if with each throb of him against her tongue and the roof of her mouth she was able to draw upon the virile strength that flowed from him and be nurtured by it.

With this feeling, she wanted only to be as comfortable as possible and with a little experimentation she hit upon the fact that if she cupped her breasts and held them in her hands, the strain came off her shoulders and she could relax with her head resting on his inner thigh. As she did so, she once more became deeply aware of how she now looked — the helpless slave, transfixed upon her Master's cock, offering up her breasts for his pleasure, whilst apparently ignored by him. His pleasure toy — his slave. Kate moaned around his cock despite herself as this image lingered in her mind, and she knew there was nowhere else that she would rather be.

After what was for Kate a very long and deliciously frustrating time, James sighed with regret as he slowly withdrew his cock from her hot mouth. By contrast, the time had been filled for him with the soft waves of pleasure as his cock hardened and softened fractionally before her attentive tongue had teased him back to full erectness. He doubted she had noticed that he had hardly turned a page of the book he had supposedly been reading. Despite appearances, his attention had been solely upon her as he followed the gradual process of her internal surrender — the journey from struggle to acceptance and then enjoyment.

Though she did not know it, her body and especially her face had mirrored each phase of the transition as slowly the tension she held had been replaced with ease until finally her features had completely softened as she began to suckle.

James reflected that whilst some men used sex as they used drink — to be consumed until intoxication overwhelmed their senses, he loved to appreciate his pleasures unhurriedly and sensually, allowing each moment to be fully savored.

Chapter Twenty-Three
Made for Fucking

කා

Drawing himself from his reverie, James stood up, telling Kate with teasing severity that she had done quite enough lazing about for one day. Her eyes, which had been closed as she dreamily relished the taste of him remaining on her tongue and the supple languor of her body, now shot open in surprise. He was standing next to the fireplace and drawing his finger along its surface then frowning at the imaginary dust.

"Time for a slave girl to do a little housework, I think!" he announced.

James left the room after instructing her to stay on her knees, and when he returned a few minutes later, he was holding a pair of ben-wa balls and some more light chain. Telling her to assume position number two, he pushed the balls inside her pussy from the rear and then, after unclamping her nipples, told her to kneel with her arms behind her head.

"I'm going to bind your nipples. The clamps you've worn before are all well and good, but if they're too tight they can't be left in place for too long and if too loose, well you might as well not be wearing them. This binding method can be applied over many hours without harm, though of course you will feel your nipples throbbing intensely."

So saying, he took some bits of thin, red rubber that, to Kate's fascinated gaze, vaguely resembled tiny condoms. The rubber was much thicker than the latex used in condoms, however, and when James pinched her left nipple to erectness and rolled the rubber sheath down its length, Kate felt its strong elastic grip her flesh. James then produced some white cord and proceeded to wrap it round and around her nipple.

"It's important to use the right thickness of cord. Too thin and it cuts in and restricts the blood flow too much, too thick and you can't wrap it round like this," James explained as his hands worked deftly to bind her tender flesh.

Kate saw that after the first turn James was laying each subsequent turn next to the previous one so that the cord formed a seamless spiral from the base to the tip of her nipple where he tied it off to leave two dangling ends. Then he did the same to her right nipple until, looking down at herself, it seemed that her nipples were twice as long as they would normally be, even when erect.

The sensations surged through her. Her breasts swelled and her nipples throbbed with a burning ache that seemed to transmit directly to her belly. Her breath was coming in ragged pants and her eyes closed as the myriad feelings overwhelmed her. Then she heard James' voice gently pulling her back, telling her softly to open her eyes, to breathe more deeply. She felt his hand on her belly, felt his fingers slip between her pussy lips, brush her clit and then move down farther until he was pressing firmly into the band of flesh between her cunt and ass.

Somehow the pressure there brought her back as it sent tendrils of pleasure shooting down her thighs. Her eyes came into focus, and then James was kissing her passionately, his tongue flicking against hers. She moaned as he pulled away but did not protest more for she knew he was determined to torment her with pleasure.

Kate looked down and saw that James was tying very light chains to the binding cord that hung from her nipples. He then fastened each chain to her wrist cuffs. These longer chains allowed her a certain freedom of movement—she could lift her hand to her mouth easily, but they were just too short for her to touch her pussy—as she discovered when James asked her to try.

Even when stretching her nipple and breast as far as she could, her fingertips barely reached her pubis and James expressed his satisfaction with a grunt of approval. Then he handed her a duster and polish, and told her to get going.

It was only as she clambered to her feet that Kate realized a wire was hanging down between her legs to mid-thigh. She turned to look questioningly at him, and saw him smile as he flipped a switch on a remote control that sent the balls buzzing inside her. Unable to suppress a groan of sheer lust, she moved hesitantly, not quite trusting the strength of her legs which seemed about to give way at any moment. Eventually, she managed to adjust to the wonderfully powerful vibration, and she began distractedly to dust the shelf above the fireplace.

"I want you to repeat a little mantra as you work, Katie. Just repeat over and over, 'I'm a beautiful slut, my body is made for fucking and I love myself just as I am.' Say it out loud so I can hear you, and then feel the feelings the words provoke, allow them to be. I'll be watching you," James instructed.

At first, Kate struggled to say the words distinctly. It felt very strange to be saying anything at all in the circumstances, yet there was nothing she could really take exception to. When she stumbled over the words, James knew it was not a problem with her memory but with the surging feelings attendant to what she was declaring. He coached her patiently until she had them straight and then told her to carry on.

He smiled to himself as she moved around the room with utterly unconscious grace. Every move she made was profoundly sensual despite, or possibly because of, the mundanity of her chore, and she drew his gaze magnetically as he absorbed every curve of her. At the same time, her voice cast its own spell as he heard the timbre of her voice change over time, as slowly she became accustomed to the multiple sensations coursing through her.

James sat and watched her for a while before he was forced to close his eyes in order to concentrate as he reviewed his plans for the week ahead.

It was imperative that the oasis of sexual freedom he had created here in the farmhouse did not serve to completely divorce Kate from reality. This was partially why he was making her do something so dreary. This was the process of integration he was guiding her through...fantasy and reality, the normal and the mundane interweaving with the erotic and explicitly sexual. Worlds that most people went to great lengths to keep separate, James was determined to make overlap and even merge as one in Kate's mind, just as they did in his own.

Later, he would continue her training in public places, so that she was forced to come to terms with the degree to which her present status conflicted with everything she had previously held to be normal. This was very important, for though this was a week in which all manner of fantasies would be explored — he hoped very enjoyably — there was a deeper purpose that was not about the enactment of fantasy, though it was served by it. The forging of a bond of such intimate and extraordinary trust that it would remain intact when they resumed their normal lives outside of this idyllic setting. There were many unknowns to consider, and James knew how incredibly important it was for him to remain responsive and flexible as Kate embraced the transformational process he was guiding her through.

When she had finished the room, James took her back to the kitchen and had her tidy up the breakfast things, then upstairs to the bedroom to make the bed and clean the bathroom. All the time requiring that she repeat her mantra.

Aching for some respite from her all-consuming arousal, Kate obeyed him, her mind functioning on at least three different levels as her body went through the motions.

First the intensity of physical feeling — a body-centered thing that seemed to have a life of its own as it ran in leg-weakening jolts from her belly to her breasts and back again, as every movement of her arms pulled with sweet agony on her engorged and throbbing nipples. The beat of her heart echoed by the now steady rhythmic contractions of her inner muscles as they spasmed around the vibrating balls. Her clit protesting neglect by sending tingling yearnings that seemed at times to strip away her breath.

Second was the intensity of emotion, the interplay of her mounting frustration, a flickering ghostlike shame at the manner in which she was made to do her tasks. A feeling that could gain no firm hold upon her against the forceful assertion of her whispered words. Their contradiction, their possible meanings, where was the truth and where the lie? This incessant self-questioning formed the third level, though the mantra ensured that the thoughts were not sequential, still they intruded powerfully.

Other questions encroached but were beaten back to irrelevance as the words she spoke triggered ever-fresh associations. A beautiful slut—a slut—why did that word haunt her so? Made for fucking—why *made*? Was she beautiful *because* she was a slut? Weren't they opposites? Did she love herself? Now, as she was? What did the words *mean*?

The words, the feelings, the glimpses of understanding and the fractured internal debate continued as James led her from one room to the next, and then suddenly none of it mattered for she saw James' intent. Saw that the words had dual meanings— then and now. James wanted her to love herself *now*! Now— amidst the tumultuous storm of thoughts and feelings.

She was beautiful to him *now*, and she must love everything about herself that he found beautiful, including most especially, what he had called her "inner slut". That wanton and unashamed, provocatively sexual woman she had previously only allowed herself to reveal for an hour or two between the sheets, and then normally only with the assistance of a few glasses of wine. Then there was the counterpoint understanding—her body was literally made, grown, evolved, designed and purposely built for fucking!

Yes, a resounding yes!

Intellectually it was nothing new to her, but inside, the feelings ignited something marvelous and raw as if she could sense each minuscule cell in her body in microscopic detail and feel each one as a tiny engine for pleasure, life-enhancing pleasure.

She hung between two simultaneous states. Outside herself and looking in, and within, deep, deep within her core as she had never been before, looking out and seeing herself, as if for the first time, as beautiful, *as she was.*

This beauty she now perceived so clearly was not a visual sense but a vibrant feeling that dispelled all doubt and fear, and made her feel she must explode with joy, tinged with relief. Kate knew with utmost certainty that everything would be *all* right. She was all right—there was nothing wrong with her and everything right, even the "bad" bits—especially the bad bits.

She felt James' arms come around her, gentle and strong and realized she must have stopped moving, had lost all sense of time, could not say when or how long ago the balls had stopped buzzing inside her. He turned her slowly and looked into her eyes, and kissed her softly on the lips.

"My lovely Kate, you're quite amazing! You look like you've been lit up from the inside."

She leaned into him, wanting to feel his strength and at the same time wanting to give him hers. This limitless ocean of giving within her, previously glimpsed, but now plunged into and claimed as her own.

She felt his eyes sink into her as if they could read her mind and she welcomed him in, opening joyfully and enormously pleased with herself and for herself. Though the bright incandescence of the feeling was slowly dwindling, Kate still sensed the pulsing strength of her new self-awareness burning like a steady flame. She pushed herself against him, needing to feel his hard cock pressing into her belly.

"Fuck me, please fuck me, I need you to fuck me, I need you inside me." She writhed against him, her lips hungrily seeking his. As she spoke the words, she knew them to be a simple truth and felt not the tiniest hint of shame saying them.

James swept her up in his arms and carried her to the bed. He lay her down and as he withdrew the ben-wa balls, she moaned and her hips bucked as if her cunt were a hungry mouth searching for something to feed upon. The rest of her body followed its lead—her whole being sought only pleasure, brazen and demanding. James might deny her or fulfill her—it did not matter. All that mattered was that she surrender to the passion that consumed her, that she honor it and surrender—not to James, but to her own desires.

Everything whirled as James grabbed an ankle and turned her on her front, then took her hips in his strong hands and drew her back towards him so she kneeled with her pussy pouting from between her widespread thighs. He leaned forward to take a handful of her hair and with this purchase, he pushed her face to the mattress and in the same instant he thrust inside her.

Kate screamed, and her hands clutched violently at the bedsheets. She writhed back, pushing with her hands, convulsing as her exquisitely tender nipples were stretched by the outthrust of her arms. She did not care—she needed him deep, deep inside her, wanting to feel him distend her to the utmost.

James knew what she craved. The time for teasing and the torment of denial was over. He hammered her cunt with merciless powerful thrusts that shunted her down the bed so that he had to drag her unresisting back to him again and again. He let her come a couple of times before he withdrew and fell onto the bed next to where she knelt.

"Your turn to do all the hard work, Katie," he gasped, smiling as he unfastened the chain that linked her nipples to her wrists before rolling onto his back.

She did not need a second invitation and with one sinuous writhe of her body, she was astride him and seconds later had impaled herself fully.

James let her use him. He was thrilled by her transformation, and wanted her to be selfish so that she would utterly lose herself in sweat-soaked pleasure. Even so, her sheer endurance shocked him and forced him to release himself in a dozen miniature orgasms that felt sublime and yet allowed him to stay hard for her.

He felt her frenzied movements beginning to slow and knew it was from simple physical fatigue rather than true satisfaction. Without warning, he grabbed her behind her neck and with his other hand in the small of her back he rolled her over and began to fuck her in earnest. The moans and cries became delirious screams as he took her with savage intensity. Then the screams doubled in volume as he lifted her knees over his shoulders and thrust still faster. But it was only when he gripped her wrists and held them encircled in one strong hand above her head that the pleasure-pain ripped through her in one final all-consuming sundering of ecstasy, and as she felt the hot jets of his come flood her womb she fainted dead away.

Hours passed as they lay together, their tangled limbs entwined. James was the first to stir and when he looked at his watch, was astonished he had slept so long. Not that he had any regrets.

He woke her as he was removing her nipple bindings, for the returning blood seemed to sear her tender flesh. Her moans were throaty and lustful, her body once more brazenly eager for him even though she was not really awake. James hushed her and carried her still half-asleep to the bathroom where he ran the shower and soaped her all over. As his hands roamed her body Kate began to feel more awake, and she was quite alert in a blissfully relaxed way by the time he was rinsing her off.

They did not speak as she washed and rinsed him, though the hundreds of kisses she planted over his body as she dried him spoke volumes. She felt so unutterably peaceful inside that any sound would have intruded.

After James had dried her, he replaced her bracelets and thigh hoops though he left her wrists free as he intended her to cook for them. He led her down to the kitchen by her leash and sat at the table while she made them both some pasta. As they ate, they talked of trivial things, neither knowing how to express the intensity of what had occurred between them. Yet both knew nothing need be said. Their silence on the subject was mutual and the understanding perfectly shared.

As the late summer sun dropped behind the western hills, James fastened her bracelets to her thigh hoops and then draped a coat around Kate's shoulders, tied it at the waist and took her out for a stroll. The garden was not especially large and they had hardly begun to stretch their legs before they reached the small stream that marked its farthest boundary. A little wooden footbridge took them over the stream and into a three-acre paddock bordered by a wood.

They walked easily along the grassy path, James' arm around Kate's shoulder, listening to the evening chorus of songbirds in the hedgerows and woods. It was so idyllic and she felt such a quiet sense of safety that it did not occur to Kate to be concerned at her bondage and nudity beneath the coat. James was with her and that was all that mattered.

As the heat of the day slowly dissipated, James led her back to the farmhouse, and after a quick visit to the bathroom, he fastened her to her sleeping chain and watched as she curled up at the foot of the bed. He smiled at himself, knowing how much he would like her to snuggle into bed with him, yet that would only lead to one thing, and he sensed how thoroughly exhausted she was by the day's events. *Better*, he thought, *that they both got a good night's sleep and made an early start tomorrow.*

Chapter Twenty-Four
Belonging to James

80

The next morning Kate woke before James. She stretched sensuously and then lay quietly for a while, smiling as she fingered her collar. She had never known such peace on waking. Her body felt delightfully relaxed and her mind was clear and empty, waiting to be filled with whatever new experiences the day would bring. How different from her normal mornings with a hundred and one things to be juggled, plans made, endless lists to draw up so she would not forget something vital to the efficient running of the company she worked for. She was not naturally given to worry, but her work was demanding, and not a day went by without her having to manage some minor crisis.

Even on the holidays she had taken, she had never felt anything like this kind of inner tranquility. There was no point in planning or even thinking about planning the day's activities, nor was there any point to speculation on what may be in store for her. James and only James would decide. She smiled softly to herself, feeling freed and unburdened by her status. She did not know how long such a total lack of autonomy would remain enjoyable. Weeks? Months? Frankly, if she felt this good every morning, she would not mind if it lasted for years!

But she knew it would not remain the same forever, knew that this return to a childlike loss of power felt wonderful because it was such a temporary luxury. Surely, in time it would come to feel as restrictive as it now felt freeing. That was why she thought James so wise to insist that they perceive it as role-play whilst immersing themselves completely in the role. *In any case*, she thought, *what was a role but an expression of something innate?* At least if the role were to feel authentic and for it to be emotionally satisfying—a role was only trivial if approached without due respect, if done half-heartedly…

She laughed softly at herself as she recognized her tendency to overanalyze what was happening and renewed her determination to just let go and relish the moment.

She stretched again and sat up, the faux fur pooling around her waist. By turning her head and stretching her neck, she could just see James' sleeping face and her heart seemed to squeeze inside her chest at the sight of him. Unconsciously, her hand smoothed down her belly, but at the first touch, she drew it away. She would be obedient even if it killed her! She smiled as she felt the now familiar torment of need flood her pussy.

It was frustrating of course, yet the frustration was also a form of pleasure, at least of anticipated pleasure, and it felt glorious to be so utterly possessed, so completely controlled. She felt bathed in his attention, knowing that, perhaps with the exception of now when he was fast asleep, not a second of the day went by without him being as intensely aware of her as she was of him.

Yet she realized she did not *need* James watching over her to take an active pleasure in her submission. In a moment, she would stand up. Since he was fast asleep, James would not see and would never know how she did so, whether she staggered to her feet or did so gracefully. It did not matter for like so much of what he had taught her it was her choice—to fill her life, her every waking moment with pleasure, and with beauty or to be lazy and uncaring. It was a form of conscious narcissism, but narcissism born from the deep well of sensual pleasure within her, rather than from her superficial exterior.

How extraordinary that simply standing up could be so charged with eroticism that it sent a flush of pleasure through her, that it forced her to see herself in an entirely different light, where nothing she did was unimportant and that everything was an opportunity to express her joy in life.

She rose to her feet, gathered her house chain in one hand to stop it from rustling and possibly disturbing James' sleep, and walked into the bathroom. After using the toilet, she washed herself carefully, then shaved as best she could until her mound and pussy lips felt silky smooth to her touch.

As she ran the razor over her skin she noted how clinical, almost detached, her movements were. It was as if she were not touching her own body, but someone else's. No sooner had the observation occurred to her than she nodded and felt a sweet stabbing ache in her heart and belly that was nearly orgasmic in its intensity, though far more fleeting. *That was right*, she thought, *her body belonged to James. Her body was his property, given willingly to into his care.* He would return it to her only when she loved it completely and unconditionally.

Kate rinsed and dried herself, and then walked back to the bedroom. Seeing that James was still sleeping, she crept quietly to the bed, lifted the cover at the foot and slipped her head underneath. Careful not to wake him, she let her lips brush his feet, needing this time in which she could privately adore him.

Slowly she moved up his legs, covering them in tiny kisses, until she drew level with his waist. Without using her hands, she curled her tongue beneath his cock head's sleeping weight and sucked him gently into her mouth. Then she did nothing more, she did not want to wake him, only to be with him, to savor him and feel the throbbing life of him on her tongue.

Even so, it seemed only moments before his cock jolted in her mouth and began to swell. Then she pressed her face into him, wanting him to swell inside her, to push deeper into her mouth and into her throat as he grew. If possible, she would have loved for him to keep growing so that she might swallow him and feel him in her heart and stomach and all the way down to her pussy. She slid her hand behind his back to keep her mouth pressed to the soft curls of his belly.

"Mmm, my beautiful Kate." James' voice was deep and husky, as was his chuckle. "At least I assume that is my lovely Kate under there…or maybe some other girl turned up in the night…"

She bit the base of his shaft gently but firmly.

"No, I definitely think that's my Katie," he laughed as his hands came down to caress her face and run his fingers through her hair. She giggled around his cock and the vibration made him groan throatily.

Kate felt him begin to move as his stomach muscles tensed. She withdrew her mouth enough to whisper, "No, Master, please let me bring you to pleasure...please..."

James sighed and relaxed back into his pillow, and she gratefully swallowed him down again. He smiled both from the delicious sensations and sheer contentment, extremely pleased that she knew to trust her instincts. There was a time for sweet passivity, for acquiescence to his demands and a time to be demonstrative, to be lusty and demanding. She was taking in the guise of giving, just as he loved to give her pleasure in the guise of subjugating her to his will.

He gave himself up to the wonderful feelings that raced in tingling bursts through his cock and spread through his body like a gloriously soft and heavy weight.

Chapter Twenty-Five
Object d'Art

න

An hour or so later, after he had showered and dressed, James led her down to the kitchen. He had asked her which type of bondage she preferred for the morning, and she had requested that he place her in the tight-fitting thigh hoops with the matching bracelets.

Kate prepared breakfast according to his instructions while James laid the table, and then she came to kneel by his side as he ate. She pressed her bracelets against the tiny catch on the outer surface of her thigh hoop until with a slight click they snapped into place, securing her wrists to her sides. As always, she felt the delicious thrill of being so helpless before him.

James fed her by hand, sharing a portion of everything he ate until she smiled and shook her head when she was full.

"You're probably wise not to eat too much," James said. "Later I am going to dress you and take you out for something to eat. When we're out, you'll follow the same rules as on the day we first met—you will do exactly what you are told as you would here. You will under no circumstances cross your legs. You will keep your knees at least twelve inches apart when seated. You will stand and sit with your back straight and your breasts thrust forward, no matter who may be staring at you. When you sit, you will lift your skirt so that your bare bottom is in contact with the seat. You will address me as 'Sir' instead of 'Master', other than that you may speak freely. If you've got questions, then would be a good time to ask them. Free time begins from the minute the car door closes until it shuts on our departure from the restaurant. Do you understand everything?"

Kate nodded, excited at the prospect of going out with him and then quickly said "Yes, Master," before he commented on her lack of courtesy.

"This morning I want to use the time before lunch to introduce you to something new."

James lifted her head to look into her eyes. "You know I find you beautiful, and I know that you're beginning to appreciate your beauty more than you used to…"

Kate nodded, her eyes shining. She knew James found her beautiful, and that fact combined with the extraordinary sensual and sexual pleasure she was learning her body could give her in his hands, allowed her to cherish a sense of her inner being as beautiful even though she knew that really her face and body were at best averagely attractive.

"This morning," James continued. "I'm going to help you appreciate your body in a new light, as art. I'm going to pose you as a living sculpture. You know, or at least you're learning, that the essential you is not an object and never can be because it's intangible. Call it consciousness, spirit, soul — call it what you like — you definitely can't make an object out of it. On the other hand, your body *is* an object, and I want you to appreciate the distinction and see that object as it really is." James grinned suddenly. "It'll be fun!"

He led her into the lounge and told her to kneel and not to move until he returned. Upstairs in the bathroom he collected some large towels and grabbed his small suitcase from the bedroom, then hurried back to her.

James moved the coffee table and pushed back a couple of chairs to make some space and then spread the towels on the floor. Then he disappeared out of the room again only to return five minutes later with every single mirror he could find from around the house. These he proceeded to place around the lounge, sometimes having to fix a small hook into the wall to get a mirror in the right position. When he was finally satisfied, he told Kate to come and stand in the middle of the towels.

"I want you to see yourself very differently, to see your body without identifying with it, at least not at first. So first, I'm going to blindfold you and then I'm going to paint you with body paint. That's all you need to know for now, so let's get those cuffs and bracelets off you."

James stripped her of her bondage and even removed the tiny earring studs she wore. He hesitated, considering removing her collar, but decided to leave it in place—it seemed a part of her now.

He quickly arranged her hair into a long ponytail, which he wrapped in black ribbon. Then he slipped the blindfold over her eyes and told her to stand with her legs straight and shoulder-width apart with her arms out by her sides.

The next thing Kate felt was the sensual touch of a wet brush against the skin of her belly as James started to apply the paint. He worked carefully to ensure the paint was evenly spread, working the brush into the folds of her sex and between her buttocks to make sure every inch of her was painted save for her hair and the portion of her face covered by the blindfold.

The luscious, wet softness of the brush moving over her skin contrasted with the tightening tingle as it slowly dried and both sensations made her intensely aware of her whole body, somehow knowing she was being painted made her feel more acutely aware of her nakedness. It was blissful torment, and she longed for the brush to return to her pussy and especially her clit for its fleeting visit had felt exquisite and tantalizingly gentle.

It was tempting for James to use different colors. He longed to use the topography of her skin as a three-dimensional canvas on which he could accentuate the multiple curves the brush revealed, but he knew that would defeat what he was trying to achieve. He wanted Kate to see her body as art rather than merely a canvas that art was done upon. He therefore used a glossy black paint, spreading it thick and even until it covered her from head to toe.

When James was finished, he told her to keep her eyes closed, and then he removed her blindfold. Where the blindfold had been, he very carefully painted the skin around her eyes and then had her open her mouth so that he could paint her lips. Then, telling her to remain absolutely still, he plugged in a hair dryer and began to direct the hot air over her body.

As the special paint dried, it remained supple and set into a thick, gleaming ebony second skin that followed and perfectly mirrored every detail of Kate's naked body.

As a finishing touch, James used some white paint to trace fine lines around her lips and eyes, her hairline and the angle of her jaw. Then he stepped back and examined his work critically.

He was very pleased. She was no longer immediately identifiable as Kate. The paint had hidden her features whilst revealing and enhancing everything else about her body. Warning her to keep her eyes closed he drew the curtains and then experimented with the room's lights until satisfied that he had the desired effect. Then he switched the lights off again and parted the curtains just sufficiently to allow a dim sunlight to filter into the room.

Now it remained only to arrange her body in a pose that truly gave full expression to every delicious curve of her. He knew she would lose her balance if he demanded she keep her eyes closed so he gave her permission to open them, but instructed that she look only towards the gap in the curtains. James walked around her and told her in minute detail how he wanted her to stand.

Kate could not fail to grasp some sense of the transformation that had occurred. It would have required impossible self-control not to steal the occasional downward glance at her body, but it was not until James had arranged her limbs and turned her torso just so and had switched on the lights that she saw the full effect.

Now in half-a-dozen mirrors she saw a stranger, gleaming black and unutterably feminine. It was as if by preventing her from seeing herself James had revealed some inner core of her being that was the essence of *woman*. It was disturbing but she felt an extraordinary reverence as she beheld this stranger. The image seemed to cut through her mind and strip away all her negative preconceptions of her shape and form. All the hours of tedious self-deprecation were erased in one blinding flash of perception.

James stood there smiling and not a little awed. "Move around, explore your shape, play with the images." He encouraged her.

Kate moved, slowly at first, and then with increasing confidence as she found that her will and this ebony goddess were indeed one and the same. She experimented with different poses, her body feeling strangely fluid stripped as it was of inhibition. Some poses were undeniably erotic, but they occurred almost by accident as she bent and stretched and twisted, discovering angles and curves that seemed inexplicably right, that pleased and somehow nourished her visual sense.

"Wait, don't move!" James spoke urgently. "No, go back, raise your leg and point your toe again as you were. Good, now your right arm above your head with your hand relaxed and your left arm in front across your body with your palm down, fingers straight. Perfect! Now what do you see?"

Kate wanted to smile, but she froze her features to maintain the image. "It's like I'm one of those Indian statues…I don't know the name, is it Kali? Shiva? I can't remember…"

James laughed. "Nor can I, it doesn't matter. I just wanted you to see yourself this way. To see that *within* you is what every artist has striven to capture down through the centuries."

"Yes, she is…I am…" Kate was lost for words.

He came to her and looked into her eyes. "Now to finish. I want you to find a pose that you find so beautiful you really struggle to believe it's you. Forget about me, it's not about what you think I want to see. Understand?"

Kate nodded, and once more began to move until she suddenly gasped. Her arms were above her head and her left foot pointing forward her body one continuous curve.

James nodded. "Yes! You're right, that is perfect. Now hold still."

He approached her with a slender chain, and kneeling before her, he parted her pussy lips, drew back her clit hood, and secured a soft rubber-toothed clamp to her clit and let the chain hang down between her legs. To the end of the chain, he attached a small bell. As her clit took the small weight of the bell, she moaned loudly, as she felt her belly melt inside.

The sudden implosion of aching pleasure seemed to suck Kate deeper inside herself so that she was forced to bear witness to the stunning reflections that surrounded her and simultaneously sink into the concrete physicality of her flesh.

"Now don't move a millimeter. If you do the bell will ring."

Still kneeling before her, James slowly pushed a finger inside her. Kate's thighs trembled but she managed to stay still. Then he started to explore her cunt, his finger tracing all her internal surfaces. It was an exquisite torment to have to stay absolutely still and she was doubting she could take much more when James removed his finger and began to stroke her cunt from its apex, where the clit chain dangled, down between her labia and over her perineum to her ass where he dipped his well-lubricated finger into her.

"Good girl, don't move, just feel the pressure build inside you. Keep watching yourself in the mirrors. Tell me what you see?"

"Oh, James, I mean, Master...I don't know... I see myself, I see you touching me, and yet I see this other person's body, so beautiful, so alien. They can't be the same and yet I know they are..."

"You need to *feel* they are the same, Kate," said James as he began with his free hand to peel away the paint from around her pussy. It came off in long continuous sheets so that only a few minutes later James had peeled off all the paint from her legs, bottom and belly. Then he had to stand to peel away the rest, leaving only the paint on her face, outlined in white, so that she looked like she was wearing a mask. As he worked, his hands constantly returned to tease her and all the time he insisted she keep looking at herself in the mirror and hold the pose exactly.

For Kate, it was extraordinary to watch her own flesh emerging. It was as if her eyes refused to believe it was her own body that held her spellbound with its beauty, incredible that she had never seen herself this way before. She was no different — nothing had changed. And yet, as James removed the last remaining traces of the paint, she realized that something deep inside her *had* changed. It was an extension of her previous experiences. Indeed, it would not have been possible had they not preceded this moment.

She sobbed and fell to her knees, the bell tinkling briefly. For once James was not tender and did not seek to comfort her. Instinctively he knew such gentleness would be misplaced. He tore off his clothes and entered her as she knelt before him, driving his cock deep in a single thrust that turned her sobs to moans and then cries of pleasure as the power of him filled her.

Even as one part of her mind dissolved away as she embraced and floated high on the waves of pleasure that enfolded her, another part of her awareness sank deep inside her core and rested effortlessly in an ocean of contentment. There was no struggle anymore to be anything other than she was. James loved her, though he had not said it, because he saw a truth she had been blind to, and nothing mattered more to him than that she love herself as he loved her.

She turned beneath him and lifted her face, needing to feel his lips on hers, wanting the taste of him on her tongue and the roughness of his cheek against hers. He moved inside her, and though the physical feeling was exquisite, still more wonderful was the light that shone in his eyes when he looked into hers.

That alone was enough to send Kate spinning over the edge to plunge headlong into an abyss of molten pleasure. She clung to him as he possessed her, and she gave him all she had to give.

James gave an exultant shout as the electric pleasure erupted inside, and Kate held him still more tightly, never wanting him to leave her, wanting him always to fill her so beautifully, so completely. Deep inside she felt him come, and though transfused with joy, she wished she could taste his cream on her tongue, and she laughed and writhed her hips for the sheer glory of knowing herself so insatiable.

Then struck by the idea she wriggled off him, moaning as if he had deprived her, as if to blame him for not possessing the means to fuck her pussy and mouth simultaneously, and then stifling her own moans as she took his cock into her mouth and reveled in the combined tastes of their pleasure.

Chapter Twenty-Six
Dressing for Lunch

&

They lay together in quiet, exhausted contentment for some time, and then James gently stirred her to wakefulness and eased his cock from her mouth.

"Come on, we're going out, remember? Let's get washed up and then I'll get you dressed."

James clipped a lead to her collar and led her upstairs. In the bathroom, he ran the shower and carefully washed away the remaining traces of paint, then washed her hair, before allowing her to wash him. When they had dried each other, he had her sit at the dressing table and watched as she blow-dried her hair. He smiled to himself as it occurred to him that he liked her hair much better when it dried naturally and hung in damp curls about her face, but today he wanted her to feel elegant, or at least to know that she looked elegant and stylish, the very image of a respectable young woman.

As she finished drying her hair, James tidied up downstairs and replaced the mirrors he had taken from around the house. Then he returned to the bedroom with his suitcase and unwrapped a collection of perfectly smooth metal rings. He held them up one by one as he glanced from her breasts to the rings and back again. Finally he chose a pair he thought would fit her well and told her to come and stand before the long mirror, for he wanted her to watch everything he did.

He held her firmly by the nipple, stretching her breast into a cone as he slipped first one and then the second breast hoop into place so that it sat snug against her rib cage. The hoop acted rather like an under-wired bra to hold her breasts out from her body, especially when he attached the fine chains that linked the top of each hoop to the front of her collar. Yet, unlike a bra, they were slightly constrictive and made her breasts ache and her nipples tingle.

Standing behind her so she could watch his hands manipulate her tender flesh, James made her already erect nipples even more prominent by twisting and rolling them between his fingers. Then he used a small brush to apply a solution that instantly dried into semi-hard translucent latex, which shrank to force her nipples into a state of permanent erectness.

He then had her sit at the dressing table again and watched her carefully as she applied her makeup. He told her which shades he wanted her to apply and how much he wanted her to wear. The effect he sought was a natural one, a simple enhancement of her lovely features. Before allowing her to put her makeup away, he told her to rouge her areolas and the lips of her sex.

When he was satisfied, James had Kate lean back and pushed the ben-wa balls inside her once more, then reattached the soft rubber-toothed clit clamp with its hanging chain and delicate bell. He held her ankles to raise her legs, making it easier for him to roll the shining metal thigh hoops up her legs until they fitted snugly at the top of her thighs. Then he told her to stand and walk around the room.

"The bell will tinkle as you move, you will hear it and you will feel it, but no one else will know the source of the sound except you and I. Now walk naturally, as if it were not there, good — that's much better. I want you to feel the dangling weight of it pulling at you, but to keep your poise no matter what you feel."

Kate smiled. It was quite a challenge to keep herself from responding to the insistent sensations that churned inside. Every movement made the fine chain swing and pulled deliciously at her clit, as if a tiny mouth were randomly sucking on her. If she moved too abruptly then the bell bounced and the tug became a jolt that made her knees go weak and made it hard not to moan out loud, so she tried to walk as smoothly as she could.

Next James gave her some sheer, black hold-up stockings to put on, which stopped just an inch short of her thigh hoops. When she had put on the high heels she had been wearing when he picked her up from the station — shoes that he had obviously cleaned and polished at some point in the last two days — he brought her to stand before the mirror once more. There he teased her while she watched his reflected hands move over her body. Her breath becoming ragged, as she felt herself helplessly respond to his knowing touch.

When he knew she could not take much more, he went to the wardrobe and selected a cream cashmere roll-neck sweater and a classic charcoal two-piece suit. Kate had never seen the clothes before — she realized James must have bought them especially for her, for they fit her perfectly. The skirt was knee-length and flared enough to allow her to lift it from beneath her bottom when she sat. James had her practice a few times sitting on the dressing table chair until she could do so gracefully.

Kate was grateful that he did, for the dangling chain tended to catch on the edge of the chair as she sat. The first time it happened, in the super-sensitized state James had brought her to, she nearly came from the sudden and unexpected tug, as it was she moaned loudly and gripped the arms of the chair until eventually the pleasure receded.

The roll-neck sweater hid her collar and the chains that ran to her breast hoops, though her nipples almost poked through the super-soft wool, which felt delicious against her swelling breasts. James snapped her delicate bracelets onto her wrists, lifted her skirt at the side to secure her bracelets to her thigh hoops and finally he placed the jacket over her shoulders.

After permitting Kate a last look in the mirror — for he wanted her to appreciate exactly how she now looked — James led her downstairs and out to the car by her leash.

Somehow being led by her leash while so elegantly, even formally dressed felt even more arousing than when she was naked. Apart from the way her skirt was hitched up at the sides—and of course the leash—Kate knew she looked like any properly dressed businesswoman being taken out to lunch by her boyfriend. She smiled as she reflected that this appearance was not untrue—he was her boyfriend and she was a well-dressed professional woman, but she was also his slave girl and his very willing slut.

Helping her into the front passenger seat of the car, James lifted the rear of her skirt before she sat on the leather seat and Kate blushed in the knowledge that her pussy juice would inevitably seep slowly into the leather during the journey. After a moment's thought, she realized James must know this and want this, and so surrendered to his wishes.

James unclipped her leash and put it in his pocket before walking around to the driver's side and settling himself behind the wheel.

As he drove away, James lifted Kate's skirt in front and moved her knees a little farther apart, telling her to slump in the seat to expose more of her pussy to him. Briefly, he touched her heat and pulled teasingly at her chain, until she moaned and threw her head back with her eyes tightly shut as she struggled to control the imminence of her pleasure. She was saved by the narrow, winding country lanes obliging him to concentrate on driving safely.

At irregular intervals as the lanes allowed, he would touch either her pussy or thighs especially where her soft flesh emerged from the tops of her stockings. Playing with the remote control of the ben-wa balls, sometimes turning them to full power so that she struggled to suppress the fevered moans that arose from deep within or turning them off so that she sat torn between frustration at the lack of stimulation and gratitude for the respite.

All the while she stared rigidly ahead, terrified and excited by the thought that her nakedness would be observed by a passerby and wondering how she would possibly cope with the sensations in the restaurant. In fact, they were well into the small town before he moved her skirt to just barely cover her pussy. And only then did she realize that she had not asked a single question or made any use of her free time.

When they eventually found a parking place, he had her sit up straighter and lean forward so he could detach her bracelets from her thigh hoops and help her into her jacket, then once more acting the gentleman, he got out and went to open her door for her.

"I think the seat needs cleaning, Kate," he said quietly. "Use your tongue... Quickly!" She hesitated and looked frantically around. The nearest people were twenty yards away...maybe it would just look like she was bending to get something? Not daring to look at him, she quickly bent and licked her juice from the seat, not really believing she could be doing this at all. Standing directly behind her, his hand lifted her skirt as she bent over, to slide up the soft flesh above her stocking along the inside of her thigh to her sex, she froze, torn between the constant need she had for his touch and the terror of discovery.

Finally, James relented and taking her arm, he escorted her towards the restaurant. As they walked, he told her, "You are a very beautiful young woman, you are elegant and poised, you will walk with pride and look with disdain on those who cannot tear their eyes off you. There! That's better...feel the power your sexuality gives you...use it! Feel those eyes feasting on you and relish the knowledge of your difference. The only people who will sneer are those who will never have what you have...let them! Be yourself!"

As Kate walked, the bell and chain swung between her thighs and even with the noise of the traffic, she could hear its faint tinkling chime. She scanned the faces of those they passed, certain that somehow they must see through her façade and perceive her as the wanton slut she knew herself to be. How could they not when she felt their gaze linger, she drew their eyes compellingly, and yet when she dared to look, their eyes flicked away, as if they were the guilty ones, not she.

With James, tall and strong by her side, she felt the aura of his confidence and authority extend to her. At first she felt it externally, like a thick coat being wrapped around her shoulders, protecting her and wrapping her in his strength, but then as they walked, her sense of confidence grew stronger still and now it seemed to come more from within herself and, despite the erotic pleasures that if anything intensified, she walked with more assurance, her head held high.

The words James had just spoken echoed in her mind...*relish the knowledge of your difference*...were so true. She had spent so much of her life trying to convince herself that she was not different, hiding who she was and what she wanted even from herself — *especially* from herself, that now, walking down this crowded street, she felt a joyous sense of release from all pretence. It did not matter that people could not see the bondage beneath her clothes — in fact, other people's opinion did not signify in any way. All that mattered was the glorious thrill of knowing herself to be radically apart from the mundanity of normal life. In her concealed bondage, she was free and unfettered in a way few people imagined possible.

Chapter Twenty-Seven
Internal Friction

ഇ

They entered the restaurant and were met by a waiter who showed them to an alcove table. When they were seated, he handed them both menus and then asked if they would like to order drinks. With her newfound confidence in herself, Kate opened her mouth to speak, but James raised his hand to stop her.

"You have forgotten your skirt, my dear, please attend to it while I order."

She flushed and sat rigid, desperately hoping that the waiter would look away. Instead, he was staring at her in some confusion and clearly wondering in what way she had forgotten her skirt? The silence became quite tangible, as she found herself unable to move even though James was clearly waiting for her to obey.

Thankfully, the waiter came to her rescue and again asked what they would like to drink. In the few seconds reprieve this gave her, she quickly snatched up the back of the skirt to sit herself, her pussy tensing in reaction, on the smooth cold of the leather-padded bench. Kate flushed at the tinkling of her bell, and then flushed still deeper at the thought that James might make her lick this seat clean, too!

When the waiter went to fetch their drinks she composed herself to ask a question, struggling to frame it properly and going over and over the words in her head. So much had changed since that day just over a month ago when James had taken her and made her his own.

Kate felt she was riding a roller coaster—exhilarating, exciting, sometimes terrifying, but always arousing and deeply satisfying. James was her Master, her mentor and guide. He was the reinforced steel of the track along which her personal roller coaster hurtled, immeasurably strong and completely reliable.

Though he was unquestionably the most physically attractive and adept lover Kate had ever known, it was his mind and his understanding that truly intrigued her...that made her sure this was not just some crazy lust-filled adventure, but something very much deeper and more significant, perhaps even more so than she yet realized. Here then was another chance to understand him better...and she found herself tongue-tied like a silly schoolgirl!

Finally, she managed to say, "Sir, what will you be doing with me over the next few days? I know we've talked in general terms about the week's purpose, the objectives of my training, but can you say more? Perhaps I should just wait and see?"

"Don't worry, Kate, for sure there are some things that are better not discussed in advance...because you need to approach them without expectation, without any preconceptions of what the experience will feel like. When I think a little anticipation will enhance your experiences I will tell you, though."

James paused, and with a sudden grin said, "I am going to continue what we have already started. I will be making you feel a powerful internal friction." He gazed deeply into her eyes as he said it and despite the obvious innuendo, Kate blushed and looked down. Then after a moment, looked at him questioningly.

"You're not talking physically are you, Sir?"

"Well, let's just say I am not talking *just* physically. Do you know what draws you to submission?"

"It's many things, it arouses me of course, but I also love to please, to be found pleasing."

"Yes, those things are true, but there is also a feeling of respite, is there not, the relief of being able to surrender control?"

Kate nodded. "Yes, it feels wonderful to give up the control to you, Sir, not to have to worry that I am not pleasing you since you do not allow me to displease you, or what you think of me because you tell me exactly what you think and want without subterfuge." She paused. "So what did you mean, Sir?"

James smiled admiring her insight. "In order to understand the dynamic of Master and slave, the allure of dominance and submission, you must first understand the need for this internal friction I mentioned. It is a friction between the many, sometimes contradictory aspects of yourself. Even now, we are exploring one such friction. There is the self within you who has dined out in countless restaurants, and then another who enjoys bondage—the toys you hold inside you, but in coming here, we bring them together. This generates a form of psychological friction, which releases sexual energy and lots of feelings. You might say it is the friction between the everyday mask you wear and the core of your being. How do you feel?"

"I feel sexy, desirable, horny—very, *very* horny." She smiled, and then laughed. "I feel wonderful in fact."

"Ah, but how did you *think* you would feel on the drive here when you imagined yourself sitting dressed as you are in a busy restaurant?"

"I thought I'd feel ashamed and embarrassed, actually. I was terrified, but excited, too."

"And yet you now feel all of those feelings at once, the good ones and the bad ones," he said, and casually turned up the ben-wa balls vibration so she gasped.

"You wouldn't have closed your legs would you?" He raised his eyebrows questioningly though he knew the answer.

Kate tried to breathe deep and allowed her legs to move back apart again, biting her lip so as not to moan.

"Isn't it interesting that when your body feels pleasure you try to stop it? Why should you do that?"

She fought to concentrate. "I suppose because I would fear shaming myself, Sir."

He smiled. "Take a look around the room. Know anyone? Care about anyone's opinion of you? Even if they could see you in this alcove, which they cannot. If we were alone would you have closed your legs?"

"No, Sir, I don't think so, and no, I don't care what they think, it's just automatic."

"Yes precisely, it is a *conditioned* shame and a *conditioned* denial of pleasure. That is what this week is about changing, or beginning to change. And we do it with friction, by making you feel contradictory things simultaneously and making sure that the feeling that wins out is the one that connects you to your true self, to the source of pleasure within you and not your conditioning."

James looked at her closely again, and held out his hands palm up so that she placed her own in his. "I want you to know that the more you surrender to your body's pleasure, the more you will please me." He held her eyes in his. "Including right now, Kate," his voice just a whisper. "Give in to the pleasure now."

Kate felt herself melt inside, and her nails dug into his hands as her inner muscles squeezed on the balls inside her and her buttocks tensed on the seat. As her awareness sank into her belly she felt the urge grow stronger to close her eyes, an urge that fought against the instinct to break contact with him and glance around to ensure she remained unobserved. James gently extracted one hand from her grip and placed it reassuringly on her thigh.

She shivered at his touch, her breath becoming ragged, but she allowed herself to be held in the still strong calm of his eyes and surrendered to him. This alone made the sensations that rippled through her seem to double in intensity. Then she felt his hand upon her thigh as it slid beneath her skirt and the exquisite jolt as he took the chain between his fingers and pulled on it with gentle insistent tugs.

The sensations were just too much for Kate to endure. She came powerfully but almost silently, her inner self became liquid while her mind floated free. Kate dropped her head so her forehead rested on the back of her wrists as the waves of bliss washed her body from within, surrendering to the pleasure, surrendering to James.

Some indefinable time later, she felt the incessant vibration within her pussy soften to a gentle hum. At the same time he released her chain, the bell tinkling delicately, and then he kissed her softly and murmured how proud he was of her.

Allowing her a few moments to compose herself, James waved the waiter over and ordered their food. While they waited for it to arrive and when the soft, dreamy look had begun to fade from her eyes, he resumed his explanation.

"Different parts of your body and mind have been numbed by that conditioning, even the most sensitive parts of you can be made still more sensitive, can become *superbly* responsive to pleasure and that is what being a pleasure slave is all about experiencing. Becoming a slave to pleasure. Ultimately, it has nothing to do with me. I am a Master in that I have mastered my art and have so much to teach you, but your willing obedience to me in all things is, as I have said before, simply a steppingstone to greater things for us."

"Yes, Sir, that sounds wonderful, but what about you? This all seems to be about what is good for me, but my pleasure is so much about giving myself to you and pleasing you."

James smiled and nodded in agreement. "I am not just talking about physical sensitivity, however. The word 'sensitivity' means to be attuned to your senses of which the sense of touch is just one. As you become still more superlatively aware of your body so sight, sound, feelings, even taste, become more intense and alive. You will become more acutely aware of my pleasure as you become more sensitive to your own. You will notice more and be quicker to do so. For example, right now you quickly become lost in your own pleasure, often quite selfishly…"

He shook his head when she attempted to deny this.

"No, I am not criticizing you. It's a lovely thing to watch a pretty girl get lost in her pleasure, but as you progress, you will be more able to remain aware of *my* pleasure and how you may best serve me despite the intensity of your own arousal. It's not a choice between pleasing me and feeling pleasure. In fact, you will not please me unless you can abandon yourself completely to pleasure, but you will learn to serve mine at the same time. It's like surfing a wave…you cannot fight the wave's power, you have to go with it…and yet despite its awesome strength, you can learn to harness the power. The power of your own sexual energy."

James paused while their food was placed before them and gesturing for her to eat, continued. "I love how hungry you are, my beautiful slave."

Kate looked up, and realizing that he was not talking about her food, she blushed.

"You frequently become so hungry that you do, in fact, become selfishly focused on what you want. Yet my pleasure is enhanced when you are able to bring me to the brink of orgasm again and again, holding me at the edge of pleasure, but you're so wantonly greedy that without considerable self-control on my part, you would succeed in pushing me over the edge immediately, sacrificing my pleasure to feed your own hunger."

Kate grinned, and licked her lips provocatively.

"So you will learn to judge that moment very finely and you will submit your pleasure to mine and the wonderful thing is that this makes your pleasure still greater. However, such things are for the future."

They ate in silence for a while, enjoying the delicious food. Kate had so much to think about that she could not frame another question properly in her mind until he had called for the bill.

"What do you have in store for me this afternoon, Sir?"

He smiled, and lowered his voice to a secretive, playful whisper. "I'm going to hunt you down and take you by force, and you, my lovely Kate, are going to try and stop me!"

Kate looked at him in astonishment. "But...but, James, I mean, Sir, you can have me whenever you want me!" She blushed prettily. "I want you..." Kate lowered her voice to a whisper. "God, I ache to feel you inside me again! How can you possibly take me against my will?"

James smiled, and holding her hand, he kissed her palm softly. "There is something wild and powerful inside you I want to set free, and so we are going to play a little game to generate some of that friction I mentioned earlier. You'll see! Now let's finish up here and take a stroll."

Chapter Twenty-Eight
The Cellar

80

Kate had smuggled her napkin beneath the table and she used it to wipe the seat discreetly while James was occupied with settling the bill. She paid a quick visit to the bathroom having received a nod of permission from him and when she returned he was waiting by the door.

They enjoyed the sunshine, and by the time they had slowly wound their way back to the car, window-shopping and laughing at the garish rubbish on display for tourists, they were in high spirits. It was a shock to Kate when James opened the car's rear door and told her to crawl inside and lie on her back just as she had on their journey down to the farmhouse.

Once she had struggled inside, James opened the passenger door and used her bracelets to cuff her hands above her head. With her arms in this position, her jacket fell open and James tugged the cashmere sweater up and over her breasts, which stood up proud of her body with the supportive constriction of the hoops. Then he drew her skirt up above her waist and told her to open her thighs before he got behind the wheel and eased the car out into the traffic.

In the sunlight, she realized that the windows were tinted and it was unlikely anyone could actually see inside, even so, she could see out and as they crawled through the slow traffic out of town she thought she made eye contact with at least a dozen people who seemed to be staring down at her helplessly naked body. Only their lack of reaction told her that she could not be seen, even so the exposure was deeply unsettling in a way she was not sure she liked.

Kate caught herself closing her eyes in the childish delusion that if she could not see them, then they could not see her, but noticing this, she laughed softly to herself and bravely forced herself to look and feel. She had to admit that her pussy was once again hot and aching, squeezing on the balls inside her.

Unaware that he had been observing her, she was startled when James instructed, "Lift your pussy to the crowds, my lovely one, be shameless, and show your beauty to them…as if they can see you!"

Hesitantly and blushing furiously, she raised her hips and widened her legs still farther, though she saw no reaction, the movement itself caused her acute embarrassment, and a rush of arousal so intense it made her gasp.

James chuckled, very proud of her obedience and fully aware of how difficult that had been for her.

"When you were a very little girl, you raised your skirt to everyone, loving the thrill, wickedly enjoying the shock you caused…then as you grew older you learnt how bad such behavior was and shut that wicked and wanton part of you away somewhere dark inside. She's just come out to play again!" James reached over to gently brush her cheek and she kissed his hand lovingly, and by the time she looked again, they were out in the countryside once more

James concentrated on his driving and said nothing for a long time, and then as they were approaching the farmhouse, he leant back to remove her cuffs and told her to strip to her stockings and heels. In the confined space, it was difficult to comply but with a variety of contortions, she managed to remove her skirt and sweater and was naked by the time they bumped to a stop before the front door.

"Free time is over for a while, my pretty slut, so be on your best behavior," he reminded her as he got out of the car and leaned in through the passenger door to reattach her leash to her collar. She clambered out as elegantly as possible, but was unable to suppress a moan of lust as the dangling bell bounced between her thighs, its tinkling no longer muffled by her skirt.

He led her into the farmhouse and through to the lounge where he made her stand with her hands clasped behind her head and her legs apart. Her breast hoops in combination with her arms behind her head lifted her breasts in vulnerable provocation. He caressed them softly as he spoke.

"That was a gentle introduction to exhibitionism, next time you will not hesitate to obey, it is how we build the trust between us. Your obedience, and the realization that nothing I do is done thoughtlessly. I will not always want or be able to give you an explanation of 'why' before or after, that is why the trust is so important. As it is now in what we are about to explore."

James detached the bell and clit chain and then took hold of the remote wire dangling from between her legs and drew the balls out of her so slowly that her thighs trembled. Kate gasped when they finally popped out, feeling that her legs were about to give way. Then he grabbed her hair and pulling her head back, he pushed them, dripping with her juice, into her open mouth. The smell and taste of her excitement was now so familiar to her, she sucked them clean quite shamelessly.

James led her by the leash to the small hidden door leading down to the cellar. She felt her heart hammering in her chest as she walked after him down the small flight of steps, her skin becoming chilled in the slightly damp and chilly room. When he flicked on the central bulb above the workbench, Kate shuddered, beginning to guess what he intended.

James led her over to the bench and made her lie down, the rough wood against her back. Her eyes becoming wild and scared as he placed her wrists and then her ankles into heavy, cold, steel shackles and secured her tightly. Taking up a length of thick chain, he then began to wrap it around her body and her mouth opened in silent protest as she felt the touch of the cold chain against her warm skin. Finally, he padlocked the chain to the table and saying nothing, left her, switching off the light as he went through the door.

Grinning wickedly to himself, now the grin would not spoil the impact he wanted to have, James sat at his laptop and pressed the keys to activate the recording hidden in the cellar.

For the first few minutes Kate heard nothing, her thoughts were racing as she tried to guess what this was about. Why was he doing this? He had spoken of a game? Was this it? It was not much fun...none at all, in fact!

Kate started as suddenly she heard something move beneath the table, a skittering scratching of tiny feet, a high-pitched squeal. Then abruptly the noise stopped, though her ears strained to hear in the darkness and her heart thumped loudly in her chest. She had to scare it away! But if she shouted James would hear her...dare she? Perhaps it was nothing after all...then the noise again, seemingly louder, closer. Maybe it was climbing up the table leg? She moaned and lifted her hands...her shackles knocking against the table...that was it! She banged the shackles hard into the table, a sudden shockingly loud noise that felt strangely comforting. Kate banged again and then lay completely still, straining to hear once more.

Abruptly the light came back on and James was standing there, looking down at her with a stern expression on his face.

"You hate it here, I knew you would..." James paused, and gently stroked her hair, calming her, reassuring her with his presence.

"In a while we are going to play a game called 'resistance', the rules of the game are simple. You will attempt to stop me from fucking you. If I succeed in fucking you within the next thirty minutes, you will be chained as you are now—but instead of it lasting only a few minutes, I will chain you here for hours, in addition you will be blindfolded and gagged. On the other hand, if you manage to elude me for the full thirty minutes then you don't get put in here at all. However, if I catch you immediately, that's six hours in here...every five minutes you stay free equals an hour taken off the time you lie in here. Understood?"

Kate nodded, her heart pounding in her chest. James continued. "You are restrained here now so you will be properly motivated to resist me. You must fight with all your strength and determination. You may try *anything* you can to protect yourself. You will lose eventually, but maybe you can hold me off for that half an hour?"

James bent to release her from the chains and unshackled her, removing her breast hoops, bracelets, thigh hoops and even her heels and stockings until she lay there naked but for her collar.

"I suggest you run," he said grinning wickedly, looking at his watch. "I'll give you five minutes head start!"

Kate lay still for a moment, stunned by the impact of his words and then, pushing herself off the table, she ran for the door half expecting to find it locked. Jerking it open with relief she raced up the steps and stopped in panic in the hall wondering where on earth she should hide.

A brilliant thought crossed her mind and summoning all her nerve, she ran to the front door, and out to the car, for a second quite sure he had left the keys in the ignition. Looking inside, she saw they were not there and that the car was locked, with her crumpled clothes in the back where she had removed them earlier.

Looking up, she saw James at the front door, smiling and waving the jangling bunch of keys in his hand. Swearing to herself, Kate set off around the side of the farmhouse as quickly as she could, though her bare feet made her progress slow, but he didn't seem to be chasing her. He had said he would give her five minutes...but she had no watch!

Kate headed towards the back door, very aware that she could not stay outside for too long without clothes—now that clouds had blown up from the south and covered the sun, the wind had turned bitingly cold. She was okay so long as she kept moving, but she needed to try and find somewhere to hide for as long as possible, and the old farmhouse held no such hiding places.

She crept through the kitchen, ears straining to hear where he might be. Arriving back in the hall, she moved stealthily up the stairs intent on grabbing some kind of clothing, even a towel or blanket would do if she could find nothing better.

Hoping James would still be looking for her outside amidst the tumbledown outhouses that surrounded the farmhouse, she began to rummage through the suitcases he had brought. Discarding the one full of his toys, she found the smaller one containing his clothes and quickly grabbed a sweater and a pair of jeans.

After she had wriggled in to them, she paused only to roll up the legs of the jeans to avoid tripping over them before she walked cautiously to the top of the stairs. She grinned, almost enjoying herself and suddenly feeling much more confidant now that she had some clothes on.

As Kate crept down the stairs, James was in fact sitting by the fire in the lounge, not even attempting to discover her whereabouts as yet. In fact, he was pretty sure he knew where she would go—there was only one hiding place outside that he thought would appeal to her—unless she dashed off into the surrounding countryside, which he thought very unlikely with nothing on her feet.

In fact, it took Kate only a few minutes to discount the other buildings. Whilst they afforded some refuge from the wind and the rain that was sure to start soon, they were barely more attractive than the damp cellar she was trying so hard to avoid. When she found the stables and noticed the ladder leading up to the loft she at first discounted it as too obvious, but then inspiration struck and she climbed the ladder and with some difficulty pulled it up behind her.

Peering through the broken roof tiles, she checked that James was not in the immediate vicinity and then lowered herself down through the hole to check the stable door, it opened outwards and a quick glance assured her that there were plenty of long timbers available with which to wedge it closed.

Kate hid herself behind a couple of bales of hay and waited. Wondering how much of the half hour had already passed? With a moment to collect herself, she realized how excited she was at this game of hide and seek. Her hand slipped down the front of her jeans to cup her pussy, her thumb automatically rolling her clit as a finger stroked the lips of her cunt—one and then two fingers slipping inside her. Kate made no attempt to bring her pleasure on, it was simply an act of comforting defiance in this world turned upside down, where avoiding him, and disobeying him was what he wanted from her. Even so, it felt so *good*.

Kate heard him approaching and slowly withdrew her hand. Looking from behind the bales, she saw him grin as he spied the drawn-up ladder, and was stunned when he simply jumped straight up, almost as if levitating. He gripped the edges of the hole in his strong hands, and effortlessly pulled himself up.

Now panicked that she would miss her only chance, Kate leaped from hiding and ran outside, slamming the stable door closed behind her. She grappled with a length of timber and frantically, breathing hard with the effort, she managed to wedge it into place, terrified that he would understand his mistake before she had the door firmly barred.

Kate added a second piece of wood to the first and was beginning to breath easier when she saw the door move as his weight crashed into it from the inside. Then she grinned, and then laughed as the door held firm despite the tremendous battering and curses that were coming from the other side.

It was therefore with stunned incredulity that she observed the top half of the half-door swing slowly open to reveal him standing smiling and looking at his watch.

"Ten more minutes!" He shouted, backing up to vault the half door.

Chapter Twenty-Nine
Ravished

∞

Cursing loudly, Kate turned and raced back to the house. His laughter followed her and drove her on faster. Desperately she racked her brains for somewhere to go. She only needed to hold him off for a few more minutes.

The second bathroom! Maybe it had a locking door? They had never used it so perhaps James had not bothered to remove the bolt? She hurtled through the kitchen, up the stairs and along the landing. She crashed through the bathroom door and whirled to slam it shut as her fingers searched frantically for a key or bolt.

There was no lock of course. James was nothing if not thorough. He arrived at the bathroom just moments later and though she put all her weight behind it, the door was forced open slowly inch by inch. Finally, she was forced to let go, and Kate prepared to defend herself. James approached her with his arms casually by his sides. She saw his supreme confidence and nearly gave in then and there. Then she remembered what was at stake and she steeled herself to resist with all her might.

James moved closer and Kate looked frantically around for some kind of weapon as she backed away from him towards the bath. Groping desperately behind her, whilst never taking her eyes off James even for one second, she felt something solid beneath her hand. It was the wooden handle of a back-rub brush, and with a surge of hope, she gripped it tightly and held it in front of her. Whilst looking slightly silly, it was made of a heavy varnished wood and its large brush head made it a useful cudgel. Kate began to swish it as hard as she could to and fro in front of her to keep James at bay.

Kate was therefore utterly dismayed when, with consummate ease, James stepped inside the arc of her swinging arm and made her drop the brush with a simple wrist lock. He let go of her wrist as his other hand caught a handful of her hair and he dragged her struggling and swearing out of the bathroom and along the landing towards their bedroom.

Haunted by memories of that horrible cellar room, Kate felt one last surge of adrenaline sweep through her and she let fly with her feet and fists, hitting out as hard and furiously as she possibly could. Though she knew she must be hurting him, her blows seemed to have no effect. This more than anything drove her completely crazy. She struggled and spat like a she-demon unable to resist being dragged by her hair but otherwise impeding him in every possible way.

When James had finally managed to wrestle her into the bedroom, he let go of her hair and threw her on to the bed. Making sure he steered clear of her flailing feet he ripped the buttons of her jeans open and began to pull them down her legs. Kate's face was a snarling mask of fury as she struggled to keep them on. She kicked for all she was worth and tried to rake him with her nails so viciously that only the speed of his reflexes stopped her from shredding his face, though she drew blood on his hands and forearms.

James realized he would have to deal with her differently if he wanted any skin left intact, and so he grabbed her ankles and held her legs out straight so that he could use them as long levers to turn her helplessly onto her stomach. Then kneeling on her calves, he once more grabbed a handful of Kate's hair and used his other hand to bring first one wrist and then the other within the confining circle, entrapping and entangling her in her own hair.

With her arms thereby controlled, he began once more to wrestle off her jeans, and finally succeeded in ripping them by sheer strength down to her ankles.

Kate's bare bottom lay temptingly before him, but he didn't have the time to indulge himself in giving her a spanking. James sat astride her and, briefly letting go of her hands, he twisted her arms so that her hands were now palm down on the top of her head, one on top of the other. Tangling them once more in her hair, he lifted the baggy sweater up over her head to trap her arms and at the same time blindfold her as if she were held within a large woolen sack.

Only then, did he tug down his jeans and flip her writhing body back over by her ankles, dragging her towards him as he stood by the side of the bed, his hands holding her legs widespread. Kate had very nearly got her hands free from her hair when he finally got the head of his cock centered on her cunt so he let her legs go and fell on top of her crushing her even as he slid inside her.

With a long wailing moan, Kate realized she was sopping wet and extraordinarily aroused. James plunged into her easily and she continued to fight him, not wanting to admit that he had beaten her and wanting still more to feel his strength overwhelming her. Giving her no choice.

Keeping himself deep inside her, James wrestled off the sweater and with some difficulty recaptured her hands in his — not trusting that in her passion she would not still go for his face with her nails. Slowly and inexorably, his strength trapped her hands beneath the small of her back where just one of his hands could hold both her wrists and leave his other hand free to roam

James drew her back, half lifting her until he had both his feet on the floor and her bottom was perched on the edge of the bed. Then he began to fuck her in earnest, with his free hand now working her clit and now rolling her nipples. Occasionally he slapped her breasts lightly to make them bounce as they were thrust forward by the arching of her back. The energy of their fight transformed by the second into a frenzy of hard, physical all-consuming lust.

Kate's struggles to escape became confused with a deeper instinctive struggle to impale herself ever more forcefully on his cock. To suck him in to her — to devour him with her heat.

She was dominated and yet she was capturing him. This was nothing like the tamer submission she had previously experienced. This had a raw primal force that thrilled her even as it scared her and aroused her more. She was free—free to struggle, free to beg, free to scream, free to use her utmost strength to resist him and free to experience the futility of that resistance. Her submission was complete because the choice to submit had been made irrelevant.

As Kate lost herself in the increasingly powerful waves of pleasure, she found herself somehow floating above herself. Feeling how she writhed to take more of him into her. Watching her body go in to its spastic catharsis as yet another orgasm racked her. Hearing the whorish voice that begged him for more, to fuck her, to split her with his cock, seeing the insensate animal passion in her own eyes oblivious to everything save for him and the use he made of her body. With this shocking image electrifying her senses, Kate felt herself rush back into the mind-eclipsing frenzy of her own passion, wanting it all, wanting to drown in this sea of desire.

As James picked her up with one hand beneath her waist, her thighs gripped him tightly as if she were terrified of losing this tremendous strength inside her. Holding her hair at the back of her neck he arched her back until she was literally balanced only on her head, each thrust of his cock now compressing her whole body, forcing screams from her throat, she could not have held back had she wished to. Kate lost herself even more completely and in her total surrender, James took supreme delight.

James withdrew from her and dropped her, letting her fall in a tangle of limbs wantonly open and glistening with sweat. The moan that escaped her lips despairing and denying the experience of his leaving was deep and pleading in its tone. He bent to his case, retrieving a flogger, its long, soft leather strands brushing the ground as he returned to stand at the head of the bed.

"Come here, slave, and take me in your mouth," James commanded, and she dazedly struggled to comply. "No! Not like that! Turn on your back and tilt your head back, look up at me, look at my cock, you may kiss the tip and no more."

James stood with his cock tantalizingly brushing her mouth, she ached to gorge herself on its hard flesh, but he denied her.

"Tell me what you want, slut?"

"Master...I want your cock in my mouth." Kate replied, her voice lustful and pleading.

"Beg me for it!"

"Please, Master, I need your cock in me, I need your cock in me anywhere you like, Master, please fuck my mouth, Master, please..."

"You are a delicious little slave." He wet his fingers in the copious fluid that soaked her thighs and spread it over her breasts and then her face, even the pressure of his fingers on her mouth made her involuntarily open and suck them, she trembled as the need grew inside her.

"I am going to flog your belly, your thighs and your breasts while you suck on my cock. Beg me for your flogging, and I will allow you to take my cock into your mouth."

Not quite believing that she was doing so, Kate heard herself beg for the flogging, her eyes saw nothing. Transfixed solely upon his cock and the desperate need she had to have it inside her. She felt one strong hand slip beneath her neck to tilt her head still farther and then the silken, hard head of his cock was between her lips, and then more of him as he took her throat. Kate closed her eyes and tried to relax to make his access easier, imagining that if only she could swallow him deeply enough, she could feel him once more inside her cunt, now hungrily open, seeping desire.

The flogging James gave her as she sucked on him was nothing harsh, in her super-sensitized state it did not need to be. He simply loved the extraordinary lust-filled rapture that consumed Kate and wanted to give her every possible flavor of sensation so that she could surrender ever more deeply to pleasure.

James flicked the soft strands at her belly and breasts, occasionally catching her nipple or clit, sometimes stinging the soft, open petals of her pussy. Mostly he simply trailed the strands over her skin. Kate felt the fire in her belly grow stronger as he fucked her mouth and soon without any control or ability to resist she was coming, her hips arching and writhing, the only point of stillness her mouth wantonly closed around him, sucking hungrily.

As Kate groaned ecstatically, James felt the vibration of her orgasmic cry through his cock and the fire leapt within him, resonating with her pleasure. The sight of her body thrashing in the throes of ecstasy making him surrender his own control and come deep in her throat, then withdrawing to splash her face and breasts before plunging deeply inside her mouth once more.

James groaned loudly and pulling her head with him by her hair, he fell onto the bed to let her suckle on him as he let the waves of pleasure suffuse his body.

They lay entwined in a happily exhausted daze for an hour or so before he took her with him to the shower and had her wash him before in turn soaping her all over.

In contrast to the previous few hours of lustful passion this, by some mutual sense of the different level of intimacy now binding them, was soft and gentle, a closeness in the almost silence of water, steam and soapy warmth. James said nothing about the winner of the game—this was now understood by both to be an irrelevance, a means to an end now accomplished.

Drying her, he noticed Kate was nearly asleep on her feet, not surprising after the emotional and physical trials of the last twenty-four hours. Taking time only to replace her bracelets and then attach them by a short length of chain to her collar, he bundled her into the bed and held her closely until they both fell deeply asleep.

Chapter Thirty
The Cleansing

The next morning Kate was dozing quietly contented, her head pillowed on James' firm, flat stomach, when she felt him shift and tell her not to move, whispering that he would be back soon.

She drifted back off to sleep and was dreaming softly when he next awoke her by gently trailing his fingertips over her skin to draw her back to consciousness.

"Wake up, sleepy, I have everything set up for you in the bathroom. Follow me."

James walked off, and Kate struggled to wake herself up, staggering dozily after him to the bathroom. He had been busy. There was a board of some sorts, one end propped on a small stool, and the other positioned over the toilet. A very large bucket hung from the ceiling. It must have held about five gallons she guessed, her insides knotting as her still half asleep mind began to figure out what this was about. The urge to turn and run was powerful, but she could not stand the thought of James losing respect for her so she willed herself to stand still, determined to confront her fears.

"This is a colema board," explained James. "It's for doing colonic irrigation at home. For my purposes, it's to give you one hell of an enema and to allow me to massage you at the same time. You will lie on your back on the board, your bum snug against this hood." He patted the raised cowl. "Your legs would normally simply rest either side of it, however I want you to feel more intensely controlled and helpless so I'm going to raise and spread your legs using these restraints and the hooks you can see there and there in the ceiling beam." James pointed and she followed his gesture, beginning to see the whole picture with alarming clarity.

James spread a towel on the smooth board and told her to lie down on her back. Then after pulling her a little way towards the hood that would direct everything down into the toilet, he parted her legs and placed first one and then the other into heavy ankle restraints.

Though made of strong leather, the ankle cuffs were beautifully soft and padded inside so that when James tightened them and spread her legs far apart, Kate felt her body react wantonly to the helplessness of her position, despite what she knew was about to happen. James took her hands and cuffed them beneath the board, forcing her chest to lift and thrust her breasts vulnerably upwards.

The next thing Kate felt was his sudden forcing of a generously lubricated finger into her ass. Her whole body jolted, her eyes widening with the shock as she gasped. Then the movement of his finger began to register, and she felt him massaging the inner surface of her ass, and her pussy indirectly through the soft connecting internal wall, as his finger curled upwards inside her. He continued the internal massage for some minutes and Kate's breathing became heavier, her chest heaving and her face flushing. The sensation beginning to spread through her belly familiar, and yet, new and strange.

After a while, he withdrew his finger and she felt him insert something inside her. It was much smaller than his finger, the sensation of it barely perceptible. James drew her whole body down a few more inches until she could feel her bottom fit snugly against the curvature of the hood.

James knelt beside her, his hand resting lightly on her trembling belly as he spoke quietly, explaining what was to happen.

"I am going to start the water now. There's about five gallons this first time, though in the future you'll take much more. This is how it works—you will feel the water fill you and as it does I will be massaging your belly from the lower left-hand side up to your ribs and then across and down again, following the course of your bowel. When you're full, you will not be able to hold it in, so don't try! Just relax and it will come pouring out of you and straight into the toilet. As you empty, I will reverse the way I'm massaging you to encourage the evacuation. Whilst this is mostly being done to prepare your ass for the fucking I'm going to give you later, it's also extremely good for you and gets rid of all kinds of toxicity that may have built up in your system. I am not remotely turned on by shit or anything to do with it, therefore the best and most freeing way to experience anal sex is for you to feel and know yourself to be completely clean inside."

Out of sight, James must have released some sort of valve as Kate almost immediately felt a curious sensation deep inside. It did not feel like water, more like sparkles and tingles rushing around her thighs and belly. James told her to breathe deeply and when she did, the sensation changed once more so that now she could feel the beginnings of the distension. His hands moved rhythmically over her belly and she closed her eyes. Unable to resist, she told herself to relax.

The feeling of pressure grew and grew. Not unpleasant, yet not exactly pleasant either. Then she felt her ass begin to spasm as she struggled to control herself. Kate heard James telling her to let go, to relax, but she felt suddenly deeply ashamed and resisted with all her might. James laughed, not unkindly, but reading her completely misplaced determination in the set of her jaw, he pressed gently on her belly.

"You cannot hold in all five gallons, Katie, so let go. You will have to sooner or later. I can't see anything if it makes you feel better, I repeat I am not remotely turned on by shit, however, nor am I bothered by it, it's just natural stuff!"

He laughed again and pressed more deeply into her belly, and as he did, she felt something give inside her, and the water came pouring out.

Kate half felt the movement of soft stools escaping, yet almost as soon as she registered this, she heard him move to flush the toilet and relaxed.

"Now you begin to fill again...this will take some time, at least an hour I would think, so just relax and give up control, not to me for once, but to your body — let your body do its thing!"

Kate did as she was told. What choice did she have? The filling and releasing became a cycle. James' hands working on her belly, his voice occasionally reminding her to breathe, sometimes telling her to hold more in and other times telling her when to let go.

After a while, she was no longer feeling any stool come out and felt much easier with the process. The sense of shame dwindled away and she became once more deeply aware of the complete control James had of her body. Or the complete *lack* of any control she had, for really the water and gravity were in control. In some way she could not understand, their combined mindless insensitivity to her needs aroused her deeply. Nothing would stop this except the water in the container running out — she had rarely felt so helpless and she began to admit she was enjoying herself.

Perhaps it was that in this moment she had passed beyond and through some psychic barrier — now nothing was concealed, and instead of shame and embarrassment, she felt nurtured and cared for. Whenever she opened her eyes, she saw James' kind and handsome face filled with an infinite tenderness as he caressed and massaged her.

Kate loved to feel his hands on her, knowingly sensing everything that occurred within her. Even to the outline of her internal organs. Nothing was hidden from him. She felt utterly exposed to him, and yet with his gentle ministrations, she also felt held and comforted.

As James saw her relax and begin to enjoy the experience, so he began to massage her differently. His previous, entirely clinical, movement became increasingly sensual as he caressed and explored her intimately. He poured some musky scented oil onto her belly and began to work it from there all over her body. Working deeply and powerfully from her hands and feet back to her belly until she felt herself beginning to float free, drifting on the waves of sensation inside and out, surrendered and vulnerable, yet warm and basking in his attention, nothing withheld, everything given to him.

Slowly James started to bring her back, interweaving featherlight touches to her nipples and pussy with the strong deliberate strokes down her arms, legs and torso until her pleasure-glazed eyes opened and her lips parted, yearning for his kiss, which came with surprising softness.

When it was finally over, she felt him release her legs and wrists, remove the probe and turn the shower on. He told her to be quick, to use the toilet to eliminate any last water and then shower and return to the bedroom when she had finished.

Kate climbed unsteadily to her feet as he removed the board, sitting to use the toilet as he left, and then when she was sure she was empty, Kate stepped under the welcoming hot water. She bent over to let the powerful jet work between her legs, feeling it split her pussy lips and hammer at her little asshole. It felt delicious. So much more so now that she knew herself to be completely clean, in a way she had never felt before, curiously light, a buoyant feeling inside, energized and refreshed.

Chapter Thirty-One
Dissolving Shame

මා

Back in the bedroom, James was waiting for her and told her to kneel before him as he sat on the edge of the bed.

"Feels good, doesn't it?" he asked, reading the answer in her face before she could respond. Her eyes were shining and clear, and she knelt before him with a grace of movement that took his breath away.

"Some women," said James, "actually feel greater pleasure from anal penetration than vaginal. My guess is that's because some kind of past trauma or bad experience has left their vagina relatively numb compared to what it should be—and that is happily not the case with you!" James grinned, and Kate blushed and smiled in return. "But in any case, it goes to show just how much pleasure a woman can get from anal sex."

Kate dropped her head, quite certain that she would be one of those women—the telltale signs were already apparent to her now she was honest enough with herself to recognize them—an inner turmoil, the anticipation of shame, and the thrill of erotic fear as once again James steered her into uncharted waters.

"The point is," he continued, "that it's possible for any part of our bodies to become desensitized, some people refer to the phenomenon as 'armoring' because it's as if tension has built up in order to protect us from feeling the emotional hurt we associate with that part of our body. With the tension comes a gradually increasing numbness until the person doesn't feel the hurt anymore—but then nor do they feel any pleasure. Think for a moment about all those women of your mother's or grandmother's generation who were brought up to believe that sex was something only men took any pleasure from—that a woman's role was simply to endure it—and their belief *made* it true for them. I think it's fair to say that in many cases this was because their lovers were pretty ignorant and unskillful, even selfish, but the fact remains that when you bring a child up to hold strongly negative beliefs about their body it leaves scars—emotional ones, of course, but also physical in the sense of an area that's become numbed-out, or which simply isn't conceived of as being a source of pleasure."

Kate nodded. "I guess I was lucky—my mum is really great with stuff like that, she's always been very open-minded. Not that she'd approve of me right now, mind!" she giggled.

James smiled. "Yes, happily that kind of deep negativity about female sexuality is becoming increasingly uncommon—but the same can't be said for things anal, which remains beyond the pale for most people. People confuse the fact that shit is dirty and unhygienic with the idea that therefore there is something inherently dirty about their ass—even when they're scrupulously clean as you are now. Which of course brings me to what I'm going to do with you..."

He paused as Kate looked up at him, her expression a mixture of excitement and apprehension.

"Simply put, I'm going to give you an internal massage using lots of oil." James took a large plastic syringe from behind his back. "Obviously there's no needle—and equally obviously this is going to get a little messy because I'm going to be using a *lot* of oil. So I want you to stand up and bend over and grasp your ankles while I prepare the bed."

As Kate obeyed him, James stripped the duvet, pillows and sheets from the bed, and then went to his suitcase and took out a square of folded rubber sheet. Kate watched from between her legs as he unfolded the sheet and spread it over the bed. She felt a submissive shudder run through her whole body as she imagined what she would look like moments from now, kneeling on the rubber sheet with her bottom being filled with oil.

But then James did something unexpected. He began to attach chains and soft, heavily padded cuffs to the top corners of the bed frame, and Kate began to form a very different picture of what awaited her. James momentarily disappeared from her view and then suddenly she felt the kiss of something cold and smooth around her waist.

"This is a special sort of corset. I'm going to suspend you from the bed frame and the corset, with its padding and reinforcement, will support your middle so that not all your weight is on your arms and legs," James explained as he tightened the corset's straps.

James had her stand up straight to make tightening the corset easier and then led her to the bed and helped her up. The corset was only slightly restrictive to her breathing, the effect she was most aware of was the way it pushed down on her lower belly and thrust up her breasts. Her pussy and breasts seemed somehow heavier, a soft liquid weightiness that made her ache for James to touch them.

With Kate standing in the middle of the bed, James clipped karabiners into the D-rings on each side of the corset and then used these to attach the chains already hanging from the center-point of the top frame. He had Kate experiment with lifting her feet off the mattress while he made adjustments to the height and then he supported her as she let the corset take her full weight. James rolled her forward until she looked a little like a skydiver doing a nude freefall, and then he secured her wrists and ankles so she hung in a graceful curve with her arms and legs pointing towards the corners of the bed.

After making sure she was reasonably comfortable, James said, "This next bit is strictly speaking unnecessary, but I can't resist the temptation to torment you a little more."

So saying he rolled her nipples to full erectness and then applied clamps with small heavy weights on springs. To the soft music of Kate's moans, he drew upon the weights and set them in motion, slowly bouncing up and down on the springs.

Next, he took up the oil-filled syringe and squirted a little around the entrance to her bottom before sinking its nozzle inside her and depressing the plunger until it was empty. Then he climbed down off the bed to fetch the bottle of almond oil and refilled the syringe.

Kate hardly felt the ingress of the oil the first time, but as James squirted the second syringe-full inside her, she squirmed as the weight of the oil began to make its presence known. Her belly churned and she hung her head, eyes tight shut as her entire attention became focused on her bottom.

As he injected more and more oil, inevitably, some began to spill and James knew it would trickle down between the soft folds of her pussy. He longed to touch her there, but still more, he wanted her to feel the sweet torment of the oil's caress. So instead, he reached beneath her and pressed his fingers over her pubic bone to pull back the hood of her clit. Now the oil ran between her lips and began to drip from her little bud — a tantalizingly delicate sensation that made Kate moan with frustration as she felt the aching need grow inside her.

Suddenly she felt James' finger slip easily inside her bottom and her body jolted so that the chains rattled. Her bottom mouth tightened around his finger, but the oil was so copious that his finger slid deep inside her to the knuckle and his fingertip explored the soft, spongy tissues of her core at will.

Slowly and deliberately James withdrew his finger, instructing that she bear down gently, that she let herself open. Kate groaned and relaxed only to feel a second finger slip inside her.

Now with two fingers buried up to the knuckle in her lovely bottom, James had the purchase he needed to begin the massage. He began with her anus, squeezing and rolling the ring of muscle gently between his thumb on the outside and his fingers within. He moved clockwise around her opening, moving his thumb in slow, deep circles, his other hand placed on her ass cheek to steady her.

There was a certain necessary clinical quality in his manipulation. He wanted to work deeply, to maximize the benefit, knowing that just through this focusing of her whole attention on a part of her body she normally ignored, he was awakening something powerful within her.

"I want you to feel the itch in your pussy, Kate. Feel the need, feel the desire, the potential pleasure building up. Hold that feeling and let it mingle with the sensations of my fingers inside you."

James worked his fingers deeper still so that now his thumb and fingertips pressed into the band of flesh between her pussy and her anus. He squeezed it gently and then more firmly, responding always to her breathing and the tone of her soft cries as she slipped further into helpless pleasure. Then methodically, he began to stroke her pussy from inside her bottom, feeling her internal muscles ripple beneath his fingertips. She groaned much more loudly now and James again fought the temptation to touch her clit directly and bring her on quickly.

Instead, he worked towards her clit from within, probing in full circles incredibly slowly so that he could sense from the changes in her voice and the trembling of her thighs where she was most sensitive inside. At the same time, by the lack or diminution of such responses he would identify less sensitive tissue and then his fingers would work deeper—probing, circling, enticing and enlivening until Kate's moans and soft cries, her pleadings for release became a constant impassioned stream.

Not once, had James touched her pussy or clit and, save for the delicious pulling on her nipples and the stretching of her breasts, Kate felt no familiar pleasure. This stoking sensation, this burning glow inside her, was something entirely new— recognizable only in its effects upon her mind and body. As she writhed beneath James' hands, she felt her pussy swell and drip its essence, mingling with the sweet oil. Her limbs felt boneless and her thoughts had long since sunk beneath a warm-scented surface to drown in the sensations flooding her body.

All she knew was the constant and all-consuming urgency with which she needed to feel James inside her, and—while before today she would have voiced a preference for the taste of him on her tongue or the thickness of him stretching her cunt, now there was a third and equally attractive option. It mattered not—so long as he was inside her, taking her and possessing her.

Her ass had become a second hungry mouth. James need only press his fingertip to the rim for involuntary contractions to start as if she sought to suck him inside. When a third finger joined the first and second there was no pain, not even the mildest discomfort—only a jangling of chains as she arched her back in vain attempts to impale herself more deeply.

She felt James spread her ass cheeks wide and she tensed, expecting to feel the singular thickness of him enter her, but instead, shockingly she felt the stinging slap of his fingers as he began to spank her. Not as he had spanked her before on the cheeks of her ass, now he spanked her ass directly. Light stinging slaps of his fingers to her tight little hole that sent fiery jolts through her body. At first, she felt her buttocks clench as instinctively she sought to guard against the tender assault, but then a still deeper instinct took control as she found herself offering her ass up in anticipation the next sweet sting.

Only when she hung in her chains almost entirely passive except for the slow, lascivious grinding of her hips—which seemed to have a mind of their own—did the spanking stop. James' sensitive fingers now found no resistance, only soft yielding acquiescence to his intrusion. And then Kate felt what she had craved for so long—the smooth velvet hardness of his lovely cock sliding inexorably into her ass.

She moaned loudly and her hands gripped compulsively at nothing as he entered her. His cock, which inside her cunt had always seemed to fit so perfectly, now stretched her—an exquisite invasion as he claimed the last remaining part of her body for his own.

Slowly he eased himself deeper, allowing her body to accommodate him. Hanging in her chains, Kate could only surrender to the burgeoning sensations — her desperate struggles to thrust herself onto him made unnecessary as she felt herself begin to swing on the chains. She felt James' hands on her bottom as he pushed her away from him, simultaneously the void within as he withdrew — then the grip of his strong fingers around her thighs as he pulled her towards him, and the rippling power of him entering and distending her once more.

Still, he had not touched her pussy and yet the imminence of her orgasm was obvious to James by the passion of her cries. He shook with pleasure as he felt her tighten around his cock. Instinctively his cock pulsed strongly in response as if their bodies spoke a private language whose only words were lust and pleasure.

James slid his hand beneath her thigh, the angle was awkward but he wanted her to have no warning of the sudden intensity of pleasure he intended to inflict upon her helpless body. Feeling delicately, he centered his hand and then abruptly brought his palm sharply upwards, slapping her pussy's swollen lips in the same manner as he had just spanked her ass.

At first, Kate froze — but only for the count of two heartbeats before her whole body convulsed, making it impossible for James to administer more slaps. Though he had been anticipating a strong reaction, he was amazed by the power of the orgasm that now took her by storm. The chains securing her arms and legs creaked and rattled, even the stout timber frame of the bed seemed to groan as she thrashed in her bondage, screaming all the time for him to fuck her, to fuck her hard.

In fact, James had only to hold her tightly, so as to ensure that her frantic writhings did not dislodge him. Despite the lack of purchase, her body's sinuous and wanton convulsions, combined with the greedy contractions of her inner muscles made any movement on his part superfluous.

As one part of him surrendered to the incredible pleasures that surged through his loins, another beheld Kate with awe, even reverence. Her surrender to pleasure was so absolute it was breathtaking—she had far exceeded his expectations. Her courage and the trust she placed in him moved him deeply and never more so than when she was helpless, abandoned to lust and utterly uninhibited as she was now. Even as he reveled in the gloriously erotic spectacle of her luscious body so lewdly displayed, so voraciously lusty and so extremely arousing that it was all he could do to stop himself from coming immediately, he also felt the sweet pain in his heart as he acknowledged himself to be completely captivated by her extraordinary spirit.

Suddenly James felt their relative positions to be far too impersonal. He needed to look into her eyes, needed to feel her arms around him. He carefully withdrew and then quickly released the chains so that Kate fell the short way to the oil smeared rubber sheet. He flipped her over on her back and was just about to enter her when a wild thought struck him.

Leaving Kate moaning ecstatically, he slipped off the bed and moments later returned with a large vibrating dildo. Despite its girth, it slid easily into Kate's pussy, accompanied by the sound of a renewed chorus of frenzied and lust-drenched moans. He knelt between her legs and effortlessly lifted her lower body, pushing her legs back towards her head to center his cock head on her ass. Once again, he eased inside her, his way superbly lubricated by the oil, but now he could feel the bulging outline of the dildo in her pussy pressing on his cock head and—as was obvious as Kate's moans became screams of lustful pleasure—her ass felt exquisitely tight around his cock.

James began to fuck her slow and deep. Each time his pelvis came forward it pushed upon the base of the dildo, nudging it deeper into her pussy so that she was doubly fucked with every thrust. Kate's eyes shot open, incredulous that there could be an entirely new level of sensation previously undreamed of. And though her eyes were glazed with lust, deep within their black pools there was a smoldering fire that seemed to scorch James to his core.

He fell forward, grasping her hair so that he could turn her face to his. Now there was nothing restrained about him—she had ignited a force in him that nothing but the cataclysm of orgasm could subdue. He kissed her passionately, crushing her lips and licking her tongue. Impossibly, his cock seemed to grow even longer and thicker and the itch inside its head could find no relief within her oil-slicked ass except by almost complete withdrawal to plunder her tender ring again and again.

Kate relished the rampant fury let loose upon her body. She welcomed his devastation and soaked up his power. Her nails running electric trails down his back, served only to spur him on until, unable to match his pace, she could only surrender to the hurricane of passion she had unleashed.

Chapter Thirty-Two
Puppygirl

ร๏

An hour or so later Kate groaned as she stirred beneath him. She did not so much awaken as return to consciousness, for where she had been could not properly be termed sleep.

In that brief moment before the clarity of remembering faded to leave only a series of vivid images, she thought she had been transported to another world where only she and James existed. It was a world of multiplicities where she lived a thousand-fold life—for every Kate a James, and for every couple a facet of their love portrayed. One of her selves laughed as she held his hand on a long ramble across a ploughed field beneath an autumn sky, another screamed as she writhed in silver chains. A third gazed up into piercingly kind blue eyes and felt the warm strength of protecting arms hold her close and safe. Another ate a meal by candlelight—though her arms were pinioned to her sides and each mouthful was spooned tenderly into her open mouth, while still another danced lasciviously with golden sand beneath her feet flaunting and enticing with every sinuous movement of her naked body.

Kate squeezed her eyes tight shut, not wanting these images to ever leave her. But inevitably they faded and in their place, as if the thought had bubbled up from the depths of a clear well to float upon its shimmering surface, she recognized that for once her dreams held true meaning. That with James she could be all she was, that no single aspect of her being could not find happiness with him.

She felt him move, his weight lifted off her body as he rolled onto his side, and she was torn between relief and the absurd desire that she might spend her life so entangled. She opened her eyes and found him staring at her intently. Immediately though, his eyes softened and he leaned down to kiss her softly, his hand trailing a path down her belly, through the still moist folds of her pussy to delicately touch her ass.

"Are you okay?" he asked as his finger probed gently.

Kate nodded and lifted her head to his, needing to be kissed again.

James kissed her, but when her arms came around his neck and her hips wriggled as she sought to trap his hand between her thighs, he laughed.

"No, my beautiful and insatiable slave, we must get something to eat and then you have a busy afternoon ahead of you, so save your energy for later!"

James disentangled himself and ignored her mews of mock protest as he led her to the shower.

Half an hour later, Kate was kneeling by his side on the kitchen floor as he fed her a very belated breakfast. As he selected choice tidbits from the food he had prepared, he explained what he intended for the afternoon.

"Yesterday and again this morning," he said, valiantly fighting the urge to sweep her into his arms and carry her back to bed, "you connected with an aspect of your sexual self that had been buried somewhere deep inside you for a long time. From now on connecting with that kind of primal sexual energy will be much easier for you, and in turn that will give you much easier access to the level of truly uninhibited pleasure that—as you will have gathered," James grinned, "is what makes me so crazy about you."

Kate returned his smile, but had no words to express the extraordinary thing that was happening between them so she just leant forward and kissed his hand. James' fingertips brushed her cheek lovingly as he continued.

"But the thing is that it's only one aspect of many, there are others, equally desirable but very different. Whereas the woman who emerged yesterday was aggressively sexual, surrendering herself only to an equally fierce and aggressive lover, this morning you discovered that intense pleasure could lie buried beneath feelings of shame that were probably instilled in early childhood. There are other such pleasures to be revealed and each one needs a slightly different approach to bring them out."

James laughed and leant forward to kiss her. "Don't look so worried! I'll be there loving and encouraging you every step of the way...and I think you'll really enjoy yourself once you get into it."

He stroked her cheek and gently brushed away a loose strand of hair that had fallen over her eyes.

"Yesterday was about adrenaline, primal fears, escape, pursuit. A very physical form of domination that allowed you to find inner strengths you didn't know were there, whereas today is all about connecting with feelings of helplessness, weakness and vulnerability. A good way to do that is to let yourself sink fully and completely into a role that embodies those qualities — in this instance you're going to be a puppy!"

Kate looked up at him in surprise. "A puppy? How..."

James raised an eyebrow and Kate realized she had spoken without asking permission, but James did not seem to mind given the circumstances for he made a gesture that encouraged her to speak.

"Why a puppy? I'm already your slave girl..."

"Yes, and that's part of the problem. You are really strongly identified with being my slave girl, even though that's also a fantasy because after all you're free to leave whenever you wish. The one thing you can *never* be, no matter how hard you try, is anything other than a human being. Therefore putting you into the impossible *role* of a puppy helps you make a very clear distinction between your real self and the feelings that arise whilst in role. The idea is that you can really feel those feelings intensely without losing your *self* entirely. It's a way of keeping things clear. Anyway, that's one reason, and it's a very good one — another reason is that by playing a role — an animal role —

it gives you a sort of license to sink into your animal instincts. Somehow it just shortcuts a lot of inhibitions…"

James saw the confusion on her face and leant forward to kiss her again.

"Kate, just trust me on this okay? You'll understand through the experience of doing it rather than intellectually beforehand. Just remember to try and sink deep into the feelings—how would it *feel* to be a puppy? You're tiny and weak, you cannot fend for yourself, and you are totally dependent on others and incredibly anxious to please them. Yet at the same time you are fun-loving and playful, with an enormous appetite for life and you are curious about *everything…*"

She nodded as she allowed herself to begin to slide into those feelings. There was an immediate attraction to the innocence of the role that seemed to pull at her from deep inside. James led her upstairs to the bedroom before he said anything more.

"Let's not forget that you're this curious hybrid puppy-*girl*, and that we want to make this as erotically charged as possible!" James grinned wickedly and told her to bend over and grab her ankles.

"If you're going to be my puppygirl you need a tail to wag…" As James spoke, she felt his finger probing once more at the entrance to her ass. She was still quite well oiled, but James administered another syringe full before she felt something harder begin to penetrate her. She felt the by now familiar sensation of her ass stretching and she moaned as she tried to relax and let it enter her, wanting it inside her for his pleasure and her own.

"I'm putting a small inflatable butt plug in your ass to which I'll attach a tail. Just relax again…"

James attached a little air pump to expand a small rubber balloon within her so that the butt plug would be held firmly in place, then after closing the valve he attached a long semi-rigid tail to the part of the plug that still protruded. As he released it, the tail hung down between her legs and in front of her face, and she saw that it was the same color as her hair. James told her to stand up straight and as she obeyed Kate felt the tail plug move inside her and the tail itself brush the inside and the backs of her thighs.

Instructing her to go down on all fours, James walked around her and made a few adjustments until he was happy with the angle of her new tail. Kate moaned softly as the plug moved inside her bottom.

"Very pretty!" he remarked with a wicked smile, and then went to his case to get a few more things. The first items he showed her were a small waist cincher corset in tan leather and a matching pair of kneepads also made of leather.

These he buckled into place before instructing her to crawl around him to make sure the fit was right. As she moved, she felt the tail move inside her, and glancing over her shoulder saw it was swaying to-and-fro in a gentle wag. Kate also noticed the kneepads were fastened by chains to the corset, slightly restricting her movement, and she glanced up at him curiously.

"They will stop you from standing upright, slut-puppy," James explained as he turned to select the next items from the case. These resembled gloves…except that the fingers and thumb of the material were stitched together, effectively binding her hands into "paws". These he secured in place with tiny padlocks at her wrists.

James then told her to roll over on her back and fastened leather cuffs high on her thighs. They were similar to the hoops she had worn previously—they fitted her snugly and their circular cross-section meant they stayed in place without needing to be over-tight. In addition, these cuffs had three light chains ending in rubber-tipped clamps. With her legs spread wide he clamped each of the chains in turn to her pussy lips, then he made adjustments to the length of each chain until, by moving her thighs in and out he made sure that spreading her legs also served to open her pussy wide.

Glancing at Kate, he noticed the flush in her cheeks as she grasped their purpose and teasingly he ran his finger up to her clit making her whole body tremble and her breath become ragged.

"You will be a depraved little bitch-slut all day today, so let's not pretend you're not loving it already!" James spanked her bottom lightly and told her to roll back over on to all fours again.

From this position, James added nipple clamps to complete her "puppy" bondage. These clamps were attached to a short length of chain, no more than three inches long, from which hung glittering, faceted glass balls that sparkled in the afternoon sunlight. Their weight pulled deliciously on her nipples and when he made her crawl again, they bounced from side-to-side.

Happy with Kate's transformation into a slut-puppy, James fastened her leash and telling her to "heel", he walked downstairs, enjoying her sensual whimpers as she struggled to keep up with him. Her arousal was heightened by the fact that each movement of her legs pulled slightly on the chains clamped to her pussy and caused her moist lips to rub lubriciously together before they were pulled apart again as she took another step.

In the kitchen, James told her to kneel back with her hands on the floor, sitting upright. As he poured her a bowl of juice, he reminded her that as a puppygirl she was no longer allowed to communicate in words. She must use her body and simple sounds to express herself. Of course, he admitted casually, she would make many more sounds than normally available to a puppy!

James placed the bowl on the floor before her and was pleased to see her look up for permission to drink.

"If you want it, you'll have to show me how pleased you are, little bitch!" he said, watching her puzzled expression change to comprehension as she lifted her bottom to wag her tail from side-to-side.

Smiling with pleasure at the speed with which Kate picked things up and entered in to the spirit of her new role, James gave her permission to drink and watched as she bent over the bowl to lap and lick it up.

After the first bowl, he filled a second and then a third making sure every drop was licked up. Kate struggled so much to finish the third bowl that he did not think it worthwhile to try and force another on her, so when she had finished he pushed the ring gag into her mouth and then secured her to the table leg. After quickly making himself a hot drink, James sat down at the table, telling Kate to take his cock in her mouth as she knelt between his legs. Once more, she was only to hold and not to tease him with her tongue.

As before, Kate found this demeaning and arousing at once. The taste of him in her mouth always aroused her and it was very hard to stop herself from sucking and using her tongue on his lovely hard cock.

Kate imagined how she looked squatting there between his legs. The unavoidable strands of saliva dribbling down her chin from the ring gag and flushed with a delicious shame as unseen she moved her knees as far apart as possible to make the clamps pull on her pussy and squirmed on the dildo in her ass. Quickly she found herself longing and aching for some sort of touch to her clit, or to be able to rub herself on something to relieve the mounting tension of her need. The torment was exquisite…to need so urgently and yet be denied. To be held in this suspense of wanting and to revel in it rather than deny it or attempt to distract herself from the desires that flooded her body.

Inevitably as all the fluid she had drunk made its way through her system, Kate became very urgently aware of a need to pee. A need that Kate was determined would not interrupt this excessively pleasurable moment and so she tried instead to focus on James' warm, hard cock. Remembering and daydreaming of how deliciously he tasted when he came into her mouth.

Chapter Thirty-Three
A Walk in the Garden

ഛ

Kate had successfully lost herself in her own wonderful inner world of desire, control and denial when she felt James move and withdraw his cock from her mouth.

"Time for a walk I think, little puppy-slut!" he said, looking down at her. He considered taking the ring gag off, but then decided to leave it on since it obviously made her feel more sluttish and she looked so incredibly desirable with her mouth held open and available all the time. Further, it reinforced the prohibition on speech and so served several purposes at once.

Picking up her leash, he headed for the door and after a momentary resistance at the thought of going outside in daylight as she was, she followed him very nervously, struggling to keep up once more.

James knew she would not be able to crawl very far without becoming tired and sore, so he walked her towards the small garden set to one side of the farmhouse. Here there was soft lawn on which she could move more easily and also another feature useful to her training as a puppy.

It was now that the extra bowls of juice should pay a dividend. He had no specific idea what the experience would trigger. If she was holding on to some old hang-ups and shaming about peeing then he knew she would soon show him signs of distress as the feelings began to shift. On the other hand, if there was nothing there this might just push her exhibitionist buttons or she might find it "dirty" in an erotic way, alternatively she could find the whole thing tedious and that sort of boredom would signal that there were no inhibitions to release. Any other response, from tears to anger, would tell him that he should follow through. Whatever happened, he would remain totally focused and aware of her responses and be ready to support her in whatever she needed from him.

As he led her over to the first small tree, he explained that she was to lift her leg to the side, thereby opening her pussy by her chains, and pee. Except she was not to let it all out! Just a squirt and then stop...there were other trees and she must anoint each one before they left the garden.

Mortified, Kate lifted her leg dutifully though she felt intensely aware of the conflicting urges within her. There was a strong desire to please him, to be obedient however bizarre the instruction, there was the counter-urge, not to run but to seek clarification, to want to understand *why* before she obeyed, to delay the shameful experience for as long as possible, and then there was something within her, incomprehensively perverse, that felt aroused, not despite, but *because* of the degrading act she had been told to perform. Then of course there was the increasingly urgent need to relieve herself. Crawling across the lawn had done nothing to ease the pressure on her bladder.

The humiliation of actually performing like an animal in front of him generated equally contradictory feelings. That being controlled aroused her she had long since accepted, yet he had previously always controlled her as herself, not in the role of an animal that she could never be. Wait! That was what he had said...she was *not* a puppy, she was playing the role of a puppy—he had told her to sink into the feelings of being a puppy...how embarrassed would a puppy be to pee against a tree? Not at all...but she was not a puppy...

The circular arguments went round and round Kate's head whilst all the time James stood waiting patiently for her to obey. All she could do, Kate reminded herself, was to trust and obey, and hope that the understanding would come later.

At first, Kate thought she would not be able to do it, and then to her eventual relief she felt her pee spurt forth. No sooner had it started than she felt his hand slap down on her bottom commanding her to stop in mid-flow. With great difficulty, she did and gasping through the ring gag, she lowered her leg feeling a trickle run down her inner thigh as she did so. She felt degraded and dirty. The first hot tears began to run down her face.

Flushing crimson and deeply ashamed, she knelt with hunched shoulders trying to assimilate what she had just done. James crouched beside her, kissing her eyes, he stroked her hair, and then down her back, understanding what this was doing to her emotionally, but knowing that it was important to overcome this. He comforted her to a point, lending her his strength, encouraging her and praising her as much as possible. He dare not dispel the emotional charge completely for that would defeat his essential purpose, and then he would have put her through it for nothing.

He took her farther down the sloping lawn watching the beautiful way her lithe body moved. Paradoxically it was James and not Kate who fully appreciated the exceptional courage and inner strength it took to obey and trust in such circumstances, when raw and potent emotions were running wild. When the conditioned responses from the long-ago past were overlaying and obscuring the grounded simplicity of her actions and behavior.

Every time she demonstrated the combination of her superb sensual eroticism and the courage to venture that little bit further into the shadow-side of her sexuality, he loved her that little bit more. She was exceptionally beautiful to him and an exceptional girl, never more so than in those moments when she felt, as she did now, most ridiculous and foolish.

James walked her slowly to the next tree and knowing his wishes, Kate raised her leg again, this time controlling the spurt much better. The urge to pee was still very strong and a part of her mind now realized the reason he had forced her to drink so much juice.

Kate was also getting the hang of walking on all fours. In truth, the problem was not so much the physical movement since she was reasonably fit and healthy, but the feelings generated with every step. From the rubbing of her pussy lips and the trickle of dampness down her thighs to the bouncing of her nipple crystals that pulled so exquisitely on her breasts with every movement. She felt torn in two — humiliation, the sense of looking absurd and just plain ridiculous pulling her in one direction, and the deep and inexplicable arousal pulling her in the other.

Another tree and another burst of pee sprayed on it, and the feelings of turmoil grew deeper, the urge to get up and flee was mounting rapidly, especially as she looked ahead and saw the next tree looming before her. Why was he doing this? It was so cruel! She felt so stupid!

Even amidst her turmoil, she became aware that it was not just the peeing that created it. If it were not so difficult just to focus on keeping up with him she would have been able to think more clearly...but then what had he said? To try and let her body do the thinking...how was she feeling? Not how *should* she feel, just tuning into what *is*, not what ought to be...

It was then that she realized what was haunting her was not this moment but the past. The feelings that had been raging inside her crystallized in an instant into the most vivid and unexpected memory...a memory that started to run through her mind like an old home movie repeating itself over and over, though she knew no such movie had ever been taken

James seemed to have sensed the change within her because he led her away from the next tree and towards a garden bench situated to afford a view down the valley. Here he sat and softly as if not to disturb the process of her remembering, as if he knew, he told her just to kneel and sit quietly. To take all the time she needed to be with herself.

The movie replaying in Kate's mind was of herself as a little girl playing with her friend in the garden, they giggled and tickled each other. Her friend, being slightly bigger and stronger, had pinned her down. The taller girl's hands were merciless and the tickles had made Kate writhe and shriek in an unbearable ecstasy of pleasure...so much in fact that she had peed in her panties. Her friend did not realize what had happened and so had continued tickling and imprisoning her. The hot wetness, the continued tickling, the helplessness, a sense of being wickedly naughty and yet innocent of bad intent...all had combined into a delicious pleasure. And most importantly a *shared* pleasure—intimacy, helpless laughter and the thrill of sensual pleasure free from guilt.

The raucous laughter of the two girls had attracted Kate's mother's attention. Irritated by their shrieking, her mother had come out to tell them to be quiet and then noticed the stain on her dress.

Disgusting dirty girl! Didn't she know how naughty she was! She'd ruined her dress! She was wicked and she should be so ashamed! Her friend must go home at once...at once! Naughty, dirty girl! She would go to her room, and she would wash and change! She was bad...such a bad child! How could she embarrass and disgrace her mother so?

Blurred images followed of her being dragged, shocked and crying into the house, there to be stripped and bundled into the bath, her tired mother angry with her, and then finally angry with herself for losing her temper. The awful feeling of shame and guilt for making her mother, normally so kind, so cross. The willful childish determination, never, never to do it again, and the powerful connection seared into her memory—what she had felt, the delicious, helpless, intoxicating pleasure was *dirty*. She was a *disgusting* girl for having enjoyed it. In her inability to recognize how bad the act was—she made her *self* irredeemably bad.

Kate felt the tears run down her face and almost immediately, James' strong arms came around her and his voice soft in her ear, soothing and calming her. After a while, the vivid images and feelings began to fade and she leaned into him seeking his strength.

To her surprise he said softly, "You're not a little girl now, I want you to pee for me now where you kneel, do it now, for me!"

Kate felt his hand pass underneath her bottom and cup her sex. He wanted her to pee on to his hand! She shuddered and went tense throughout her body.

"Trust me," he said. And she did, moaning softly, part in shame and part in relief to finally let it go. Her pee trickled warm between his fingers and onto her thighs and calves as she knelt. She felt the stirrings of shame begin, then felt them evaporate like a dark cloud lifting off her as she heard him whisper, "Good girl, that's my Kate, let it flow, good girl, my special Kate."

There was no hint of disgust from James. To him it was just exactly what it was—a sterile fluid. It did not arouse him—it did not repel him. All that mattered to him was that a source of shame and self-disgust had been expunged and, with his love, would be banished forever. Along with the pain and hurt from so long ago went an idea of herself...a belief that something inside her was dirty and unlovable. And in that moment, Kate was able to believe in James and his love for her, though as yet unspoken she felt it like a new awakening in her heart.

James began to press his hand deeper into her pussy and told her to relax into the pressure, to open to him. Breathing heavily, she did and as his fingers entered her, she turned her face to his and he removed the ring gag to kiss her deeply, possessing her.

Kate felt herself melt inside—hot, liquid and aroused, all confusion leaving her as she surrendered herself to him and to the knowledge that there was nothing, no part of her too shameful or too dirty that this man did not want or that he would ever try to make her feel bad about.

The long, passionate kiss lasted for a timeless moment before James led her farther down the garden to the small stream and told her to crawl into the cold water, laughing at her shrieks and, in helping Kate get clean, getting thoroughly soaked himself.

The fierce cold of the pure mountain water as it bubbled over its gravel bed seemed to wash her spirit clean as well as her body. Kate felt herself light up inside as she played childishly, splashing James and taunting him with an entirely new level confidence in and comfort with her naked body. Striking poses in her chains, rolling on her back as the water beaded on her breasts and the sunlight glittered off her body.

Inflamed with desire, his heart pounding in his chest, James found himself caught in the magic of the moment. The sheer joy, delight and sensuality Kate exuded, wrapping around him like a spell. James brought her to lie in the sun-warmed grass and told her to roll over on her back.

With her knees drawn up by the chains James fondled and stroked her as she dried in the sunshine. Soon Kate was moaning and whimpering, struggling desperately not to speak and beg him to enter her and fuck her.

James knelt between her legs and placed his strong hands on her thighs, opening her to the fullest extent of the chains before detaching them so that he could plunge himself inside her without restriction.

The heat of his cock was electric within her pussy, still cool from the water, he quickly melted her. His thick cock moved within her slowly, savoring her, and exploring her, his eyes gazing down into hers capturing her more powerfully than any chains could ever do.

As always sensitive to the moment, James realized this was not the time for self-restraint and subtle love play. His lovemaking was powerful, direct and forceful. He took everything Kate had to give and gave her everything in return.

Kate felt herself surrender to him as never before. Not that she had ever consciously withheld from him…but now she had so very much more to give. She felt him move inside her with an extraordinary clarity as if all her internal senses were amplified a thousand-fold.

Every movement James made sent tendrils of pleasure shooting hardwired through her body. Each thrust, triggering a ripple through her that began with a responsive tightening of her pussy muscles and the bucking of her hips to meet his thrust, to push her swollen clit against him as if she could pierce him in return. Then a reflexive tightening of her thighs around his hard-muscled waist as she sought to pull him still deeper inside her.

Kate's heart seemed with each thrust to leap in her chest, to explode with the joy of being his, of being herself in this beautiful moment. And in the center of her mind, so bright that James looking deep into her eyes saw the brilliance of it shining up at him, glowed an incandescent star of ecstasy shooting solar flares of pleasure through every nerve in her body.

James felt himself consumed by her fire and dived headlong in to its molten core. The possessor was possessed and, filled with fierce passion in the savage raw energy of their common fire, he exploded into her, enfolding her in his powerful love as he flooded her from within.

Long moments passed as the aftershocks of pleasure rippled through their fused bodies and James kissed away the tears that washed Kate's face. Loving her with an intensity he had never known before and only dreamed possible. In that moment, James knew that she was his all, had surpassed by far his most optimistic expectation. His search was over and yet their journey together had only just begun.

Later after Kate had tenderly licked him clean, James led her crawling back up to the farmhouse, steeling himself to keep her in role when every part of him screamed to release her and carry her to their bed.

He put her to doze in front of the fire, curled up on the rug while he sat contentedly in his chair, admiring her delicious body as she slept away the rigors of the afternoon, both emotional and physical.

The complete transformation of deep shame back into uninhibited sexual and sensual pleasure energy was not something you could possibly achieve in a single afternoon, not even in a month...yet something extraordinary had happened.

Kate had broken *all* the rules, had leapt from novice submissive to adept in just a few days.

There was a catalyst at work that James had no prior experience of at this incandescent level, though he recognized it full well. He loved her and she loved him with every atom of her being.

Tomorrow would have to be completely rethought. The games he had previously had in mind, though as erotically charged as only his imagination could make them, would seem like an anticlimax after today. It was time, James thought, to engage her consciously in the development of her sexual energy. From now on, he must work *with* her and not on her. To do otherwise, would be to disrespect the wonder of what they had discovered in each other, and that he could never do.

This decided, he woke Kate gently and led her into the kitchen where he prepared them a late supper. Since she was so obviously at ease with her role, she ate from her bowl on the floor and then suckled on him as he ate his own meal. After he had cleared things away, they spent a quiet evening—James reading with Kate curled in his arms or dozing contentedly in front of the roaring fire, looking more like a self-satisfied cat than ever she did a puppy. Occasionally, James felt the urge to talk to her, to bring her out of role and discuss the day's events, but whenever he looked at her, he saw such soul-deep peace and warm contentment in her eyes that he could not bring himself to disturb her.

Before bed, he took her outside in the dark of the evening for a walk and a pee. Kate crawled after him eagerly, now clearly relishing her role and her complete freedom from the restraints of acceptable human behavior. With the burden of shame and inhibition gone she giggled as she raised her thigh and was so obviously taunting him with the excessive wagging of her tail that he laughed out loud and spanked her playfully.

In the future, he knew he would give her many more such role-play experiences, maybe as a kitten or a pony girl, it did not really matter though they had different mindsets and lent themselves to different experiences. Sometimes it would be just for fun, for the sake of the freedom she now enjoyed to be a purely sexual animal without a trace of shame. At other times, he or she would identify some issue that their sexual games would simultaneously evoke and amplify so that their love might heal them.

Ultimately it would be Kate who chose the role. She would follow the promptings of her unconscious mind as revealed in her dreams or in moments of self-reflection. Where there was erotic charge, however perverse, however dark, there was a way to bring love and light to bear upon it, to release it, befriend it and embrace it. When there was no more charge, there would be no further point...it would simply become dull and repetitive, so they would let it go and move on to higher planes of pleasure.

With some slight regret caused only by how extraordinarily sexy a puppygirl Kate made, James realized that tomorrow he must take her training onwards or lose a precious opportunity.

Both of them exhausted from their day, he led her upstairs and placed her on her furs before climbing wearily into bed himself.

Chapter Thirty-Four
Fusion

ॐ

In the morning, James unshackled Kate and removed all of the puppygirl gear, noticing that she had obviously grown to like it from the playful pout on her face. Slapping her bottom good-naturedly, he urged her into the bathroom and went through the agreeable routine of shaving and plucking her. As always, teasing her as he did so.

This morning instead of using the colema board, he administered a large enema while she bent over the side of the bath. He instructed her to hold it in for ten minutes while he continued to tease her, before allowing her to release into the toilet bowl. He then ordered her into the shower. Beneath the hot jets, he soaped her all over, teasing and tormenting her once more until her legs were trembling so much she could hardly stand. Then he climbed into the shower with her and made her wash him, fully appreciating the many opportunities she took to take her revenge as her hands wandered soapily over his body.

When Kate had dried him, James led her downstairs to the kitchen, enjoying the pleasure of watching her prepare their meal. When it was ready, he had her sit on his lap so he could feed her morsels of food with his left hand whilst his right hand stroked and played with her.

He loved to watch her face as she responded to the synchronized movements of his hands. His fingers opened her pussy when she opened her mouth and then slid inside her as she swallowed. It was deliciously cruel to watch her struggle to concentrate on chewing her food while all the time anticipating the next movement of his fingers deep inside her. He did not allow her to come, despite her pleading. He wanted to build her pleasure layer upon layer so she would be ready for what would follow.

When she had finally finished eating, James had her lick his fingers clean of her copious juices, and then Kate went beneath the table without needing to be told, to suckle on his already hard cock while he ate his breakfast and read the morning paper. Occasionally, James would read her some interesting or funny piece of news, and he enjoyed the fact that her response could not be more than a happy mumble. Indeed, she clearly was not listening very closely, just savoring the taste of him, her submission to his pleasure and the sense of constant satiation she experienced whenever she held him in her mouth.

When he had finished his breakfast, James told her to tidy up and then follow him upstairs. It was the first time that Kate had been left alone without being bound since the first evening, and she relished the trust she had regained.

"Today," he told her when she arrived in the bedroom. "Your training enters a new phase. Today you will learn what being a slave to pleasure is really all about." A statement that left Kate excited and wondering what all her previous training had been for?

James had been standing with his hands behind his back and he now revealed that he had been holding a huge catering size roll of food wrap. Hesitantly, she walked towards him and he said nothing as he gently took her shoulders and positioned her in the center of the large open space beside the bed. James placed her ankles together and then picked up three soft leather pads. The first he put between her ankles, the second between her knees and the third much larger one between her thighs about six inches beneath her pussy.

"Stand so that you hold them in place while I wrap your legs," James said as he started wrapping the plastic wrap around her ankles working his way up her legs. More intrigued than frightened, Kate stood very still and watched as he deftly moved the roll up and up until he reached mid-thigh. James paused to position her arms with her hands flat against the sides of her thighs before continuing upwards, now walking around her to unroll the film. Within a few minutes she was encased from ankles to neck and quite unable to move.

Standing back to look at her James warned her to stand still lest she fall. He then took a pair of blunt-nosed scissors and cut away a panel of the film to allow his hand access to her pussy and then two more small sections were cut away to expose her nipples, which jutted forth erectly as soon as they were released. Satisfied, he picked her up and laid her on the bed.

"What I am going to do with you is a little conditioning, some sensory relocation and sensitizing you all at once. I know you are presently aroused by your helplessness and all the teasing you have already endured this morning, however, so far you haven't even tried to move so I want you to do that now," James watched as she tried to wriggle and encouraged her to try harder. He noticed she was getting some very slight movement of her arms, and so he picked her up and balanced her on her feet again to add a little more wrapping in a figure of eight shape around her shoulders and arms before placing her back on the bed. This time, she could not move anything even half an inch.

"Good! Now you really feel and know how helpless you are. However there's a little more to do yet." James walked over to the chest of drawers where he had put various toys and brought out a half-hood.

Holding it up so she could see he explained. "This has integral headphones and will blindfold you, and yet leave your mouth accessible, most of the time you will hear just soft, soothing, nothing noises — waves on a shore, that kind of thing — through the headphones. Should I need to, I can also speak into the microphone and tell you what I want you to do. The point is to have you completely focused on what your body *feels* by taking away meaningful input to your other senses."

James slipped the hood over her head and adjusted it until it fitted comfortably, and then speaking into the mike continued to explain.

"In a moment, my lovely Kate, you will feel something very gentle touch you. It is a soft brush dipped in oil and when you feel it I want you to very precisely follow my instructions. I want you to imagine that your mouth lips are your pussy lips. Wherever you feel the touch of the brush on your pussy lips you will put your tongue. When you feel the brush touch to your outer lips you will run your tongue on the outside of your mouth and when you feel me touch your inner lips you will run your tongue inside your lips. Occasionally, I will touch the brush to your clit and then you will gently bite your tongue. Now we will begin."

With the leather pad snugly between her thighs to hold them apart, he had easy access with the small brush and began to move it in slow circles around her pussy while he watched her attentively to make sure that her tongue followed exactly. From the start, she was very accurate and only occasionally did he have to correct her.

Doing this forced her to concentrate hard on the subtle sensations of the brush. James could hear from her breathing that she was becoming very aroused. He knew that this must be contained if the process was to have the desired effect, so after some ten minutes of slow circling, he rested the brush against her clit and as Kate gently bit her sweetly protruding tongue, he switched the mike back on to talk to her.

"Now I am going to use my hand to massage you very deeply, I want you to breathe into your belly for me while I do this."

James placed one hand on her lower belly to make sure she breathed deeply while his other hand went in through the gap in the food wrap and he began by pinching and rolling each outer labium and then her inner labia in turn. Exploring her responsiveness, noticing exactly where his touch had most effect and where it seemed to have less, then working deeper with the massage on those slightly less sensitive areas, then doing the same to the entrance of her pussy.

All this was in stark contrast to the previous sensation, and though it was extremely arousing and deeply pleasurable to her, as he could see from her face and the continuous moans and sighs she uttered with each breath, he knew that the totally different type of touch would initially bring her down away from the edge of orgasm only to approach it from a completely new direction.

James slipped his finger inside her, and once more began to explore, watching her, sensing her response. The soft elastic walls of her vagina were revealed to his sensitive fingers in every tiny detail, each small contour magnified under his touch and still he worked his fingers deeper in a slow spiral. Kate's voice, always expressive, was now a steady low moan on both the in and out breath, while her tongue licked her lips, questing unconsciously. Her head tossed from side-to-side, sometimes lifting so that cords of muscle stood out in her neck as she groaned and panted her way through an especially strong wave of pleasure — her face and voice were expressing everything her tightly bound body could not.

James' fingers reached her G-spot and pressed forward deeply into the bone making her back arch, even with the restriction of her bondage, and her tongue protrude from her mouth as it opened in a silent scream.

The feeling Kate now had, James knew, was close to feeling an urge to pee, which is why yesterday's training had been so important. Softly, he spoke to her, reminding her that she need feel no shame, to just accept and surrender to any pleasure she felt whatever its source, whatever happened.

James continued to massage, and her hips began to buck despite the food-wrap restraint and he knew she would soon be helplessly slipping into a powerful orgasm if he continued. Knowing Kate could not sustain such pleasure, James quickly withdrew his fingers and pushing one slippery finger into her ass and his thumb into her pussy he squeezed the bridge of flesh and rolled it between his thumb and finger making her cry out.

"Do you feel the sensations in your legs, lovely slave? I want you to sink into them, allow the trembling, even though your legs can't move, your muscles can still shake...so let them!"

Little shivers coursed through her legs and he could see the muscles of her belly contracting, feel the spasms under his fingertips as the sexual energy coursed through her as it sank down through her body. Now the pleasure current was reversed, the spiral upwards became a spiral down and where only moments before Kate felt that she must explode with pleasure, now she felt that she must surely drown in it.

When James was sure Kate had contained the pleasure, he picked up the brush again and began the slow circling once more. He instructed her to move her tongue as before. Though now knowing she would be even more sensitive he touched her even more lightly with the brush and noticed that she followed his movements exactly.

James was determined to put the considerable time and patience needed into this aspect of her training. Though apparently selfless, he knew how wonderful the eventual payback would be for him. His aim was to teach her to ride the waves of pleasure, the subtle light sensations of the brush causing her sexual energy to rise, enhanced by the movement of her tongue. Then the deep massage that enclosed her pleasure, forbidding its dispersion, so that it must sink down deep, and in doing so re-sensitize her for the next upward wave. They were different pathways of pleasure that opened ever more powerfully with each cycle. James thought she would manage five or six cycles this first time, though he knew this was only the beginning, for soon she would be consciously able to do it for herself.

James finally stopped an hour later when Kate's breath was ragged, and her moans were incessant pleadings for release into orgasm, for more, for less.

"Oh, PLEASE, James let me come, no more...oh, my god...not again...pleeeeeease... YES...oh, fuck, oh, fuck, oh, fuck..."

He left her to fetch her some water though Kate was moaning as if he were still touching her when he returned. James knew she would only realize later that the pleasure she was now feeling *without* coming was, in fact, several orders of magnitude greater than she had ever previously known, even when lost in the multiple orgasmic ecstasy that she submersed herself in so enthusiastically. However, she was far too far-gone to appreciate this now.

James smiled down at her, loving her, and feeling intensely proud of her, and took an ice cube from the glass in his hand.

Switching the microphone on, he spoke gently but firmly to her telling her to focus her attention on her pussy and open her mouth, and stick out her tongue. Carefully, he allowed one drop of ice water to drop on to the tip of her tongue. She gasped, and a shudder ran through her body, her thighs gripped the cushion as if she was trying to crush it. James smiled at this proof that the sensation on her tongue had connected directly to her clit and pussy. It was a crude test, but it demonstrated how wonderfully sensitized she had become.

James then alternated the ice with kissing her deeply, knowing now that as his lips crushed hers she would feel the sensation right through her body, even though he had not once touched her pussy since returning. He knew she was close to coming no matter what he did, the pleasure energy was now spiraling upward so incredibly powerfully that only the most advanced adept would have stood a chance at containing it— and Kate was only just beginning.

James ached to be inside her as she came, the last hour had taken all his self-control as he beheld his love writhing in the throes of her wanton passion. Quickly, he ran the sharp edge of the scissors through the food wrap down from the hole above her pussy to her ankles. He tore away the film so that just a fraction of a second later Kate felt her legs, immobilized for so long, suddenly spread wide. She felt his hand enter her, first two then three then all four fingers and the palm of his hand, stretching her and opening her without resistance in her superbly relaxed state.

James fingers sought and found her G-spot while his thumb pressed into her swollen clit and instantly she began to buck and scream as the force of the orgasm shook her like never before.

His hand no longer needed, James withdrew it. Grasping her ankles to lift them to his shoulders, he entered her swiftly forcing the head of his cock into her G-spot. His hands tore away the film to release her breasts first to his hungry mouth as his body arched over hers, then as he fell forward to crush her unresisting body, his mouth devoured her lips. He sucked her tongue deep into his mouth, biting down and triggering a rushing flood of pleasure energy down the core center of her body to melt her womb and send implosions of all-consuming ecstasy rippling through her cunt.

Catching the force of her pleasure like a surfer riding a wave, James felt himself swept up and up, impossibly high, before he plunged joyfully over the edge into La Petite Mort, the little death, the never-ending spiral of pleasure into oblivion, knowing that in this moment of indescribable bliss, the fusion of their love was sublimely complete.

Chapter Thirty-Five
The Torc

ഇ

Hours later, Kate moaned softly as she began to stir, not yet quite conscious but nearly so. Waking instantly, James quickly divested her of the last remnants of the film and carefully removed the hood. Taking her into his arms he rolled her over gently until she faced away from him and then he held her closely, their two bodies spooned together.

Holding her so tightly, he could not fail to be aware of the tension in her body. Acutely sensitive as he was to her internal state, James knew she was experiencing the emotional contraction that inevitably followed such a powerful expansion. So, when without asking his permission, Kate whispered, "What is happening to me? What are you doing to me?" he understood exactly what she meant, and he reached out and enfolded her with all the love he had to give.

"How do you feel?" James asked quietly, knowing the answer, but wanting her to voice her fears.

"James, I'm scared… This is changing me in ways I never expected—" whispered Kate, in a quavering, small voice.

"Where in your body do you feel the fear?" asked James, interrupting her before she gave in to panic.

Kate paused for a few moments and said, "I don't know, everywhere… I feel it more here and here." Her hands moved to her stomach and chest as she spoke. Shifting his body slightly, James placed his hands over hers. Immediately, she felt tremendous warmth begin to seep through her hands and into her body.

"It's okay to be scared, just feel it. You are not the fear you're feeling, it's just a feeling you're stuck in right now, so just feel it, be curious about it, what does the fear *feel* like?"

Kate's immediate reaction was that this was a stupid question, but somehow as the intense warmth from his hands penetrated deeper into her body, the fear began to soften its paralyzing grip on her mind, and she began to understand what he meant.

"It feels like two really tight places inside me, the one in my chest makes me feel like I can't breathe and the one in my stomach like I feel a little sick."

James kissed her just behind her ear, and speaking quietly he said, "You *can* breathe, my love, so breathe like I showed you before, deep in your belly and just notice the feelings, see if they change. Don't try and make them change, just breathe and feel. You're safe, completely safe."

Kate did as he told her and after a few moments, she shivered, the tremble running right through her body.

"The cold sensation you feel is just the fear leaving, feel my warmth, breathe in my warmth." He held her and felt the tension slowly release under his hands until finally it had completely dispersed. Then gathering her to him, he pulled the duvet snugly over them both and held her until he felt her whole body relax once more into his. Then he turned her so he could look into her eyes as he spoke.

"Pleasure and pain get mixed up inside us. When pleasure energy washes through you powerfully, it stirs up old feelings, things we have locked away inside for a long, long time. They need to be released and as you let them go you feel them, though only for a little while. Sometimes the feelings are very old or very strong or both, and then it's easy to think that they are about now instead of belonging to the past." He paused. "That's what you felt, isn't it?"

Kate nodded. "Yes." She looked into his eyes, and then turned her face away and whispered, "I'm still frightened, not like I was, but I'm still scared." She waited for the expected question. Scared of what? Instead, he just kissed her then lifted her chin gently and spoke quietly and as a statement not a question.

"I know, falling in love *is* scary, our hearts are so vulnerable and we're so afraid of being hurt again...so let's just do it this one last time together, and then we won't have to do it ever again."

A moment's confusion, the slightest frown creasing Kate's forehead before she understood, and then her eyes crinkled with her smile as her heart leapt inside her and she came to him, tender kisses all over his face until he laughed and held her away from him.

"I do, you know," he said, gazing in to her sparkling eyes.

"I know," Kate said smiling.

James rolled off the bed and padded across the room. Moments later he returned to her and drew her close to him. In his hand, he held a torc. Not the one she had worn before Kate realized as he passed it to her. This one was much heavier and had no tag. Instead, it was engraved in a beautiful flowing script across the platinum outer surface.

It read simply—

Loved by James, Trained to Pleasure

Kate kissed him and gave it back to him as without a word, she spread her thighs wide and offered herself, body, heart and soul to him. Giving herself utterly and in the same instant, claiming his love for her own.

James' hand cupped her sex with infinite gentleness and his heart swelled to bursting in his chest as he slipped the ball ends inside her and squeezed the torc closed upon her tender, moist flesh.

For a long while they lay watching the shadows moving across the room, so entwined that neither knew where each began or ended and neither cared. As the shadows lengthened, Kate said quietly, "Permission to speak, Master?"

"Yes, Kate?"

"What's for lunch?"

"Me," said James. "You're dessert."

Author's Afterword

ಐ

I hope you enjoyed reading Training to Pleasure. Much of the new material in the extended version of the ebook and the paperback was written in response to the many thoughtful and intelligent questions sent to me by readers of the original ebook. I want to take this opportunity to thank everyone who wrote to me.

In this novel, I have tried to show how the exploration of sexual shadow, through bringing fantasy to life in responsible role-play, may engender trust, love and mutual understanding. At the same time, I wanted to emphasize that the erotically playful can have profound consequences and therefore needs to be treated with the utmost respect.

I have attempted to demonstrate how a person may conscientiously take a dominant role and use their power to empower, and use control and restriction to liberate. If this is not a person's ultimate intention when in the dominant role then, all too easily, the submissive may be harmed, and negative emotions such as shame and self-disgust will be at least perpetuated, if they are not worsened. In either case, an opportunity for deepening intimacy and trust has been sadly missed.

I have also tried to show that, contrary to the stereotypical calloused sadist, a responsible dominant needs to be extremely sensitive and empathic. Such a dominant is only worthy of the power given them if they seek to enhance the submissive's self-esteem and self-respect. Critically, a dominant needs to feel humbled by the extraordinary trust bestowed upon them. Only such genuine humility effectively guards against the misuse of such power.

As a work of fiction, I hope that Training to Pleasure affords the reader a glimpse of the possible rewards for daring to own and acknowledge their own sexual shadow. What the novel does not portray — and could not do so and remain an entertaining story rather than a textbook — is the innumerable occasions when delving into our shadow evokes painful memories and unresolved emotions that are utterly un-erotic, and which cannot be resolved in the course of a single afternoon. Such memories and feelings need to be responded to with understanding, wisdom and love by both submissive and dominant if they are to be transformed into loving self-acceptance and be resolved.

Should this novel inspire you to explore your sexual shadow, I encourage you to be extremely cautious in your choice of partner. An open heart, a discerning mind and an enthusiastic willingness to learn and keep learning are far more important than any number of years of experience as a "dominant" or "submissive". Indeed if you have understood a central theme of this book, you might question why such a person remains so heavily identified with one limited aspect of themselves after such a long time?

Nor does the novel adequately describe — since it would be a lengthy novel in its own right — the process through which a responsible dominant develops their skills and sensitivities. To avoid being too long-winded, I will simply say that it is only possible to guide another safely down a path if you have already walked that path yourself.

Julian Masters

Why an electronic book?

We live in the Information Age — an exciting time in the history of human civilization, in which technology rules supreme and continues to progress in leaps and bounds every minute of every day. For a multitude of reasons, more and more avid literary fans are opting to purchase e-books instead of paper books. The question from those not yet initiated into the world of electronic reading is simply: *Why?*

1. *Price.* An electronic title at Ellora's Cave Publishing and Cerridwen Press runs anywhere from 40% to 75% less than the cover price of the exact same title in paperback format. Why? Basic mathematics and cost. It is less expensive to publish an e-book (no paper and printing, no warehousing and shipping) than it is to publish a paperback, so the savings are passed along to the consumer.

2. *Space.* Running out of room in your house for your books? That is one worry you will never have with electronic books. For a low one-time cost, you can purchase a handheld device specifically designed for e-reading. Many e-readers have large, convenient screens for viewing. Better yet, hundreds of titles can be stored within your new library — on a single microchip. There are a variety of e-readers from different manufacturers. You can also read e-books on your PC or laptop computer. (Please note that Ellora's

Cave does not endorse any specific brands. You can check our websites at www.ellorascave.com or www.cerridwenpress.com for information we make available to new consumers.)

3. *Mobility.* Because your new e-library consists of only a microchip within a small, easily transportable e-reader, your entire cache of books can be taken with you wherever you go.

4. ***Personal Viewing Preferences.*** Are the words you are currently reading too small? Too large? Too… ANNOYING? Paperback books cannot be modified according to personal preferences, but e-books can.

5. ***Instant Gratification.*** Is it the middle of the night and all the bookstores near you are closed? Are you tired of waiting days, sometimes weeks, for bookstores to ship the novels you bought? Ellora's Cave Publishing sells instantaneous downloads twenty-four hours a day, seven days a week, every day of the year. Our webstore is never closed. Our e-book delivery system is 100% automated, meaning your order is filled as soon as you pay for it.

Those are a few of the top reasons why electronic books are replacing paperbacks for many avid readers.

As always, Ellora's Cave and Cerridwen Press welcome your questions and comments. We invite you to email us at Comments@ellorascave.com or write to us directly at Ellora's Cave Publishing Inc., 1056 Home Avenue, Akron, OH 44310-3502.

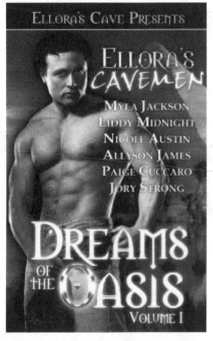

MAKE EACH DAY MORE *EXCITING* WITH OUR

ELLORA'S
CAVEMEN
CALENDAR

WWW.ELLORASCAVE.COM

erridwen, the Celtic Goddess of wisdom, was the muse who brought inspiration to story-tellers and those in the creative arts. Cerridwen Press encompasses the best and most innovative stories in all genres of today's fiction. Visit our site and discover the newest titles by talented authors who still get inspired - much like the ancient storytellers did, once upon a time.